D. HALE RAMBO

HARD BOUND

THE PLANAR PAGES

ISBN: 978-1-960123-05-3 (Hardback)
ISBN: 978-1-960123-01-5 (Paperback)
ISBN: 978-1-960123-00-8 (eBook)

Cover Design by Fantastical Ink
The Planar Page Logos by Grace Lewis
The Book of Larrakane art by Rick Hertel Art

Contents

IT TOOK EVERY OUNCE of Fiona's self-control not to dump her drink on the scribe currently intruding on her space. It wasn't that she didn't love a good verbal sparring match—she certainly started those enough. Or even that in the past she hadn't daydreamed about giving interviews about her work like all people who wanted someone to notice their intelligence. But here, in the tavern that was like a second home, one of her favorite places in the Book of Larrakane, she simply didn't want to be the one who started the fight. First because every page turner in the place would gossip about it like the hens they were, but second because Mac, the fae proprietress, would tut and look disappointed. Fiona never wanted to trifle with the bond of friendship she had with Mac. Especially not over something as small as this.

The Book of Larrakane, or the Book for short, was the way everyone grouped the seven known pages in the universe that could be traveled or "turned" to by people with the ability to do so: page turners. Fiona was one of thousands or so creatures who had the power to walk through the stacked worlds, turning the page from one to the next. It seemed like a big number until compared to the vast ocean of people who were not page turners. That was somewhere in the millions.

With a deep sigh and a tight clutch on the clay mug holding Mac's latest concoction, Fiona answered another exasperating question as reasonably as she could: "What was it like to help the Guild with Blaze? I didn't help the *Guild* with Blaze. I helped Blaze with Blaze. The citizens did it for themselves. They were quite extraordinary." She motioned with her mug to punctuate the last sentence.

Format had been decided on what had happened a couple of weeks ago, when the dying page of fire, Blaze, suddenly flared back to life, and it was all tangled. She had returned a previously stolen fire artifact to its rightful place in the dimmed page after recovering it from its hiding place, Cobbles, the page of earth. That was true. And though it had been quite the endeavor, she'd had help along the way. Once she got around to asking for it. Fiona liked to think of it as a team effort now. But naturally, the *Card* would get it wrong. The printed booklet was best at spreading the word of everything the Travel Guild did. Made sense, as they were owned by them.

The Travel Guild was a powerful organization that regulated, administrated, and profited off the Book and the page turners who traveled it. They supported them too, of course. When page turners started to travel across the Book two hundred years ago, there was a heady mess of conflict, page versus page, on what permissions the page turners were allowed, who they could take with them to another page, and much more. The first turners quickly dived into the fray and established order out of the chaos, all at a reasonable cost, and quickly the Travel Guild was born. But Fiona knew who to trust when things truly got tough, and it wasn't the Guild.

The reporter, his young voice belied by the crinkles around his eyes and mouth, nodded as he scratched on the paper. She had seen him on the edges of her vision as she moved around the city in the last week or so. It wasn't until he turned up here that she realized he had been dogging her steps closer than expected. If she hadn't been irritated, she may have been impressed.

He scrunched up his face, a habit familiar to Fiona from other humans like herself when trying to puzzle out a scheme, and said, "But the Travel Guild expressed that it was *their* jacket working with you that solved the broken page. Indeed, we made that the headline the next day: 'Guild Saves Blaze.'" He said it quite loudly, making sure to accentuate the headline with his hands as if it were written in front of him directly. The turners on the stools next to him nodded and raised mugs happily. He smirked, seemingly pleased that his show was well received.

"Well, when you print it, you can write what you like, can't you?" Fiona said through gritted teeth. "But I assure you, the Ashborn working together with the other fire denizens are really the ones who saved Blaze." Fiona knew that trying to pivot the story to the exact version would be a lost cause. But she wasn't going to let the Guild earn all the honors just because she had used some of their resources. They would take the recognition and use that for undue influence elsewhere. Well, not if she had any control over it.

Though the Guild worked to regulate the Book of Larrakane, sending jackets from page to page and stepping their foot in every negotiation they could, they were not an altruistic bunch. Dodger, one of her closest friends, and Rockcruncher, a salamander she had gotten to know well chasing down the stolen fire artifact, were about the only worthy jackets she knew. She tried to find the angle the scribe was coming from. Had been for a few minutes. But he was being elusive and wasting her time. "Why are you talking to me if you have all the facts?"

The scribe looked up, blinking. "Format has it you work for them now. There were sightings of you coming and going to the Hinge the day before. A little birdie told me you were offered a job in regulations. And your partner"—he consulted his notes—"Marcius was the one who traveled with you to Cobbles and then turned in the smilodon tigress culprit."

Curse her to the dark edge for writing his name down on the logs. At the time it was to cover her tracks in case anyone was following her. She didn't think it would be evidence that the Guild had retrieved the artifact. An artifact that enabled the fire page to be what it was and had, to her surprise, been part of a friend she dearly missed, Soots. So much had been uncovered by the simple act of restoring Blaze. So much still to discover. Fiona had many questions but so little time in getting to research exactly what a Guardian was, besides what Soots called themselves. Protector of a single page who could control it completely. The page was roiling fire currently, so hot that no one mortal could turn back into Blaze at the moment, so further questions to Soots were on hold. Fiona reasoned that this was Soots fixing the page after she left, but her curiosity made her itch to confirm it with the Guardian herself. She had given full reports to her client, the Elder druid, briefed Dodger, and filed information (obfuscating Soots's involvement naturally) so that the trial for the smugglers of the artifact could begin. Interruptions to research that would answer her questions crowded her like a swarm of ants to sugar, and the scribe was just the latest one.

"Well, format is wrong," Fiona said, turning away from the scribe and back to the counter where Mac stood eavesdropping quite openly. The honey-skinned older fae winked at her, which eased some of Fiona's tension. Though the fae looked like humans, apart from the wilting ears and taller height, their natural beauty made one captivated for a brief second, no matter how long you had known them. She focused on the barest of wrinkles on Mac's face, then sighed. "I don't have anything else to impart and I'd rather like to finish my drink alone. I've said all I'm going to say," she said over her shoulder in a nicer tone.

"If you think of anything else," the unswayed, chipper scribe said, "feel free to stop by the *Card*'s office at any time." A calling card landed beside her on the bar. "And, nice scarf," he said as he departed.

She ignored the card and looked up at Mac, letting out a deep breath.

Mac squeezed her lightly on the shoulder, her perpetually warm hand decorated in swirling cream, indigo, and olive tattoos, like a kite's tail spinning in the air. "Was answering his questions truly that hard? You should've talked yourself up a bit more."

"But it's not about me. It's about Blaze. Or it should be. People should be talking about what matters, not who saved what," Fiona said, her shoulders slumping. She had wanted the connection to the Ashborn for larger cases and a little renown with the leaders of the pages, yes. It would help her expand the investigative work she could do and the people she could help. But she couldn't see anything good coming out of having her name spread across the Book like this and linked with the Guild so tightly.

She had disliked the Travel Guild for most of her time as a page turner. They often made her job more laborious than it needed to be. They touched everything and were an obstacle in just getting a good job done. But she had to admit her grudge against the Guild could make it easy to judge them before their due, as it had in the case of Blaze's stone. She had been so focused on the Guild being the culprit, she'd almost lost Dodger as a friend and fallen into the trap of the real thieves. She wouldn't let that happen again.

She tilted her head. "Besides, the ones I want to know about my work don't even read the *Card*. No sense using that to make an introduction." Fiona wanted to get to know the leaders of Spine, the one place connected to every page in the Book. She often thought it was better to know the people in power so one could help them do better or hinder them from doing worse.

"Well…" Mac started wiping down the polished wood bar like it too was being stubborn to her words. "If it makes any difference, I think what you did to help Blaze is invaluable. I know for a fact that one or two people in the Book are impressed with you, and that may lead to bigger things, you know."

Fiona smiled. Mac was usually so forward and blunt. Why not say who? "That's quite cryptic. Who're you talking about?"

Mac shook her head, her sunglow-gold hair swinging across her ethereal azure-robed shoulder. "Nope. I've said more than I should've as it is. You're too clever, and some secrets are best kept that way—secret."

"Oh, now you're simply trying to poke my curiosity." Fiona had known Mac for the last fifteen years, ever since she was inked and brought to Spine. But somehow the fae still managed to be a bottle of mysteries as intriguing and delightful as one of her drinks.

It was a shame that the Thread was tucked so deep in the turner district. Few people outside of a smattering of page turners even knew it existed. Folks would be as awed by the proprietress as she had been—still was. Mac said she didn't mind being unknown and that those who needed the place would find it. Fiona always suspected she kept the Thread hidden away on purpose for some secret reason. The Thread housed a large first floor boding ample seating for all body types in the Book (which varied from small and winged to large and elephantine). Its robin's-egg exterior was edged in white trimming that gave the appearance of delicate lacework draped upon an elaborate dollhouse. That delicacy belied the showroom for performers, quaint guest rooms, private quarters, sitting areas and so on. With a handful of floors and so much space, there had to be more going on here than met her investigative eye. She had thought once that perhaps it was Mac's experimental concoctions, like the tipsy maelstrom she sipped on, taking up so much room.

Mac waved in Fiona's face. "Stop trying to figure me out. I know that look, and I regret every word. I'm going to go clear tables before you start asking me more questions." Her bubbly laughter trailed after her somewhat as she headed to the other patrons in the room.

Fiona took her advice, tabling her mysterious friend's antics for another time, and focused on finishing her drink. She ought to be getting home soon as it was. She had promised

Gaili that today they could discuss future living arrangements, although she didn't think there was much to discuss. Gaili had been staying in her house for the last week at Fiona's insistence that she not continue sleeping on the floor of her small smithy and alchemist shop. It was no wonder the faun was always covered in streaks of dirt and oil. Though she had only known Gaili for a couple of weeks, she felt immediate kinship with her. As that didn't happen often, Fiona didn't treat it trivially.

To Fiona it just made sense that she helped her new friend with a room. Her place was big enough for the two of them and was already paid for by the pension she received as a page turner of Restless Rise, her native home. In the last century or so, page turners from Rise were immediately lifted to nobility and put into the royal spectrum. It was more for the monarchy than them. A measurement of control. But the funds had meant she could give half to her mother, use the rest to purchase her home, and still have a small amount for basic needs set aside. She had no need for Gaili to pay for the space.

And when she could admit it to herself, it chased away the loneliness she had been feeling. That loneliness had threatened to deepen with Soots now stuck in Blaze resuming their role as its Guardian. But Gaili's chatter and inquisitive personality matched her own and made the place incredibly lively, even with Soots gone. If only she'd get over the notion of having to pay for the room in some manner. How much the faun made at her shop Fiona didn't know, but she got the sense from asking circuitous questions it wasn't enough to rent a proper room. What could Fiona possibly say to make her quit the subject?

Fiona meandered through the cobblestone streets of her beloved city. Spine was quite a bit unnatural compared to the other realms in the Book. While there was a clear indication and previous history to understand all the pages had existed separately before the Inking, the Spine had no such history. It was a large city buffered on four sides by an evergreen forest. Aqueducts were spread out far throughout the huge city, as the only source of water came from Depth's Door, a lake in the north. There were over a dozen districts, some dedicated to the seven pages in the Book and others to vocations such as crafting or farming. As more page turners were brought to Spine by their power, bits and pieces of the city refreshed over time to match their desires. Spine was at once new but also dated. For page turners, there was no other home but here. No matter how many showed up, there was always room for them, whether in a district similar to their native page or the turner one.

The turner district itself, where the Thread and Fiona lived, was home to most page turners who either had no alliance to their native page and wished to be far from the representative marks of said pages within the city or, like Fiona, had been in Spine since they were young. The mismatched dwellings that marked the uniqueness of the place were more normal to her than anything else. She passed by a small dark stone keep and a wide yellowing circle yurt on the way to her home. The area was less regulated by the Guild, so turners did as they pleased here. There were a few human and smilodon children running and laughing through an alleyway, blissful in their own little world. People strode the streets, intent on places to be and barely glancing her way. Just how she liked it when she wanted to be alone with her thoughts.

She rounded the corner of the street, swaying out of the way of a passing carriage, and went to the side entrance of her house. The front entrance, with her large Thorne Investigations sign and open-eye insignia, was for clients and when she wanted to be seen entering. The side entrance was lesser known and came in handy when she needed to get away without her nosy neighbors noticing.

Unlocking the large wooden door, she pushed it open and was assailed with the smell of fresh bread mixed with an overpowering sickly sweet smell. She wrinkled her nose, pulling up her multicolored and multi-pocketed scarf to act as a bit of a barrier. The two smells mixed together were too much, and the scarf did little to help block them. Taking a deep breath back outside, she strode into the antechamber, leaving the door open to coax the smells out into the street, and went to find the faun and her latest experiment.

Gaili sat on the wooden bench attached to the long wooden trestle table. This had recently replaced the small one Fiona had used to store various items as she passed back and forth from door to door on her way in and out. The kitchen, more cupboards than anything, hadn't seen much use before Gaili's arrival. But now it was transformed. The cupboards held dishes, the counters a mix of cooking and baking supplies on one wall and some of Gaili's alchemical equipment and clay jar ingredients on the other.

A large iron pot stood in the hearth of the open bricked stove above a smoldering fire. Thankfully Fiona had had the place modernized when she moved in a few years ago, so there was a brick-and-stone chimney attached to funnel the smoke up and out of the room. The bread smell was clearly coming from the pot, a quickly becoming usual occurrence when Gaili was working on a project. Fiona turned her attention to the kitchen table, where Gaili was focused on what looked like small hills of bright-pink sand in front of her. They almost matched the color of her curls. It was scattered on the table on one side from end to end. Larrakane help her, Fiona wouldn't be able to eat on that side of the table again without thinking about whatever it was.

Fiona's slippers made no noise on the polished wooden floor as they were meant to, so she cleared her throat to avoid catching the faun off guard.

"Oh!" Gaili said turning around. "Fi, you're back! I mean…welcome home. Sorry everything is well…everywhere. I'll clean it up right now. Do you want any coffee?"

"Please don't trouble yourself about it," Fiona said, smiling gently. Gaili could be an apologetic sort of person for absolutely nothing at all. It poked at Fiona's senses sometimes, but she would never mention it to her. She knew Gaili's strict education and deplorable professor was the cause of her timid ways. "Honestly, Gaili, there's little you could do to upset me, so don't worry so much." She squeezed Gaili's shoulder in reassurance but moved farther away from the table as the too-sugary smell invaded her senses. She took the warm kettle and buried her nose closer to it, inhaling the earthy, chocolatey scent of one of her favorite pleasures, fresh coffee. Though these were the last beans from Rise, they had only somewhat dented the brief pleasure.

As if reading her thoughts, Gaili chirped up as she turned back to the bright powder. "You got a letter today, sent by a postman from Rise."

"Rise?" Fiona repeated, surprised. A letter from the page was most unexpected. She picked it up, examining it. It was thin and nondescript except for a vine of thorns, her family's crest, on the opening. Larrakane be kind, it was from her mother. She hadn't heard from her in months. She dropped it back on the table as if it had bit her. She'd read it later, alone, or perhaps whenever she needed to remember what it was like to be frustrated and young for a moment.

The smell wafted again from the table as Gaili shifted the sand around with a scraping tool, interrupting her thoughts. Fiona said as politely as she could, "So what have you here? It has quite the interesting smell."

Gaili's rose eyes widened in barely suppressed excitement. "I went to the market this morning to get a few things for dinner, and I came across something I'd never seen here before. Fae rose! Well, the stems. It's from the Court. I haven't had access to any since I was inked. Once it's chopped into dust it's great as a binder to other elements for experimentation and creating potions." Gaili scraped up the sand and funneled it into a jar. "It was fairly rare back home too. Only the old fae knew how to grow it."

"I'll take your word on it." An alchemist and inventor, Gaili could see a great many uses for a thimble if given the time. Fiona moved closer now that the sand was gone. "I'm glad you were able to find some if it'll help you."

"And help you too. I'll be able to find plenty uses for your work with this."

Fiona wasn't quite sure when she'd need to clear out a place by stinking it up, but she was sure Gaili already had several ideas for it. The way her mind worked to take something mundane from another page and make it a valuable tool or weapon was amazing. She had met Gaili when trying to find a solution to keep her then flame sprite Soots from burning down the house. Gaili's work had already helped her more than she could properly express to the faun.

"Gaili, I've been thinking about your request to charge you something for the room."

Gaili's hands stilled as she was cleaning up and then started again. "Oh good, did you come up with a price? I'm happy to pay what you think is fair."

"No, no that's not it. I simply want to say once and for all that you don't need to pay me. The house is paid for," she mumbled, feeling odd about it, "my clients are somewhat steady, and I'm happy just to be helpful."

"But that's not the point, Fi. I need to do my fair share around here. The occasional meal cooked or jelly breath for the fire page can't possibly cover my expenses while I live here."

"Your expenses?" Fiona said, raising an eyebrow. "Are you worried that I'll think you costly at some point?"

"Well, yes, of course. Not costly exactly, but I..." Gaili wiped at her bottom lip, smearing pink powder off her hand to her chin. "I simply want to be on even footing if there's ever any particular disagreements between us in the future."

Ah, so it was a matter of equality that she was worried about. Fiona knew the basics of how things ran in the Court of Copper. She had learned during her few years of turner training and personal study on her own as a tour guide that the levels of hierarchy in the Court were very real and very felt among the people there. But she thought it better than the social order of her own native human page. At least in the Court if you worked hard and could show you were educated or intelligent you could rise to prominence and even be elected to their page council, the Order of Seven. When all the pages opened up some two hundred years ago, it upended the lives of everyone, not only turners. When the Court of Copper was revealed, the Order of Seven was created to preside over the Court's connection to other pages. Each member from one of the seven regions in the Court's page. And they had worked hard since the Inking. They were the ones who prevented the Travel Guild from having outposts in the Court of Copper and oversaw all relations between the faekin page and the rest of the Book.

There were not many methods for escaping the status one was born into in Rise. The only guaranteed way was to be inked. And even then, some people would always remind you to mind your betters.

But if Gaili thought she needed to pay rent to be equal to Fiona then she probably thought herself inadequate in some way. Well, Fiona would certainly not let that stand.

"Alright then. We should be equal partners while you're living here." She leaned back, gauging the faun's reaction to her words to make sure she was on the right track. "But you paying rent would be a waste of your paper. So instead I suggest an agreement. You help me run Thorne Investigations. Assist with the clients. Create resources at a discounted cost. Many cases have needs. And most importantly, combine your considerable talents with my rather mischievous ones to do the very best we can at helping others." Fiona held out her hand, a lightness in her chest. "This is where you take my hand and shake it, agreeing to our deal."

Gaili's took a step back, eyes widening. "You can't be serious."

"I absolutely am," Fiona said, waving away the faun's words. "I should think that a bit obvious, given the circumstances."

"Fi, I don't—You barely know me."

"I know enough to understand that you are quite capable, and capable is a good person to have at your back."

Gaili paced the floor, her golden tattooed hand rubbing her face. She sighed. "You're very sweet, but be reasonable. I can make some minor concoctions at best. That's not enough for you to be offering a partnership."

Fiona straightened up and grabbed on to Gaili, stopping her pacing. As if she was reciting the facts of a case, she said, "You have a knack for languages that is entirely useful. I pay quite a bit in the artisan district for potions to travel to the elemental pages, maintenance of my gear, and so on. I must spend time hunting down information and doing research that your thorough education may have already taught you. And your ability to create items of use for unpredictable situations is exceptional. You are invaluable, Gaili, and I'd very much like to work with you."

Gaili shook her head, bright-pink curls swaying side to side. "Oh. But..." She dropped her gaze. "I don't want to bring you down."

Fiona dropped her hand and tried to think of how she could solve this. If telling Gaili that she was valuable wouldn't work, she'd simply have to show her. "At least give it a trial run. What do you have to lose?"

The faun looked up, but whatever she was about to say disappeared as a bell sounded from the front of the house. Gaili turned to answer it, wiping her hands on her apron as she went. Fiona sighed but followed. She would bring the conversation up again later at her first chance.

A faun, tall with gold-leaf skin, deep-brown eyes, and curved black horns stood staring open-mouthed at Gaili's presence in the doorway. Her hands, less tattooed than Gaili's, held the sides of her simple rust-colored woolen dress, fidgeting. She seemed on the verge of running away.

Fiona called out to set her at ease: "Hello there. Welcome. Do please come in."

The faun's attention snapped to Fiona. There was a wobble of the mouth, but it was gone as soon as Fiona registered it. Raising her chin up, she asked, "This is the home of Investigator Thorne?"

Fiona motioned to a large padded chair by her desk. "Please sit. I'm Investigator Thorne."

Gaili took a step back and the faun walked slowly into the parlor-turned-office.

"Would you like some coffee?" Gaili said.

The faun cleared her throat. "Yes. That would be nice." She smoothed her dress as she sat down. "Er, I've never had any before."

"I know the precise way to make it for a first timer," Gaili said, avoiding Fiona's eyes and heading to the kitchen.

"Have we met before?" Fiona asked. There was a lilt to her voice that sounded a little familiar, but Fiona couldn't place her.

"No, no we haven't. I'm Elinor." She played with her dress, entangling the fabric in her fingers. "Format has it you helped some of those fire creatures get back home when the smugglers had taken them. That you didn't think twice about setting them all free."

"That's true." Fiona sat, trying to ease the faekin's anxiety. "Do you need help with something?"

She nodded and broke into fresh tears as she said, "My sister's been arrested by the Order of Seven, and I think you're the only one who can save her."

"THE ORDER OF SEVEN!" Gaili said, coming back in the room. The coffee service tray wobbled in her hands and the cups rattled together. Fiona took hers before it could fall off. Spilling coffee was a travesty.

"They took her in a couple days ago. We thought it would be all cleared up by now, but it hasn't been." Elinor said, dabbing at her eyes with a produced silken handkerchief.

"Why would the Seven arrest your sister?" Gaili said, handing her a cup.

The faun took it but kept her attention on Fiona. "Some paperwork went missing and they've said it was her."

Fiona looked between two's reaction and then addressed the obvious issue. "Do you have evidence she didn't..." She waved her hand. "Commit this crime?"

She shook her head. "Orsa says she didn't do it, and I believe her. Why would she have a need for council paperwork and such?"

Fiona raised a brow at Gaili.

"The Seven are a studious lot," Gaili said in answer. "Each of them comes from a different region of the Court of Copper and are usually the brightest or best in their field. So, depending on what this paperwork is, it could be valuable."

"Or it could be rubbish," the faun said, thrusting the untouched coffee down on the desk where it clattered. "There's just as much of that as there is anything else. They sit around theorizing or creating obstacles for the Guild, and that's about it. They've fallen a long way since they came to be after the Inking."

"Hmm, and I suppose you can't go to the Guild because that would be meddling in Court business." Not that Fiona thought even she should be meddling in Court business.

"Yes of course." The faun nodded eagerly. "But format has it you're *independent*. You could ask a few questions and find out what truly happened. You'd not be thought a spy since you're unaffiliated with the Guild."

Fiona didn't think that was exactly true but didn't have the heart to point out the particulars. Unless she traveled the entire time in the Court with a faekin guide, people would mark her as an oddity and she would be forced out like some common ripper. The Seven were highly alarmed about their creations being stolen from the page and the academies were not far off from the same feeling.

Skimmers who wished to tour in the Court had to hire faekin turners. Those page turners took on the personal responsibility for their charges' well-being and any mischief they got into. That made going to the Court of Copper incredibly expensive indeed for most people. Not only would Fiona have to find a willing guide, but she'd then have to find a way to ditch said guide to do her work. Unless she could convince Gaili. In fact, this might be a perfect opportunity to show her they would be valuable as a team.

She turned to her friend with a sly smile. "If you accompany me, then you could be my guide. People don't need to know I'm a turner as well. We could do some sightseeing around the area of the theft and just pop in. Are the Seven's chambers open to the public like Rise's parliament?"

Gaili's golden face paled peach as she stammered, "I-I shouldn't go."

"Why not? Surly we can go for a couple of hours this afternoon and be back before nightfall. If you're worried about your commissions, I promise not to keep you out long."

"I just haven't been back since the last time. You know..." Gaili's voice grew quieter and quieter. "With...what she said and all."

Fiona tugged at her scarf, trying to understand. When Gaili's professor ridiculed and turned her back on her, calling her unworthy of her teachings, it had really struck the faun down. Had Gaili truly kept herself away from home because of one person? She took a step toward Gaili and lowered her voice in reassurance. "I understand what it's like going home and facing up to the withering gaze of someone who made you feel less than." Fiona's eyes flicked in the direction of her family's crested letter. "But think about what you're missing out on not staying in touch with the people who *do* care about you."

"She does live in a completely different region," Gaili said slowly. "And it would be nice to call on some old friends if we have time." The frown softened on her golden face. She shook her head though. "But you don't need me to show you around. You're more than capable."

"Capable doesn't make me knowledgeable. You are so familiar with the area and the page. You'll make the work much faster."

"Please, miss," the faun interjected, her voice overwrought. "I'd take her myself, but I'm not a turner like you and they know me around there. It won't work. But I need to save my sister as soon as can be."

Fiona frowned at the faun's words, a noted tremble in her voice, but her attention was drawn back to Gaili.

Gaili nodded. "I'll guide you."

Fiona's smile widened. "Excellent. I'd rather a friend than a stranger any day." And it could be the start of their working together. If successful, Gaili would have no objection to continuing. Fiona turned her attention to Elinor. "I don't mind asking a few questions and seeing if we can be helpful here. But you'll have to explain a few things as we make our way to the Arches district." It was the only pagemark in the entirety of Spine that was sanctioned to get to the Court of Copper. The Seven truly kept the page under lock and key as best as they could.

Elinor picked up her skirts and nodded impatiently. "I can do that. And you'll have to tell me how much your payment is. We can work out a plan, but I'm good for any sum."

Fiona murmured without directly agreeing. She really preferred immaterial things to money and so often tried to be paid in those instead. "I'll let you know a price when I understand all the particulars. Probing into the Seven's business will not be easy. Have you worked there like your sister?"

"No, she did all the filing, paperwork, and day-to-day work for some of the Seven. Bureaucratic duties. There are others who may be willing to tell you more about the goings-on there."

"Well then, there's no time like the present. Shall we?"

Gaili put a hand to her soiled apron, untying the strings as fast as possible. "We can't go there like this. I look an absolute mess!"

Fiona had forgotten for a moment the style and grace faekin carried themselves with in the Court. It was more exhausting than Rise. "I suppose you're right." Fiona brushed a brown curl from her forehead and sighed. "Do make yourself comfortable, Elinor. We won't be but a few minutes."

The faun averted her eyes. She glanced around the office, seeming to take everything in, but asked no questions.

Gaili continued up the stairs from the parlor to the landing of an informal sitting area that branched to the bedrooms. She ducked into the farther room, hooves clacking loudly on the wooden floor.

Fiona shook her head at her hasty feet. She opened one of the few chests in her room that contained fine clothes specifically for traveling the pages. She hadn't been to the Court with any real frequency since her training days many years ago so had nothing special to wear. Her regular clothes for her human page would have to suffice. She shook out her nicest smock, bodice, and royal-blue skirt donning them as best as she could alone. They were a little dusty but not too far out of fashion. It was times like this she wished she did have staff on hand to help, but such was the life an investigator who worked out of her home. One could only keep the secrets she needed to if one kept to themselves.

Gaili bounced into the room, her energy practically static. She looked Fiona up and down. "Oh," Gaili said, "that'll do, of course. Unless…" She revealed from behind her back layers of a violet gown trimmed with copper thread. The cut was exceedingly fashionable, even Fiona could tell that. She brought out a matching satin belt with more copper swirls on it and took a step forward. "I think this will go ever so well with your skin tone, and it's a fairly recent piece. I wore it for the rare meals with the professors."

Fiona sighed deeply but smiled to soften her exasperation. She begin pulling off her overdress. "I suppose it is more appropriate."

"Exactly," the faun said brightly. "You'll fit in enough to be thought of as a regular guest of the Court in this. That will carry you further than you may believe."

Fiona nodded and finished getting dressed. It was a consideration she hadn't thought of, more used to slipping through shadows than trying to blend in with others. "There, do I do you justice?"

Gaili furrowed her brow, golden skin crinkled around her eyes. "Of course, Fiona. I'm just assisting you. There's no need to make me happy."

"You have the oddest view of yourself. Don't think we've finished our conversation from earlier. It's most appropriate that this be the start of our trial run working together." Fiona tied her scarf around her hair to act as a veil. While it wasn't entirely fashionable with Gaili's loan, she couldn't leave it behind. It was like a third hand to her at this point. Its rough cotton and smooth silk patches pooled over her hair and across her shoulders. Its secrets were held safely in its various unfathomably deep pockets. She always wondered which page the pockets all went to but so far had been unsuccessful in mapping them. But to a page she was sure, having been told as much when gifted. It was one of a kind, given to her by her father, the only authority figure she had ever really trusted, and though she didn't understand all of its depths, she cherished it nonetheless.

Gaili nodded her approval (which shocked Fiona to a small degree) and the pair went downstairs, Fiona moving slowly as she reacquainted herself with all the clothing layers.

Elinor was staring out the hazy window. She glanced at the two. "You are able to be prepared on the fly, I must say. I am impressed."

"One should always have what they need to fit the situation in my line of work," said Fiona. "Of course, having a faekin partner doesn't hurt for this particular case either."

Elinor raised an eyebrow at Gaili, assessing her. Fiona noticed her eyes grow bright, but Gaili's sigh drew her attention.

Gaili began wringing her hands again, but Fiona grabbed one and tugged her toward the door. "We'll need to catch the closest carriage. If we're going to get back before this evening, we should go now." Fiona tossed open the office door, and they strode out into the brightly lit landing and down the cobblestone street. Fiona was relieved to see her friendly but somewhat gossipy neighbor Mistress Didia Humbledraft wasn't outdoors today. The better to not see her in this getup and tease her.

Quite a few people already stood at the carriage stand. It was a full ride in the large open-air carriage as they all piled in. While the body of the wooden carriage could accommodate all types in the Book, it was still a squeeze when you crammed five or six people in it. Elinor chose to ride with the driver for a bit until there was more space inside.

Once past the market district, its enticing sounds and smells surrounding the carriage as they stopped and let people off, Elinor rejoined them, and Fiona began to interview her in earnest: "What exactly has your sister been charged with?"

"Theft and improper entry. From what I've been able to gather on my own, they said she snuck into a locked room that she wasn't supposed to enter. She would never do that."

"And inside this room was paperwork she supposedly took? Was the paperwork recovered?"

She shook her head. "No. I asked a few of the people she works with, but they were vague. I gathered they were told not to talk about it."

"How did they determine it was your sister—Orsa, I mean—who may have done it?" Gaili ventured softly from across the carriage.

"They said they found something of hers inside the locked room. I can't find out what. No one will talk to me about it."

Fiona pursed her lips and said nothing. It all sounded like bureaucracy for the sake of moving right along. Although there was something that confused her. "If they've arrested your sister, are they questioning her or trying to source where the paperwork has gone?"

"She hasn't talked to anyone beyond the first day, as far as I know. And even I can't afford a solicitor who could go up against the Seven. If we don't find evidence that it couldn't have been her, then I don't know what we'll do. At best she'll be cast out of the region. At worst she'll be jailed for years. She won't survive that."

Gaili tutted, shaking her head. "None of the other six regions will take cast-outs. It'll be either the icy mountainous Wilds or the nymphs' isle for her."

Elinor said nothing but thrust her chin up, angrily staring out into the passing city.

She could start over in another page, like Gaili, but it wouldn't be easy, especially if she wasn't a turner. And from what little Fiona knew of the Wilds and the nymphs' isle, Dew, neither were survivable alone. Dew was a far-off island of steam that most faekin never stepped foot on in their lives. The ruling nymphs, different than their continent cousins, were hostile to outsiders, and as such the island was not under the Order of Seven's purview. It was unimaginable.

The carriage slowed to a stop and the three disembarked.

Elinor gathered her skirt around her. "This is where I should leave you so that we're not connected." She nervously glanced at Fiona. "You'll be able to find me at 226 Clove Lane, near the travel corridor, at any time. I'm staying with a friend here for now."

An exclusive place to be. Whoever her lofty friend was had to be taking her back and forth across pages. Fiona nodded. "I'll see what we can find." She bit back a suggestion to brace for ill news. Her face must've betrayed her though, for Elinor nodded with a grim look before turning to leave.

Fiona watched for a moment, ache seeping in. She never had siblings. The relationship with her parents had been a tug between a warm father and a cold mother. She could barely imagine what having a sister must be like. But she knew what it felt like to be powerless for those you love.

"I hope we can help her," Gaili whispered, breaking Fiona's thoughts.

Fiona shivered and tucked her arms into her chest. "Yes, me too."

They walked toward the tall stone wall; vines splayed upon it as if built into the mortar. Verdant banners trimmed in shimmering copper flew above the wall, lording over the majesty of faekin architecture. Three high arches of bramble and twisted branches gave an uncanny if magical feel to the district entrance, vaulting the walkways but blocking the bright blue sky. The gray cobblestone streets narrowed, blocking off the ability for carriages to stroll through them. This made the darkened streets more intimate and secluded with dots of lit lanterns nestled between buildings and overgrown trees throwing amber light around. It was a spectacular area designed to delight the faekin page turners who were stuck on Spine. A piece of home.

"Perhaps you should let the guard know who you are?" Gaili said as they walked toward the opening.

"No, it would be best if you do the talking," Fiona countered. "Just the basics of sightseeing and whatnot. Like you take skimmers to the Court on occasion."

Gaili nodded nervously but had no time to reply as a guard at the middle arch hailed them. The fairy, wings of dandelion and silk fluttering toward them, addressed herself to Gaili, her voice deep and somewhat gruff. "What business have you in the Arches today?"

"Providing passage to a young woman who is engaged to have dinner in the Court," Gaili replied. Her voice was a little high, but Fiona thought she had spoken quite well, unprepared as she had been.

The fairy flew around examining Gaili and Fiona. Her hands and arms had the same sort of swirls of cream tattoos as other faekin. Though she was a third of Fiona's height, she stayed above them both, an advantage Fiona could hardly deny her.

She came back to Gaili quickly. "I haven't seen you around before."

Gaili clasped her hands together. "No, I, er…don't go home often."

"So you don't do this often?" The fairy flew down to investigate Gaili's uncovered tattoo hands. "You're in trade." She narrowed her eyes.

"Y-yes," Gaili stammered out, "but I'm doing guide work on the side. Crafting doesn't pay the bills too regularly."

Her statement rang too true to Fiona's ears, and she bit back a frown. It was unfortunate there were so many crafters piled in the artisan district. It made it hard for anyone to get good visibility, no matter how great their work was.

"Do you agree to be responsible should she get into trouble within the district?"

"Yes, of course," Gaili said, starting to wring her hands again.

The fairy flew quite close to the faun. "Do you have proof?"

Thoroughly irritated by the faekin's use of power to intimidate Gaili, Fiona piped in, "I will not have myself nor my guide lowered to such standards. Providing proof of my manners? Unimaginable. You would do well to watch yourself and those you question."

The fairy fluttered back, looking her up and down appraisingly.

Fiona arched an eyebrow, doing her best to appear fashionable and formidable like the nobles she'd always hidden from growing up.

With a flutter of wings, the fairy moved aside. "Enjoy the Arches." Her tone suggested quite the opposite.

Fiona waited a beat until Gaili had walked through before following her, ignoring the fairy. She hadn't expected this many questions just for entering the district. While the Court had always been heavy handed, this was a bit much. "Well, it's good you dressed me. I suppose otherwise that would've taken even longer."

"I didn't realize it would seem odd, but I guess it's rare that tradespeople act as guides."

"And that. How did she know you worked in trade? There's not a dirt mark on you. I would have said so before we left."

Gaili wiggled her fingers. "My hands of course. Don't you know how to read faekin marks?"

"Well, no, I've never needed to. I thought they were mostly for denoting...er, social achievements or the like?" Fiona frowned. She hadn't had to think too hard about it. Besides Mac, she hadn't been close to any faekin before. And Mac didn't like to talk about her tattoos.

"They're more than that. Some are for excellence in a field of study, but they are also social markings. Depending on the patterns and placement, you could learn a lot about a faekin."

"And your tattoos show you're in trade?"

Gaili nodded and pointed to her knuckles. "This placement does, yes. And these particular swirls tell which region I'm from."

"Isn't that a bit...much? I mean if you have it on your hand, then anyone could pigeonhole you into a place."

"It's more for the important faekin than us. Most faekin you will ever meet only have these types of tattoos."

Fiona pursed her lips. "But then if most faekin have tattoos like yours, what are the others?"

"The Seven or academy leaders have them on their face as well. To show their importance."

"Ah, much like my page uses glittering gold and how close they are allowed to stand by the Queen. The higher the mark, the higher the prestige."

"Exactly. Of course, they can be changed, but not often and only by a Copper tattooist."

Fiona linked her arm through Gaili's. "See, this is exactly why I needed you here."

The faun kept walking, barely acknowledging Fiona's statement, but a shy smile crossed Gaili's face. They ambled through the narrow, twisting streets. Seldom did they pass another person, faekin or other, but when they did, they inclined their head in cordiality, walking as close as they were. Trailing vines of colorful flowers connected building to building, making the Arches feel like strolling through the Queen's premier garden.

They reached their destination, a sizeable square with wooden benches on the outer border. Here there were no arches and most of the branches had been kept back to give it a clear space. The sky was still light enough that Fiona knew she hadn't lost too much time trying to get through to their pagemark. A large verdant banner hung from the center of the square. It was stamped with the Court of Copper insignia: an outline of a noble person with high-necked collars and copper crown upon their head. Beneath the insignia was an inked decree:

> *From Arch to Arch, from Spine to Copper*
> *From dawn till dusk, in and out*
> *Whether rain or shine, we'll welcome you*
> *As long as you respect what we do*

Seek not to spy or steal what our city holds
and we shall not confine you in places yet untold
Signed—the Order of Seven, Keepers of the Court
Dragomir L. of Orchard, Bardo P. of Lucent, Dorin S. of Glade,
Cascade of Hearth, Sofia G. of Grove, Olea of Thicket, Clara T. of
Garden

Fiona rolled her eyes at the unnecessary pomp of it all. She started to make a witty remark to Gaili but noticed the faun's eyes were staring wide at the banner. "Dear, what's wrong?"

"Clara. She's my—that *was* my professor."

3

"SHE'S ONE OF THE Seven?" Fiona asked. She had assumed Clara would be miles and miles away from where they were going. Gaili wasn't from the city of arches, Calistino. "Are you sure that's her?"

Gaili didn't respond, but she took a step back.

Fiona stopped her. "It's alright, dear. I promised to protect you. We won't even see her this late in the day, I'm sure."

Gaili nodded slowly but still took another step back. "I don't know... I mean. When did she become one of the Seven? The appointments—it's not even time."

"Perhaps we can find that out as well," Fiona said, not sure exactly what the faun was thinking, but her face said she was working on some sort of process. She grabbed her hand and tried to focus on anything other than the turn of the page. She didn't want to rush Gaili or accidentally take over the turn so instead focused on the banner, memorizing the names.

Gaili clung tightly to her bookmark, a copper coin, remnant of the page's past. The sky opened up and the decorated arches folded away from them, as if a reader was turning to the next page. On the other side was almost the same scene that they were in. Instead of the blue-tinted sky of Spine, a twinkling copper one hung overhead, bright like a freshly polished bracelet. Its rose-gold hue draped like a backdrop behind a large open square edged by tall, crowded oak trees. Warm air wafted toward them with hints of a sweet lilac and honey scent. Faekin of all types traveled in the wooded paths on the other side of the trees, and in the distance Fiona could make out a fluttering banner that matched the grassy color of the one with the poem. Music played throughout this idyllic courtyard, and there was chattering and laughter among the hot air that enveloped them like a woolen cloak.

Fiona glanced at Gaili and gave her hand a squeeze, willing her to take the first step forward. The faun did so tentatively with Fiona following behind her. The page shifted to accommodate them, and the briefest sound of the wind from Spine fluttered behind them as the page turned back, as if a reader decided to review the previous page.

Firmly in the Court of Copper now, Fiona let go of Galli's hand and looked around. She hadn't been here in some time. Everything seemed to have changed. Or perhaps since she wasn't a student or a child any longer, things just looked different.

Leaves swirled in the heated breeze cascading across her dress and fluttered down to her boots. They covered the courtyard. The faraway metallic smell of water from the canals was stronger now that she was fully in the page. A troupe of well-dressed centaurs made their way forward through the tree-shaded path, not stopping to see the new arrivals.

"Do we not need to announce ourselves anymore?" Fiona said, glancing about for a booth of some sort like there was when the Travel Guild administered a pagemark.

"It's a bit more covert than that in Calistino. Since this city is a main entryway for skimmers and guides, those watching blend in with the pagemarks. If you looked like you didn't belong or you had come across alone, you'd meet someone interested in that fact soon enough." Gaili glanced around at the trees and strode off down the path away from the courtyard. "The real questions begin when you're leaving the page."

Fiona frowned and began walking behind her. The leaves crunched under her feet, mixing with the melody that seemed to come from nowhere and everywhere at once. She cast her sight about looking for a creature hidden in plain sight but found nothing. In wonderment at how someone could conceal themselves so well, she quickened her steps to catch up with Gaili, who seemed springier, if possible, on this side.

"I'd like to start by visiting the Seven's offices first," Fiona said, picking up her skirts to avoid a sudden mud puddle. "It might prove useful to think of other places we could make inquiries with our few hours here as well." There was no response. Fiona walked a bit closer, nudging her with her shoulder.

"Oh, sorry."

"Are you alright?"

"Just thinking about... It doesn't matter, never mind. I'm sorry. What did you say?"

Fiona thought it best not to delve into the professor right now and instead give Gaili something to do. "Tell me, how do we get to see the Seven's offices?"

"There are tours of the Pavilion since it's such a prominent area and skimmers pass through here often. We should be able to catch one."

"Excellent. We can ask questions of the assembly staff who Orsa may have known."

Gaili nodded, distracted again. Fiona followed her through the dirt paths that let out through a high wooden arch to the water's edge. Calistino was well known for its port arches decorated with crawling vines and carved by well-known artists of the page's past. The arches denoted the few ports that could be accessed from neighboring cities, keeping it a bustling coastal city for trade and ships. Deep copper water brushed its northern edge, making it easy to navigate to, and canals like wriggling fingers poked into the city, giving ample avenues for traveling throughout it on boat. The walking paths were for everyday use, but it wouldn't be rare to find someone who used both in the common course of their day. It was a good city to keep as a prominent pagemark for the Court of Copper, and those who cared to track such things knew it.

They kept on the edge of the water for some time. Banners, verdant depicting the Seven's insignia and magenta depicting an arch, alternated on the buildings beside them. A few posters plastered the travertine-tiled walls. Some detailed an sculpture exhibition opening, but many shouted about an upcoming performance of Carlo Gritti's *The Blue Bird*, a play unfamiliar to Fiona but clearly in demand, if the numerous dates for its first run were any indication.

Connecting over a narrow walking bridge, Fiona noticed a striking building, like a beacon, in the distance at the end of a long path. Lush brown-green trees closed in from each side dotted with empty hanging lamps. In a few hours they'd be glowing with small embers to light the path. She had forgotten how dark it could be in the Court with the copper-tinged sky. She didn't have the vision that faekin had, but luckily it wasn't night just yet.

They passed a few faekin, a fairy and a centaur bickering as far as Fiona could tell, but not many others on the way to the Pavilion. They rounded the corner and Fiona gasped at the sight before her.

Two massive trees, taller than her Queen's palace, nestled next to each other like open hands, fingers raised. A three-story structure sat in the palm of the trees, carved from its branches, and resembled a house. It certainly had corners and stone steps that led up to a grand patio underneath a twisted trunk arch. But that's where the resemblance stopped. A breeze blew a ruffle through green palm fronds that covered the top of the structure. Pink and white bursts of flowers draped down the sides, defining the roof like pearls on a long necklace. It was a marvel of architecture she wasn't quite sure was logical, efficient, or even solid. But she couldn't argue that it wasn't fantastic

Gaili stopped, her face a wide smile, worry lines erased. "Have you not seen the Pavilion of Assembly?"

"No, this wasn't here when I visited for training."

"It's been a decade or so. Commissioned by the head of the Seven at the time. People made a fuss about the cost, of course, but skimmers turn from all pages to visit it. The best ingenuities are inside though."

"I guess it won't hurt to do some actual sightseeing while we're here," Fiona said, wishing to prolong her friend's happiness. "Then it's barely even a cover for asking questions."

Gaili, face upturned to the warm copper sky, strode at a quick clop to the stone stairs, leading the way inside.

Another faun, this one older than Gaili, grinned as they came into view inside the antechamber. He doffed his attendant hat. "Good tidings, fair travelers. Welcome to the Pavilion of Assembly."

"Are we too late for a tour?" Gaili asked, looking about. The entranceway was rather empty with just the faun.

Fiona worried they might have dawdled too much with the clothes. "Hopefully not. I've heard ever so much about this place. It is most ingenious, and I can't leave the page without seeing it."

"Unfortunately, you are. The last one started about twenty minutes ago. Do come back tomorrow morning if you are staying in the city, and I shall be happy to take you around myself." He clicked his shoes together and bowed.

"Oh but...she'd really like to come in and look around. We won't be long, promise," Gaili said earnestly.

"I'm sorry. The time is upon us." The faun motioned to the watch hanging from his belt.

Opportunities to look around the area where the paperwork was stolen with so few people in attendance wouldn't come often. Fiona thought there might be one sure way to gain access. "It would be unfortunate if I couldn't tour the place before dinner with Keeper Clara. She did so want me to see it before we discussed plans of a donation to display."

Gail's mouth dropped open. Her confusion matched that of the entryway faun.

"*You're* having dinner with Keeper Clara?" he said.

"Yes, and I am running a tad late. Sometimes it can take forever to turn from one page to the next." Fiona threw a fake glare at Gaili, hoping the faun wouldn't take her act personally. "But I'm to tour here before dinner. And I wouldn't want to keep her waiting."

He sighed and began fiddling with his keys. "Yes, yes. Well, I can just pop in and tell her you're waiting, shall I?"

So Clara was in the building still? That was unfortunate but better to know now. "We wouldn't want to bother her too soon of course," Fiona started. She slid a glance to Gaili and grimaced when she said, "When she asked you to fetch me, what were her instructions again?" She hoped Gaili would understand what she was asking for, so they didn't have to actually meet with Clara.

Gaili seemed to have composed herself and replied, "Clara will be askance if she must come here to meet her guest before she's seen the Pavilion. She only likes to be called to for emergencies, you know." She glanced at her pocket watch. "It's thirty minutes before her dinner hour. If we take only fifteen minutes or so inside, we can meet her and she'll be on her way to dinner on the dot. She does like when things are on time."

The attendant nodded, relaxing. "I didn't realize you were one of hers! Yes, well, I don't want to cause her even a minute of delay. I accidentally did once, and I heard about it for a good month." He pulled away the rope ladder blocking the way forward. "Off you go."

Gaili nodded as she walked by. "Thank you."

Fiona smiled and inclined her head, letting Gaili lead.

When they were out of earshot, Fiona whispered, "Is there a way out of here that doesn't involve that door?"

"Oh yes, several that staff use, I'm sure."

"Excellent. You did extremely well."

The faun smiled but it faltered. "Do we really want to catch up with that tour?"

"It can't hurt. It'll give us a way to blend in while we look around, and if we run into any of the Keepers, like Clara, we can ignore them as much as needed. So much information to be gathered." Fiona tried to not sound so gleeful about this part of her job. While investigating was hard work, she enjoyed digging into the mysteries life brought her. "Afterward we can ask the guide some questions, depending on what we learn."

The first-floor gallery with its bright tile flooring and tall stone walls was rather large but empty save the portraits on the walls depicting past Order of the Seven members. There were so many Fiona lost count. "You were surprised that Clara was part of the Seven now. When do members typically change over?"

"Every twelve years. People apply but mainly the best and brightest are chosen by the previous Seven, one from each region. I just didn't think the time had come up so soon." Gaili glanced at the wall of pictures. "But no, I'm right. Clara is new. See there, there are eight portraits for this group."

A placard under a picture of a young fairy read, *Taliana, Garden - Retired.* "Seems there was a vacancy for her to fill."

Gaili sighed. "No wonder she didn't want me to bother her. She had moved on from teaching people like me. And rightly so. She's quite amazing."

"Gaili, if you praise her one more time, I very well may eat my scarf. She sounds abominable in how she treated you, and I won't be persuaded to think otherwise." Fiona pressed her lips together knowing she was being rude. Her friend couldn't see what she couldn't see. She smiled to soften her words. "I'm sorry. I simply want you to know she did wrong by you."

"I know you think differently, but if you knew her the way I did, you'd see."

"Perhaps," Fiona said gently. She had learned her lesson about being pushy with her friends when she had railed against Dodger and the Travel Guild. She wouldn't make that mistake again. "Come. Let's meet with this tour and get the information we came for."

Gaili nodded and motioned to a set of stairs leading up to the second floor. A ramp paralleled the circling staircase. Both ended on a landing closed off by large wooden double doors. They heard quiet voices within the room and opened the doors to see a group of travelers farther in the chamber. They each quickened their steps toward them. A couple were faekin, fauns and a fairy specifically, but others were the animal-like people from Kerus and a sole human woman. She had Fiona's height, but her coloring was pale and peach in comparison to Fiona's dark brown skin.

A centaur turned to them with a wide smile. His silky brown fur peeked through a tunic covering large parts of his body and a vest denoting the insignia of the Order of Seven, a bust with seven floating orbs around it. "Ah, latecomers. Well, bundle in, bundle in. You've missed the first floor, but there's still more to see."

The ladies nodded with apologies to the others, and the tour guide motioned to follow him.

"Unlike the first floor with its gallery of Seven members past and present, this floor holds curiosities of nature invented by the brightest of the Court. The ones in the middle are newer than the ones lining the walls. Between each set of wall displays is a door to the office of one of the Seven." He motioned to the wall of decorated doors beside him. Each was sandwiched by an alcove in which there was a pedestal and a glass case. A hanging lantern was set above each case so that the glow diffused golden light around the objects they held, setting a dramatic scene. "Thus, they may look upon the creations of this page and be reminded every day of who they protect and what is at stake should they be derelict in their duties."

"Are the Seven in there now?" Gaili asked, her gaze narrowing toward the door nearest her.

"Yes, can we meet them?" a skimmer asked with a grin.

"To my knowledge, no, but if you're lucky, perhaps one may surprise us."

Fiona thought with some mirth that would not be luck for her. She canvased the area. There were eight doors in all that she could see. She wandered toward a curiosity, a gem-studded bell, to get a better glance at the doors themselves. They were wooden with keyholes, decorated with large etchings, and each held a plaque with a name for one of the current Seven.

The gem-studded bell glinted in the flickering lights of the wall sconces, and Fiona peered in closer. It was a silver bell with a wooden handle. Inlaid were small pearls that looked practically identical to each other. While she didn't know a lot about pearls, she thought them usually unique. She shrugged, moving over to another door and another curiosity. This was a watch, or a very early incarnation of one. It wasn't egg shaped like her timepiece but was completely round, bulky and bronze in color. Instead of tin hands that ticked for hours and minutes, it used a sort of copper filigree. Fiona opened her own watch to check against it. The one in the display case seemed to be going backward.

"Should it be doing that?" she whispered to Gaili, who had come up beside her.

"It didn't used to," Gaili said with a frown, "but perhaps it wasn't tracking the time after all. Some of these are old pieces. This is perhaps sixty or so years old. It's one of Clara's inventions."

"She made a watch?" Fiona said incredulously.

"The first of its kind," Gaili said, a bit of awe in her voice.

Fiona twirled her own timepiece, wondering just how much of its design had come from this initial one. "I thought she was an alchemist, like you."

"Most high-achieving scholars dabble in different fields of study. Horology is her passion though. It's natural she'd create a portable mechanism to track time as well as study it."

Fiona glanced at it again, trying to understand what it may be tracking if not the standard Book time. Turners were hard pressed to know what time, day, or even season it was in various pages without a timekeeping device set to standard Book time. It could be night on Spine, timeless in Blaze, and morning in Kerus. Decades of work helmed by the Travel Guild went into coming up with a date and time system that the pages could agree on, tracking from the Inking of the Binder (the first recorded page turner) and Larrakane's pronouncement to present day.

The guide's voice rang out into the open room: "While most of the curiosities on this floor are worth seeing, and I'll allow you some time to look around, I must draw your attention to this one specifically. They have been unearthed recently as part of our, somewhat artistic, revival of the past. Back when we thought the world revolved around someone other than the Blessed Larrakane." He chuckled to himself. "They are beyond the best Copper has to offer and created before the Inking. *Before* the dawn of the Seven." He paused at the end of the hall, letting his words float toward the crowd.

"They didn't have those the last time I was here," Gaili said, her voice bright with curiosity.

Fiona raised a brow, a flush of heat on the back of her neck. She was always interested to hear about things before the Inking. Before the knowledge of other pages existed. Her curiosity rose and she stepped closer to the guide with Gaili.

"Made by the Summer Monarch in the Circle of Seasons, these crowns enable the wearer to become the embodiment of summer and all its changing nature. The wearer can control the temperature around them, heating up areas intensely. The fire wouldn't hurt them of course! They could shift a sunny day longer, manipulating the passage of time during the season. It was said that the Summer Monarch imbued them with some of her exuberant youth, allowing the wearer to feel and look in their prime. With the energy and speed as well." He winked and threw his hands with a practiced flourish toward the golden lit case, then pulled off a draped cloth unveiling them.

Gaili gasped, as did others in the crowd. They gathered round, circling the case while the guide took a step back smiling at his enraptured audience. Fiona followed over, straining to see with the rest. "What is the Circle of Seasons?"

"Oh," Gaili said as if she had momentarily forgotten Fiona was there. "The ruling fae before the Inking. Each of them possessed a season and could influence it when their time came. Well, the history goes deeper than that, but that's the essence of them."

"What happened to them after the Inking?"

"They disappeared and the Order of Seven was created."

Others moved out of the way one by one until Gaili and Fiona were closer to the case. It held circular bands of interwoven copper filigree with lemon and rose-gold drop-shaped gems set in tidy order around the band. There were four crowns in all. Fiona wasn't sure what she expected but was a little disappointed to see the bands didn't twinkle or dance with flames. Perhaps her week of hopping in and out of the fire page and seeing the miracle that was Soots in Guardian form dulled her senses to anything not as magnificent. She glanced at Gaili, whose face matched her own.

"Is it weird that I thought they might dance with fire?" Gaili whispered to Fiona.

"No, I had some of the same thoughts." It's possible they were just inert in the case, but Fiona made a mental note about the oddity. "Are they bolted?" Fiona asked the guide.

"Bolted?" He crinkled his nose.

"Yes, locked. To the pedestal. It seems extremely valuable to have on display."

He waved his hand, batting the notion away. "Ah, no. No one would dare steal from the Seven."

Either the guide was being obtuse, or he really didn't know. She moved closer to him. "Are you sure?" Fiona whispered, "I heard a rumor that the Pavilion was burglarized just this week for some paperwork."

Some of the guests listening in murmured to themselves in shocked conversation. Fiona noted that the faekin couple and the human woman did not.

"That was a minor event, and the guilty party has already been found and charged."

"But what about the paperwork?" Fiona said.

"I believe all the items have been retrieved as well." He turned, moving farther away from Fiona to lead the group around to another case.

If the rest of the Seven were as unconcerned as the guide, it would explain the lack of guards she had expected to find in the Pavilion. *Interesting.*

As the tour moved with him, the blonde human woman, slighter than Fiona but in an extravagant cap-sleeved amber gown and high collar, took a step back to walk in line with her, separating her a bit from Gaili. Her hair was capped by a bonnet that sparkled with gold. She nodded her head cordially. "How do you do? Mistress Sadie Stoneguard."

Fiona didn't want to give her real name to someone from her page who might instantly know all about her. Not until she had the lay of the land. So, she said the first alias she had ever used: "Mistress Fleur Oatfallow. Well, thank you."

Her smile brightened. "Wonderful to meet you then. I heard about the little scuffle that happened here as well."

This was interesting. If it got to Rise, then that would mean it was more important than expected. Fiona wondered if Stoneguard knew anything in particular and said, "Oof, the poor Seven. But their security seems to be lacking in some areas."

"Yes, they do seem to be paying less attention to the running of their page than other things. I wonder, have you heard what was taken?"

Fiona gazed intently at the woman. "Format has it as paperwork. Valuable paperwork at that. Who would want to spend their time stealing ledgers and numbers?"

"Who indeed? But that's all?" Stoneguard's question lingered.

Fiona was used to gossipy people. Page turners were the worst gossips imaginable. But gossips didn't get all their information from one source. "Do you know anything more about the theft?"

"Blessed Larrakane, no!" Stoneguard exclaimed, laughing a bit. "My guide suggested I take a tour of the Pavilion before meeting for dinner at the lodge." Stoneguard tilted her head. "I was hoping for a good bit of rumor to take back."

"Would your guide find the theft from the Pavilion amusing?"

"Quite," Stoneguard said, glancing off to the group. "We should catch up perhaps. Don't want to miss anything."

"Of course. We are here on sightseeing after all," Fiona said, smiling wide.

Stoneguard cleared her throat, nodded respectfully, and walked quickly to rejoin the group, not looking to see if Fiona followed. Perhaps she was just a lonely woman who saw someone who looked like her and wanted to connect. Fiona sighed. She did often see drama where there was none. She turned her attention back to the guide who was standing by the eighth door, which had no etchings on it like the others.

"The administrative offices are through here as well as meeting rooms. Nothing very surprising there, but this also takes us to the private open-air deck," he said, grinning and pushing the door open.

Fiona slowed her pace to match Gaili's and put her hand on her shoulder. "Let's slip away, shall we? No Seven means it'll be easier to scout the administrative offices. I'm curious as to why a person would steal paperwork when there are actual valuables with easy-to-fleece gems to pick up instead."

They walked through the eighth door at the tail end of the tour but continued down one of the halls and slipped around the corner as quick as they could. Luckily the floor here was carpeted, soaking up the noise of their shoes.

The rooms here were open with no doors to speak of on one wall and closed doors on another. "I suppose privacy for an administrator is unnecessary," Fiona commented.

She moved down the hall, but she could hear their skirts and Gaili rustling behind her. She cringed at the noise. Soon there was another sound to block out their movement: two people were clearly in a heated conversation from one of the Seven's chambers. Fiona listened at the door for a moment, motioning Gaili forward. It was muffled even with her ear pressed against it. As much as she wanted to know what they were saying, she reminded herself eavesdropping wasn't currently her mission and found the room they were looking for, named banner still hanging on the wall. Orsa's office.

It was a small room with a desk covered in papers, a chair, and scant of anything else. The treed walls grew to an apex ceiling and a dusty window sat as the only thing eye-catching in the place. "You keep watch and I will see what I can find."

Picking through the paperwork on the desk, Fiona saw nothing especially interesting. It was clear the desk hadn't been cleaned and looked as if someone had started work but not finished it. There was a small book of appointments tucked into a desk drawer. Flipping it open, she saw Orsa had many meetings with Dorin Glade. The last meeting was dated on Orsa's arrest. Another larger ledger held tasks requested of Dorin, many related to making arrangements for him. She paged through and noticed that if she flipped the book around and upside down there was another set of tasks for Clara Garden only. One lingered past the date of her arrest, with the last being tonight at the Crystal Chest. Fiona tucked them both into her scarf beneath her dress, feeling them disappear from her fingers. She could examine them later when there was more time.

"Fiona," Gaili whispered, backing up from the door, "I heard a door open. I think whoever's here is leaving."

"Well, we're at the end of the hall. There's no reason—" She cut off as voices got closer to them, not farther away. Why weren't they leaving? She looked around for someplace for her and Gaili to hide or go. The window was the only option. She ran to it and tried to throw open its double panes, but they resisted her, clearly unused.

"Gaili," she whispered, motioning to the window.

Clomping over, the faun pressed her hands against one side while Fiona pressed against the other. Though Gaili was petite, her looks belied the muscles of her arms detailing her smithing nature, and the stuck window edging cracked a bit before giving way and opening.

Gaili picked up the layers of her dress like an expert tailor checking the hem. She pulled herself through the window and landed on the deck gracefully.

Fiona picked up her own skirts, pressing them to her. She swung a leg out the window, wishing fervently that she was wearing her normal clothes. She pulled herself half out but felt a tug. The overdress Gaili'd lent her was caught on something.

Fiona groaned inwardly as the voices moved closer. She could rip it, leaving evidence behind, but she still might not manage to get through the window in time.

"I could—" Gaili started, but Fiona waved her off.

"Go and join the group," she whispered. No sense getting her in the bind along with herself. She swung her legs back over and stood up just in time to face the faekin entering the room.

They stopped in the doorway, fae and faun. The tall emerald-colored fae was dressed quite handsomely in a long verdant tunic over plum silken hose. His belt was decorated with stiches in dramatic style with small flourishes that contained glistening diamonds within the notches. They matched the ones pinned in his downy, floppy ears and the pin that tied his long honey-strawberry hair back behind his head. Though it was a typical warm end of day, he had a heavy plum velvet cloak trimmed in copper threads clasped to one shoulder. If it had been a book, the kind Fiona liked to read on breaks between cases, he would've been the dashing hero such authors wrote about.

Though the faun was shorter than him by only a foot, she didn't seem diminished standing beside him. Her horns, brown and curved toward the back of her head, were nestled within a fashionable crown of alabaster braids adorned with small grass-green gems that reflected the amber light streaming in from the window. A black lace scarf capped her hair, draping to her shoulders. She held herself upright, if not a bit haughtily, with her arms crossed over an expensive beaded velvet bodice and layers upon layers of velvet dress. She looked proud, perfect, and perturbed. Both their faces were adorned with more swirling silver and cream-colored tattoos than Fiona had ever seen in her life.

They seemed surprised to see her, and Fiona wondered if it was just her ill luck that drew them here or if they'd already been headed to Orsa's office. She smoothed down her dress, releasing the skirt on its snagged hem, then walked toward them and nodded cordially. Taking control of the situation was her best course of action. She placed a hand on her chest, "Oh, you startled me. I was trying to hide."

"Hide?" said the faun, lily-white eyebrows furrowing. The faun glanced at the fae, who looked curiously at Fiona. "Hide from whom?"

Fiona smiled as she lied, "The guide. He does prattle on."

"There are many other places to run to," the faun said. "Away from the Pavilion, for one." She advanced on Fiona. "What are you doing in here?"

Before she could answer, the fae broke in, no longer momentarily stunned, "That veil looks familiar."

This threw Fiona off. "It does?"

"It does?" the faun echoed.

"Are you perhaps Investigator Thorne?"

Fiona froze. She had never in all her days been recognized. It left her off kilter. Unable to recover quickly, she fell back on childhood mannerisms. "Why yes. How do you do?"

"Investigator?" the faun said, moving between the two. Her eyes narrowed. "Are you spying around in here?"

"I thought you looked familiar," the fae said, grinning and ignoring his companion.

She would not be ignored. She pulled his arm, and his attention snapped to her. "It doesn't matter that she looks *familiar*, Dorin. Do focus. We have an intruder coming in here to do no one knows what."

"I'm here to help you with your case, of course." Since the fae, Dorin, somehow recognized her, Fiona thought she might as well try the best tactic she had at her disposal: the truth.

Well, some of it.

"The theft of a valuable item from within these walls is highly suspicious," Fiona said, alluding in vague terms and hoping he would take the bait.

Before Dorin could speak, the faun glared at him and said, "That's *private* information. And details will not be confirmed to strangers. We don't require any help."

"The theft of paperwork or *curiosities...*" She let a pause linger before continuing, bubbling up her theory. "...unrecovered sounds like you may need help. I came here to offer my services as a consultant." She leaned in with a knowing tilt. Paperwork sounded light, and after looking at the curiosities, she suspected more than just that was taken.

"She's the one who helped the Guild with Blaze," Dorin said to the faun.

Fiona's confidence slipped. "I didn't help the Guild with anything. I did it with the fire denizens. Completely and wholly without their help." She thought Dodger would forgive her this one occasion on not singling him out.

"They said you walked around with an unfashionable scarf. Many colors and many pockets." Dorin stared at Fiona and shifted to look her up and down. "But you look taller in the sketch."

"Dorin, please quit entertaining this intruder's meaningless conversation."

"What sketch?" Fiona said at the same time. Larrakane save her, what was he talking about?

"If she's the Thorne woman, she could help us, Clara."

Clara! So, this was Gaili's old mentor. Fiona looked at the faun in a new light. Periwinkle eyes stared distrustfully at Fiona.

Fiona raised an eyebrow and shrugged lightly. "I'd be more than happy to help. It seems to me that others will figure it out soon enough. The crowns don't give off a hint of warmth, which most items imbued with elemental essence do. You haven't recovered them, otherwise the fakes would be replaced. So that means you don't know where to find them and the culprit you've arrested isn't talking. I can help with all that and retrieve them for you. If you hire me."

"I have it in hand with the wardens," Clara said. "You need to leave before I have you escorted out by them and charged with improper entry."

"I didn't break my way into anything. There are no doors here, and the tour guide will tell you I am part of the group." Fiona casually shifted to smile at Dorin. They'd been arguing or negotiating with each other before in that room. If she could get Dorin to believe in her, perhaps it would give her a way forward here. She would need more access if her guesses were right to uncover evidence freeing Orsa.

Dorin stood up straighter, his height towering over the ladies. "Prove to us you're really Thorne. Show us how the scarf works, and we can talk about it."

Fiona rubbed the edge of the scarf between her fingers. She knew it was unusual, and to expose how it worked to scholars like them might have them making other demands. But if she did acquiesce, how far would it get her in information about Orsa and the theft?

Clara countered, "She's a gawker, Dorin. Stop taking her seriously. We need to get Jacopo to escort her off the premises at once."

Fiona, thoroughly aggravated at not controlling the situation better, sighed and held the scarf out to Dorin. "Put your hand in the black velvet pocket."

Dorin glanced at Clara but put his hand forward, slipping it inside the scarf.

"Now think of gloves, soft leather, buttery to the touch. Dove-gray riding gloves."

He closed his eyes, his mouth pursed in concentration. He pulled his hand back quickly, shocked as a pair of gloves sat half in, half out of the scarf. Fiona tugged them the rest of the way out and held them out to Dorin, who took them tentatively. He rubbed them in his hand. "Marvelous. Simply marvelous. I've never seen anything like it."

Clara's mouth hung open, but she quickly closed it, her gaze intent on the scarf. Fiona had seen that look before and promptly pushed the scarf down her dress, tucking it away from the faun's sight. She didn't want to lose it again in this lifetime. Manners be blasted.

She leaned back on the desk, clasping her hands in front of her as the two Keepers' attention was captured. "Now, when would you like me to start?"

4

"NEVER," ANSWERED CLARA. SHE glared at Dorin. "As I said, we have it under control. The wardens are on it. Orsa is in jail and that's all you need to know. Thank you for your offer of services, but they aren't needed." She turned, creating a gap for Fiona to exit.

Dorin turned to Clara, face still shocked. "She already knows about the crowns and the paperwork. We might as well use her skills to look for them. At the very least agree with that."

Clara glowered. "I don't trust her."

Fiona moved slowly from the desk, weighing her options. Being dismissed was better than being arrested. But there was much here to dig into, and it would be easier if she had access to the Seven. She nodded. "The crowns seem quite powerful to be let out of your sight for long. I hope that the items are recovered in a timely manner before other people get wind of your vulnerabilities. Like the Travel Guild or the Painted Edge. Who knows what they may do." The leaders of the pages had been warned about the Painted Edge by now. With their success in smuggling fire creatures out of Blaze, stealing the fire artifact from Soots, and an airship from Restless Rise, they posed quite a menace. No one knew where they were hiding. Naturally people thought they were everywhere since the Guild hadn't yet found them. Perhaps the threat of them would have a better effect.

Dorin put up a hand, somehow standing even taller than before. "That won't do. As a Keeper of the Seven, I wield my power to do what's best for the page. It is in my right to hire you. And that I shall." He turned to Clara. "We have it under control, but a consultant won't hurt and will lighten the burden. I'll vouch for the investigator, and I know that will be quite enough for the others. Will it be for you?"

The faun said nothing, pursing her lips. Staring daggers at Fiona, she slowly nodded.

She wasn't going to be easy to work with after this turn of events. Not that she would have been easy in the first place.

Dorin's shoulders sagged, but he smiled wide at Fiona. "I'm happy to give you my time today, Investigator, but I believe my colleague will be late for dinner soon."

Without a word, the faun turned and stalked out of the room. Fiona said a quick blessing to Larrakane that she didn't run smack into Gaili. She wanted to stand good on her word and protect her friend should that occur.

"Forgive Keeper Clara. She's apprehensive about outsiders when it comes to Order business, and she's heading a large project at the moment. She feels she can't trust anyone but the Seven with most things. Finding out Steward Orsa stole from us was a shock to her as much as to me."

"But she worked for you, yes?" Fiona said, sitting properly in one of the chairs.

He nodded, his eyes bright, and sat in the other. "You do know the half of it. I'm sure you won't divulge your sources, but I hope this doesn't get to that cursed Painted Edge. Or the Guild. We were very clear that only the paperwork had been stolen to maintain control of the story."

Fiona understood that completely. Once a story set in, that became the format moving forward. "My lips are sealed, but let it be understood I only heard paperwork as well. I noticed a few things on my tour, however, that had me questioning the information. The crowns, as I noted, seemed off. It may just be my experience talking there, but it did niggle at me, and others may wonder too."

His eyes appraised her. "Yes, your intuition on that accord didn't deceive you."

Glad to have her hunch confirmed, she said, "But I wonder, do you believe Orsa did it?"

Dorin sighed, leaning back against a plush pillow. If Fiona hadn't been paying attention, she wouldn't have noticed one of his willowy ears move as if listening for other sounds. Once it came back to its original position, he said, "No. No, I do not. Orsa was—*is* more than an administrator. She's a friend to me. A valued one at that. She even granted us the right to search her home, which turned up nothing, of course. I've been distressed about what to do next. If I should find help for her or focus the Seven on retrieving the Summer Crowns. With you hired, I get to do one while hiding the other." He seemed to smirk at that, but his mood shifted and he frowned. "But if you're here with an agenda different than finding the missing artifacts, I will use the full press of this page to reprimand and ban you. Is that clear?"

Fiona nodded, a little surprised by the whiplash of his feelings. She could understand him being upset about Orsa, but the threat seemed a little much. Was he truly that worried, or was something else at play? "I assure you, my intentions are true." And aligned, although she thought it best to keep that to herself for the time being.

"Good. I would ask for your promise but that seems archaically impolite these days." He clapped his hands, all charm and grace once again, like a new fashion being thrown on quickly. "I'll have one of our stewards be your guide while in the page and—"

She rose and inclined her head in politeness keeping her questions about archaic promises to herself. "That won't be necessary. I have my own guide as it were. Can I return tomorrow to talk to you more and the other Seven? I should like to start promptly in the morning."

"Of course. I'll alert Jacopo—he's the front guard—and the others to your inquiry and ask they comply with your questions. But as far as getting real answers out of them, I can't force anyone, bound as the Keepers are to each other. You'll have to do your part."

"Of course." Fiona moved to the door with purposeful grace, trying to seem as confident as she could. "Thank you for your time." She wanted to discuss payment but didn't want to tread on Dorin's patience any longer than necessary today. She knew when the fickle nature of luck was on her side.

She headed down the hallway glancing in the open rooms to remember the layout of the floor and out to the open-air deck. The copper sky now deepened and dark held above like a veil over the tree tops. Small lantern lights twinkled in the branches and the outline of the deck, diffusing amber light like a shower around her. Such wonders like this weren't in every page of the Book. The unique feel that one got in the Court of Copper made her heady and light despite her reservations about the case, and the state of her world in general.

She didn't see Gaili, however, and was just about to turn around when she heard a light whisper: "Fi, Over here."

Fiona peered through the trees to spot Gaili sitting on a branch high above the deck. "Whatever are you doing up there?"

"I saw Clara come out to the deck. The rest of the skimmers had gone, and I don't know. I fled up here before she could spot me."

"I'm so sorry I wasn't here to intercede."

"It's alright," Gaili said, swinging from the branch back onto the deck with more grace than Fiona thought was possible in her dress. "It helped a little to see her from afar. Now if I run into her, I will probably just stammer instead of running away."

Fiona clasped her friend's shoulder, squeezing it gently. "Well, I shall bear the brunt of her personality for you if that time comes. Although I do hope you'll come back with me tomorrow."

Gaili's eyes went wide. "Why?"

"I've been hired by the Seven to investigate the missing crowns and paperwork. So I'll have to interview her and the other Keepers."

"Hired by the Seven? Do be serious, Fiona. They wouldn't hire outsiders."

"No, I thought that too. But I believe they won't hire Guild. And I'm very clearly not." And perhaps Dorin thought that gave him an ally of a sort in this mess. She wasn't quite sure if he was truthful about his intention or not. "In either case, our thoughts about the crowns paid off. They are fakes." She moved to the edge of the deck and back down into the Pavilion.

"Oh!" Gaili said, hand flying to her mouth. "That makes so much more sense. But you're to retrieve them?"

"If we can. And doing so will help us prove it was or wasn't Orsa who stole them. If Clara doesn't become a stubborn obstacle. She tried to block my investigation."

"Clara won't like that you're coming in without her approval," Gaili said as they ambled down the stone path. "Once she's set her mind on something, it's hard to get her past it."

"Yes, and I have an inkling she's not changed much since you left her. She left almost right on the time you said she would for dinner. Speaking of, I'm curious as to the woman who introduced herself to me today."

"The Stoneguard lady? She seemed intent in talking with you a great deal."

Fiona nodded, pleased Gaili had been listening in. "Yes, and I can't shake the feeling she may know something. Odd that she would hear about it when the Seven worked so hard to keep it hush. She mentioned having a very good guide and a dinner date at the lodge. Clara had to make a dinner as well, and it just so happens Orsa's appointment notes it's for a Crystal Chest."

"You think they're eating together? Why would they know each other?"

"I've learned that coincidences are few and far between. How do you feel about a bite to eat? My treat if you show the way." Fiona locked her arm in Gaili's.

Gaili nodded and gave one last lingering look to the Pavilion before leading Fiona back down the lamplit path.

They clambered into a brightly colored ferry with a few other passengers to travel to Calistino's main square. The sound of lapping waves served as a pleasant backdrop for the smooth journey helmed by a clearly experienced faun boatsman. Gaili had known the way on foot after that, although she couldn't believe they were going to such a premier restaurant dressed as they were. But Fiona didn't want to go home and change yet again. She couldn't bear the thought of evening dress. Besides, she had met Stoneguard in this outfit, and she'd leave it to making a hurried dinner date as an excuse. She did remove her many-pocketed scarf, however, slipping it comfortably around her waist inside her dress and hoping she wouldn't need it.

The path wound its way through thin streets besieged by copper water on one side and high cream-colored stone and vine-decorated buildings on the other. They passed the massive domed marble temple to Larrakane, faekin streaming in for services, more celebratory than what was seen as worship in Rise or Kerus. But at the end was the jewel that they sought: the Crystal Chest, with its rippling stained glass walls like a see-through treasure box. The Court of Copper produced most of the glass in the Book and used that to trade for items they couldn't create, such as coffee from Rise or luxurious silk from Kerus. The trade was booming, more so than it had been in the early days of the Inking, and places such as the Crystal Chest was a showcase of what Copper had to offer.

They entered a pleasant entryway; soft amethyst oil lamps hung on the walls, and lush deep-green velvet benches were arranged beneath them for any waiting parties. They were liberated of their cloaks by the server and directed toward the stately dining room. Tables dotted the floor with groups of fauns, fairies, and other like people sitting in groups. Intimate tables were toward the back where couples sat among the finery of the blush tablecloths and glass walls. Those who needed a bit more room with centaurs in the party were shown to carefully set places on an open patio. Somehow the lodge made those places seem superior. A delicate balancing act with the varied clientele, Fiona didn't doubt. She wondered how adding skimmers such as humans and elephas from other pages into the mix worked.

Glancing around, Fiona recognized Stoneguard at a table with her back against the wall next to a fireplace. She wasn't alone; a smaller faun sat next to her in elaborate purple satin dress. It was not Clara, which deflated Fiona's suspicions.

Seeming to notice she was being watched, Stoneguard's eyes met Fiona's and shuttered as she frowned.

The unexpected reaction energized Fiona to continue on despite the lack of Clara, and she tugged Gaili over to the table. "Mistress Stoneguard, yes? Mistress Oatfallow from the Pavilion. Isn't this a coincidence! I was just talking to my guide about having a sumptuous dinner, and she brought me here."

"Well, yes," Stoneguard started. She seemed flustered, her peach skin showing a glistening sheen.

Before she could continue, the smaller faun jumped up and grasped on to Gaili exclaiming, "Gails!" Hugging her tightly, the faun said, "As I live by Larrakane's light, I thought to never see you in these parts again."

"Matteo," Gaili said, surprised and bowled over by the vigorous hugging. "What are you doing out of the Garden? I thought you vowed never to be among the skimmers."

"Yes, well, duty called," he said, readjusting his dress now that he had let her go. He motioned his head to Stoneguard. "And duty must be followed. But sit, tell me of your wonderful life as turner." He grinned at Stoneguard and Fiona. "Gails is an old mate of mine from when we were kids. I do hope you don't mind, madam." He didn't wait for a word from Stoneguard but pulled a couple of chairs from a nearby table, waving off the manager and hosts running over. "Two more places, please."

He commanded the chairs, the staff, and Stoneguard with an ease that impressed Fiona. She couldn't have asked for a better invite herself and sat without any argument. After giving food orders to the server, she turned to Matteo and said. "I've never met a friend of Gaili's."

"Well, don't trouble yourself with the others. I'm the best one." He laughed and clapped Gaili on the back.

Gaili shook her head, pink blossom curls bouncing as she laughed along. "And the most mischievous. You're looking quite elegant. That dress becomes you really. Do tell, what are you doing now?"

"I'm a guide to some and a mapper to others. I roam picking up notes and jotting down descriptions of where I go."

"A cartographer?" Fiona asked. Most of the cartographers, or spotters as she had learned of them, were page turners. She didn't know of any who were pulp. She leaned in, intrigued.

"Yes, if we're being official. But only for where I have a mind to go."

"Unless you're on duty," Stoneguard said stiffly.

He turned around, including her in the wider circle of the table. "Of course, madam." He smiled but his eyes narrowed.

Fiona sensed the current of tension between the two. As much as she wanted to talk to Matteo and get to know more about his work and connection to Gaili, her curiosity about Stoneguard's reaction to her drove her to focus on the lady instead. She turned to Stoneguard. "So, what did you discover? Is the missing paperwork an act of a jealous rival or an angry assistant?"

"I'm not sure what you mean," the woman said evasively and took a sip from a tall goblet of wine.

"I thought your guide wanted a good bit of rumor to laugh at about the Pavilion theft?" Fiona inclined her head to Matteo.

"Ah, yes, well, it was discussed for a minute, but there were other matters to spend my valuable time on." She took another sip of wine.

For someone who had earlier been so talkative, Stoneguard was giving off the impression of being quite put out at seeing her again. Fiona nodded slowly, assessing the perspiring woman. There was something off, but she couldn't place it. Perhaps a more delicate advance was needed. "Do you travel often to Copper?" Fiona said in her human tongue, Schiflan. Matteo and Gaili were talking quietly to themselves, and she wanted to press without being heard.

Stoneguard hesitated but responded in kind. Her Schiflan accent deepened with a quality matching Fiona's. "No, never before actually. Simply some sightseeing, the theater, and a small holiday before I go back home."

"Having a cartographer as a guide must give you a bit of an advantage when it comes to sightseeing," Fiona said, smiling and trying to relax the woman. She could understand the trepidation, but she wanted to assure her they could talk as equals.

Stoneguard nodded but said no more, so Fiona tried again with a friendly overture: "Where are you from within Rise?"

"The Plateau actually. I've lived most of my life in Three Churches," said Stoneguard shifting away from Fiona. She rubbed the lip of her wineglass.

So, she *was* within the nobility then. Perhaps the same as Fiona's family. She had the air of a gentlewoman. "A beautiful city," Fiona said, watching carefully for how Stoneguard would react. While the Plateau was the center of Rise, Three Churches was a large city on it thick with people, noise, and discarded temples of the old religions. *Beautiful* was perhaps a word an outsider might use if they'd never visited before.

"For some," Stoneguard said with a small smile.

Fiona couldn't tell if Stoneguard was toying with her or if she was just off her game. Seeing that this wasn't getting her any further, she took a conversational step back. "I wonder who else on Rise has heard about the Order of Seven's troubles if you know of it."

"I'm sure many people. You know how page turners gossip."

Fiona bridled at the assertion, however true it was.

Before she could respond, Stoneguard rose. "If you'll excuse me."

Fiona nodded. "Of course." She frowned as she watched Stoneguard move away from the table without glancing back.

Her instinct said to follow. She tried to ignore it, but after a moment she rose herself. "I will be back in a moment. Simply looking for a privy." She moved in the direction that Stoneguard had gone, nodding politely to the owner and a young faun as she went. Why had she run off so quickly? It was as if she couldn't stand to continue talking to Fiona a moment more.

Fiona turned past the entrance, moving aside quickly to avoid bumping into another faun coming from the lone hallway in that direction. She padded softly down the amethyst-lit hall but saw quickly it would lead to a dead end. Doors to a privy were to one side. She listened for any sounds but, hearing nothing, went to the first one and opened it. It was completely empty save the modernized and, thankfully, fast becoming common box seats, bowl, and pitcher. Fiona went to another and knocked softly before opening it to find it empty as well.

She shut the door behind her and rested her back against the wall, closing her eyes. It was as if Stoneguard had disappeared into thin air. Regardless of the innate abilities of some faekin, even that was impossible. She probably had gone out the entrance to get some air from the hot dining room.

Shaking her head, Fiona went to the basin and poured cool water from the pitcher. The metallic sheen of the copper reflected her brown pinched face and she hurriedly dipped her hands in to swirl it away. She appreciated the Court's high thrumming about cleanliness and aesthetics. While her native page didn't have such modern amenities, she was glad there was a source to bring them into her home on Spine so she could enjoy the luxuries herself. Feeling a bit more in control, she made her way down the hall and back to the table. As she approached, Fiona noticed Stoneguard's bag that had looped onto her belt had fallen to the floor at some point.

"Are you looking for secrets?" Matteo said jovially nodding as the server approached with food.

She groaned internally but kept her face unconcerned. "Oh? Whatever could you mean?"

He waited until the server departed and then turned towards Fiona. "I thought you looked familiar," Matteo said good naturedly. "A friend of Gail's is nice but to dine with a famous investigator, it is a pleasure."

"You must've seen me earlier at the library in the city." She sat as a server unfolded a napkin and draped it in her lap. She thanked him and waited till he walked away before saying, "Or at least that's the format I'd appreciate people to know about Mistress Fleur Oatfallow, should anyone ask. I have a deep and abiding love for rare books." She gave a direct look to him and then to Gaili.

Matteo took a moment, glancing between the two, then nodded. "Yes, yes. Gails was recounting your trip so far. Well, well. The Book is thin, as they say, no?" He smiled and picked up his mug for a drink.

Fiona smiled back but declined to offer more information. She would need to move a bit in the Court if she was to work for the Seven and for Orsa. She would get information about Matteo from Gaili and instruct her on how to keep a cover at the same time.

Glancing about to see if the woman was returning yet, she slid her napkin to the floor. "Oops," she said before diving under the table and to Stoneguard's bag. She opened it quickly and thumbed through the contents to get a true sense of the beguiling woman. Besides a set of soft leather gloves, a small cache of papers, and travel writing utensils, there wasn't much else.

Disheartened by the lack of anything scandalous, Fiona grabbed her napkin and tucked the bag back where it was. It was heavier than it looked, and the back of it was thick and more solid than the rest of the bag. She felt quickly around the lining within and ran her thumb across a tiny button. She heard Gaili say her name questioningly.

"Just got my dress caught on something. No worries, I'm untangling."

Fiona flicked the button to reveal a hidden compartment inside the lining of the bag. A sheathed dagger with a pearl handle nestled next to a black stack of cards. Well, well, so Stoneguard *was* more than she seemed.

Slippered feet approached the table, and Fiona heard Stoneguard saying, "I simply must dine here again. The service is impeccable and the amenities quite nice."

Fiona slipped a black card in her dress, wishing she had her scarf about her neck. With any luck the card would stay. She grabbed her napkin, closed the bag, and reemerged from under the table. "Black napkins and black flooring do not go well together." She sat giving a big smile to everyone as the server placed a new napkin on her lap.

Stoneguard smiled at Fiona. "Did you find everything you needed?"

Fiona tore a hunk of bread in half and nodded, trying to hide her guilt. There was no possibility Stoneguard saw her. She assessed the woman. Her perspiration was gone, and she seemed much happier than before. The curls wrapped around her head appeared refreshed too. Had she simply found a room to tidy up in that Fiona missed?

"The owner was kind enough to share information about the play at the new theater being built here," Stoneguard said jovially. "I'm settled on attending! *The Blue Bird.* Have you heard of it?"

Slightly taken aback to being easily addressed by Stoneguard, Fiona resisted the urge to show her suspicion. Now she was as talkative as this afternoon. Why the sudden change?

"We saw posters for that show on the way to the Pavilion," Gaili said, holding her fork gingerly. "I've heard it's quite elaborate."

"Yes, but I haven't seen it," Fiona said.

"I do so love the theater. I've gotten special seats at the new venue for opening night. If you can manage, I suggest you go. You might find it surprising."

"I would enjoy it very much. Perhaps I could purchase on the night that you go?" She knew it was a bold suggestion, but it was clear Stoneguard was playing some sort of game with her now, and it would be a good way to see her again.

Stoneguard smiled wide and said, "I'd be happy to have you as my guest if you'd like to join me."

"That would be delightful." Fiona took a sip of wine to hide her surprise. She had expected at least some back-and-forth. Off balance, she said, "I thank you for the offer. What night shall I mark?"

"The end of the week. It'll be the first time the theater will have a show. I've heard it'll be a full house and expect the actors will put on their best performances."

"Excellent. It's settled then."

Stoneguard picked up her glass. "Let us give a toast to burgeoning friendships over art and theater."

Fiona clinked her goblet and drank from it deeply. Stoneguard did as well, watching Fiona over the rim of hers. Fiona felt uncomfortable but wasn't sure what to do. Everything she had thrown at the woman had been countered or matched. Was she dangerous? The dagger suggested she could be. She let out a small sigh. She wasn't quite sure she was in control of the situation. She needed to regroup and assess. "I am starting to feel a bit tired from all of today's travels. I think I may need to make it an early night."

"Going so soon? Dinner has really begun now," Stoneguard said, grinning.

"I know it's a trifle inexcusable, but it's been quite the day." Fiona pressed her fingers to her temple and winced to go with her change in demeanor. "I look forward to our next meeting." She bid her good night with a polite nod and Matteo with a warm smile.

Gaili rose and hugged Matteo tight. "It was good to see you."

"I hope there will be more to see in the future. Don't be a stranger, my friend."

They picked up their things and moved to the entrance, paying their bill and then departing.

They left the lodge, the sounds of cutlery on plates and soft babbling fading behind them as they walked in the brisk air. Fiona linked arms with Gaili and leaned into her. "There's something about Stoneguard that truly confuses me."

Gaili stopped walking. "What do you mean? Did something happen?"

"I followed her to the privy but she disappeared." Fiona tugged gently on her friend to keep moving should anyone be watching them. "I did a little digging and found a weapon and this in a secret compartment in her purse." She produced the black card from her scarf. It was simple linen, smooth, and empty front to back. She showed it to Gaili, who didn't recognize it, before tucking it back into her scarf. "And then when I thought that was odd enough, she came back all friendly. If I didn't know any better I would say she was baiting me on purpose."

Gaili pursed her lips. "What do you think it means?"

"I don't know," Fiona murmured, pushing back a loose curl from her head. Without her scarf-as-veil, her curls were almost wild. "She may be putting on a front, possibly. Maybe she's looking into the theft at the Pavilion as well. She could be working for the Queen. But I don't know. Her accent isn't quite right."

"Her accent?"

"If that woman is a noble from the Plateau, then I'm blasted Larrakane herself," Fiona scoffed. "I've practiced for years to sound like my betters, and she matched me note for note. I'm not sure where she's from in Rise, but noble she is certainly not. I'm not sure how she's connected or why she was so interested in talking to us before."

"To you," Gaili said. "She barely acknowledged I was there both times."

Fiona shook out her wandering mind and focused on her friend. "Sorry for not introducing you properly. I got a bit sidetracked with Stoneguard. I shouldn't have let her go on thinking you were just my guide, but it is a good cover. And a good cover is worth quite a bit in this line of work." Gaili shrugged, but Fiona grabbed her around the shoulder, pulling her close into a side hug. "When it's a real introduction, I'll do it correctly. Mistress of Mortar, Keeper of Potions, Ruler of Cakes, Gaili—" She stopped and frowned. "Gaili, what is your family name? I never asked before."

"Gaili Pannete. My parents are bakers."

"Do they live around here?"

She shook her head. "In the southern region. Grove."

"Have you missed them?"

"Not as much as I thought I would. It's a little like being at the academy honestly. I've been under my mentorship a while away from them. This isn't that different." At the mention of her mentorship with Clara, her golden face grew taut.

"Matteo seemed lovely." Fiona changed the subject to lighten the mood. She tilted her head lightly. "Were you two ever interested in each other?"

Though the copper sky was dark and the lamplights casting shadows as much as light, Fiona saw Gaili give a rare eyeroll at her question. "Of course not. I was too busy with my studies."

She knew all about being too busy to have a romantic life. No one she had fancied in her early twenties would deal with her desire to work as she did. So her mother had warned her often. After a few years she simply stopped daydreaming about marriage all together. "Perhaps now the timing is better? We shall have to keep in touch with him during our case."

"Your case," Gaili corrected, shaking her head.

Fiona tutted lightly as they walked back to the pagemark to return to Spine. "We'll see."

THE NEXT DAY BROUGHT renewed energy to Fiona, and she barely showed her displeasure at dressing for Copper again. Gaili was right that dressing the part had helped Fiona succeed a bit yesterday. Plus, if she did it without Gaili's insistence, she could damage her own clothes without hesitation. She kept her scarf tied from her shoulder and across her chest for easier access but discreetness. Now that Dorin had recognized it, she was a bit worried others would as well.

After sleeping on the events of yesterday, Fiona decided that while she didn't know who Stoneguard was, she did know someone who was good at getting information in short order.

"I think a quick letter with a few questions would work. Any appends on a note to the captain?"

Gaili's eyes lit up. "Captain? Do you mean Henrietta?" Pirate, coffee smuggler, and a new connection for Fiona and Gaili, she had helped tremendously the last time they needed to know how things fared outside their purview. And although Fiona didn't exactly condone criminal activity, it was hard not to find someone who loved coffee as much as Fiona did a bit endearing.

Fiona's curiosity rose at Gaili's excited tone. "Yes, I think she would be our best bet and more. She could look into some records for us. If Stoneguard is working for the Queen of Rise, then we'll know if we can trust her or avoid her."

"Give me five minutes and I can have a letter written to go with yours."

Fiona raised an eyebrow but nodded. She needed to get a move on herself if they had any hope of getting to the Pavilion before it opened to the public. She could tease Gaili about her blushing later.

Two letters, black square included, and a courier visit later, they were off to the Court of Copper and the Pavilion. Jacopo, the faun guard from yesterday, was just opening the doors and greeted them with a tight-lipped smile. "Well, I suppose I fell for your shenanigans once, but I won't fall for them again."

Fiona's cheeks burned. "I'm sorry to have deceived you."

"That's not the part that makes me mad. It's the part where the old firecracker came and yelled at me for letting you in at all. I told her about you, miss, but she said she didn't even see you."

Gaili bowed her head. "Apologies. We didn't mean to get you in a bind."

He waved them off. "Don't bother making up more things. And I'm not letting you in."

"But we do have an appointment to be here this morning," Fiona said, voice pitching and making her wince in embarrassment. "Keeper Dorin directed us."

"Oh sure. I'm not falling for that again."

Fiona looked at Gaili for assistance, but Gaili was staring past him toward a figure in the doorway.

Clara had come swanning out of the Pavilion, satin blush skirt swirling at her feet. She stopped and threw a velvet cloak trimmed with minute roses over her shoulders before scowling in their direction and marring her previously lovely appearance. "As I live—what are you doing back here?"

"I-I'm guiding Fiona," Gaili said quietly.

"Fallen to a guide now, have you? What a disappointment." She tutted, flouncing past Jacopo and dismissing them.

Gaili looked like all the wind had been sucked out of her and took a step back.

Fiona rounded on Clara, getting in her path. "Excuse me. But Gaili runs a very successful shop on Spine and is the best the artisan district has to offer."

"Well then, they must not offer much," Clara said, looking past her to Gaili. "If this is some attempt to get back into my good graces, Gaili, it will not."

"It's... I mean, I'm not trying—"

"Good," Clara said, cutting her off. She motioned to Jacopo. "Please see that the *investigator* only talks to the Seven and no one else. Do not let them out of your sight. If there are any issues, report them to Cascade."

"I can speak to whomever I like," Fiona said, staring directly at Clara. Though she felt hot, the impractical dress of the Court not helping matters, she ignored the flush of heat. Narrowing her gaze at the abominable woman, she said, "And you will treat Gaili with more respect."

"The girl who couldn't follow direction if her life depended on it? Who is squandering a blessing not even earned? I think not. Teaching people like her was holding me back. I don't need to apologize for telling her the truth of her situation. As her mentor, it's kinder than pretending she still has a place in my world." Clara turned and sauntered away from the Pavilion.

Fiona put her arms around Gaili, who was shaking. "You know what? This isn't worth it. We can drop this and go home. I'm sorry, I never expected her to be so cruel."

"She wasn't cruel," Gaili said as tears slipped down her face. "She's right. She taught me everything I know and I'm terrible at following direction."

"Absolutely not. Don't you dare agree with her."

"It's not your fault. You don't understand, Fi."

Jacopo cleared his throat and handed Gaili a handkerchief. She took it, dabbing her rose eyes. "Sorry for the display."

"No need to apologize. I've been working here long enough to know how she is." Jacopo rubbed his face. "Sorry I was so rough with you two earlier. That one's negativity leaches out to everyone else. Happy to escort you around to talk to the Seven. I didn't realize you were here because of the missing paperwork. If it helps Steward Orsa, I'm all for it."

"Did you know her well?" said Fiona.

"Not a lot, no. But she was always sweet to me and those she worked with. She had seen a lot in her life and she could still find some optimism to show." Jacopo looked over his shoulder and then whispered, "Unlike firecracker over there."

Gaili snorted, very unlike herself.

It made Fiona smile. She grasped Gaili's wrist. "What would you like to do?"

Gaili straightened her shoulders and gave a small smile. "Thank you, Jacopo, an escort would be nice."

He nodded his head and opened the door to the Pavilion. They climbed up the stairs and followed him inside, where he shut the door and locked it quietly, keys jangling from his belt.

"Which one do you want to start with?" Jacopo said.

"Tell me a bit about them, if you will, and then I can determine from there," Fiona said.

Jacopo tossed his head side to side, short cropped hair hiding and unhiding his horns. "Well, Dorin is the eldest, most established Keeper. Comes from Glade. He's very nice. Remembers all the staff names and, even before he was a Seven, used to visit with the older members of the Seven and consult with them. Cascade can be...prickly, but only if you're in the way of her achieving something she desires, I've noticed. Her full name is Rushing Water That Does Not Break Upon the Rocks, so take from that what you will. Sofia is a hard worker, always here late after coming in early, that sort of thing. Very nice as well."

They crossed to the second-floor landing and Jacopo lowered his voice. "Olea is pretty quiet, a bit uncharacteristic perhaps but doesn't bother me any. She uncovers most of the artifacts we display here. Dragomir is fairly straightforward sort of person, if a bit unemotional. Bardo is gone on a mathematical study to the Depths, so he's not available, but he can be reached if necessary. The only thing I caution is to not mention one to the other. They fight constantly." He shook his head. "You'd think the war never ended with those two."

Fiona nodded her head, trying to pull apart the implications. Jacopo was being quite nice to them, and she didn't want him to put his guard up by asking too much of him. She looked at Gaili with a raised brow.

Gaili tucked her hair behind her ear. "The centaur-fairy war. Some people just never let up."

"Of course," Fiona said, making a mental note to ask more about it later. "After the headache that graced us in twirling skirts this morning, why don't we start with whoever is already here?"

He nodded and walked over to a door that had a large engraving of a grove of various trees populated with apples and pears on it. Knocking quietly, he said, "Keeper Sofia? It's Jacopo with a couple of visitors." He motioned Fiona and Gaili forward as something clattered loudly to a hard wooden surface.

The door opened and a tall golden black-horned faun, curled hazel tattoos on the cheekbones that connected to the corners of her eyes with the largest goggles Fiona had ever seen, stopped before colliding into her. She looked down and saw that Sofia's eyes were magnified behind the glasses rather big and blinking rapidly.

"Oh," she said, mouth agape, "who are you?"

"I'm Fiona Thorne and this is my partner Gaili Pannete. We've come to ask you a few questions about the missing paperwork," Fiona said, stressing the word. "At Keeper Dorin's bequest."

"Oh," Sofia repeated. She looked back at a wooden table in the middle of the room. Fiona's gaze naturally followed to see large cylinders, about the size of a woman's belt, laid out on the table along with a burning pot of oil, a goblet, and a platter of dried sunflowers. A perplexing mix. "Come in."

"Thank you, Jacopo," Gaili said as she and Fiona traipsed inside and their attendant returned to his post.

Sofia closed the door and stood near it still wearing the goggles. She didn't say anything, so Fiona moved toward an empty chair and sat. "If I can ask you a few questions, we can leave you be and let you get back to your work." She motioned to the table.

That seemed to rouse Sofia. She started to work on the contraption again. "Go ahead."

"What did you think of Orsa?" Fiona asked first. If she could get a sense of who Sofia was, she would know which way to go about more sensitive subjects.

"She seemed nice enough. She didn't chat with me often, per se. The other stewards have been here for a while, so I suppose I know them better. And since she wasn't my steward, she didn't support me or my studies."

Gaili's brow furrowed, and Fiona took that as a question. "Was it odd that she didn't gravitate to you?"

"I suppose so. Fauns typically stick together, for better or worse. Of course, Clara probably had a hand in it."

"Does she have a hand in most things?" Fiona said.

Sofia looked up, eyes blinking behind the big glasses. "Everything if you leave it up to her," she said tersely.

It sounded no real love was lost between the fauns of the Seven then. "Were you here when the crowns were stolen?"

"I thought you said paperwork."

"That too."

"Dorin shouldn't have told an outsider about the crowns."

"He didn't. It was easy to tell something was amiss on my tour here."

"How?"

"I've a great deal of familiarity with elemental fire. I would've expected those crowns to give off some warmth."

Sofia removed her goggles. "They did. Smart of you to have noticed. They gave off quite a bit of warmth when they were first removed from the chests. It started to wane, but it was still fairly strong."

"They started fading?" Gaili said, speaking up for the first time. "I would think with the Summer Monarch's power that would be impossible."

"Yes, that's what I thought too, but I suppose with the Summer Monarch gone and a new one not born yet, the power in them is more malleable."

"What else could the crowns do?" Fiona asked.

Sofia bit her lip. "I don't see how that information will help you find them."

"I don't see how it wouldn't," Fiona said. "If we know of any other properties, we could narrow down what they could most likely be used for, hopefully leading us to them. The guide said they had the power to enable the wearer to become the embodiment of that season, control the temperature around them, shift a sunny day longer, etc. Is that true or simply marketing?"

"The Summer Crowns could allow someone to do that naturally. Let the light linger, shift darkness, that sort of thing."

"How long did you have to study the crowns?"

"About a day before they were stolen. Olea unveiled them from the chest she uncovered, and I won the right to study them first."

"Is that where you got the idea for what you're building? Can that do the same thing as the Summer Crowns?" Fiona said.

"What do you mean?"

. "It's got some of the shape of the crowns, the copper metal, although you're using gold currently." She'd have to have seen the crowns in person enough to be able to recreate whatever they did.

Sofia planted herself in front of her contraption, crossing her arms. "I think I've answered enough of your questions for the time being. My work is not for evaluation."

She'd hit a nerve with that one. Because it was nosy of her work or because Sofia was hiding something, Fiona couldn't quite figure out yet. "If you think of anything relevant, do let us know," she said.

"Why don't you talk to Cascade if you're worried about the crowns? It's most likely she had a hand in it. She's the only one who seems unconcerned about their disappearance. And she's always looking to try out something new. A theft of this caliber would be perfect for her."

Interesting accusation. Fiona nodded politely and withdrew. It might work best to let Gaili do the talking with Sofia in the future if needed. Gaili's gaze lingered. She clearly wanted to ask more questions, but Fiona ushered her out of the room, mouthing "Later."

* * *

Jacopo led them farther down the echoing chamber to a door with the emblem of a large hearth etched into it. Instead of knocking as she expected, he threw open the door. Gaili gasped a little. Fiona peered around the corner, curious.

A coral-peach young woman stood in the office in the barest of silken dresses. Though colorful in its sunflower and azure threads, it was the most fashion-forward ensemble Fiona had ever seen in the Book. Her arms were bare without the added tied sleeves that were normally attached, and her golden tattoos shown prominently over them. Her inky hair was slicked back and when she turned suddenly to face the trio, a large swirl pendant around her throat swayed shaking copper liquid. It seemed to subtly glow gray across her dewy skin. Curled golden tattoos adorned her cheekbones and connected to the corners of her eyes as intricate as the other Order members. Her toes dug into the sand that covered the floor in small tan mounds as she flowed toward them. "Oh, I've been caught out," she said, face bright with her hand shoved up to her elbow in a pot of some sort.

Fiona's eyes shot up at her choice of words, and she gravitated toward the nymph. "Doing what?"

"Experimenting," Cascade said simply. She pulled out her hand, which was being held on to tightly to by a slippery eel. It bit at her finger as she pulled it off, but she cradled it to her chest, ignoring the writhing of the creature in her hands. "You're new."

Jacopo closed the door behind them quietly, making his exit.

"Yes," Fiona said. "I'm asking a few questions about the day the Summer Crowns were taken."

Cascade pouted. "Boring. I already talked about those once before. Let's do something new."

Fiona cocked her head. "But you haven't talked to me or Gaili about them." This was the person who should be alerted if Fiona didn't follow Clara's directions? She seemed harmless, if peculiar.

"True." She squinted and shook her head. "Not enough. I've already gone over it with Clara. Talk to her."

"We can promise to make it more fun?" Gaili offered.

Fiona shook her head, but the nymph ignored her.

Cascade's gaze flew to Gaili. She looked her up and down appraisingly. "You ask."

"I don't think it's the best idea," Fiona said and moved closer to Gaili to manage the situation a little better. She was unsure of how to handle Cascade. Her mannerisms and words flowed so rapidly.

Gaili smoothed down her hair. "Well, when... I mean, what were you doing when they were taken?"

Cascade flicked the creature back into the pot. "I was at a Garden party. It was fun until it wasn't."

"Do you know what the Summer Crowns did?"

"Of course," Cascade said moving toward Gaili. "Think differently."

Gaili blinked and said, "What's better, theft or deception?"

"Ooh, that's a new question. Deception of course. Anyone can steal unguarded crowns. But how to get little Orsa blamed seems much more intriguing."

"You think someone's framing Orsa?" said Fiona.

Cascade's eyes flicked to Fiona and she grinned. "I would, if it was me. It would be more enjoyable that way. To sneak and see how far I could go before I got caught."

"But you wouldn't take the crowns or blame someone else," Gaili said slowly to herself. "It would be less enjoyable to do things you've already done in lieu of doing something new. Like a Garden party."

Cascade's skin seemed to ripple of its own accord like a pond skipped by a stone. She pressed herself into Gaili, her arms wrapping around her. "You're familiar with me and my bathing sisters, aren't you?"

Gaili nodded and tried backing away. She looked unsure and glanced at Fiona.

"I'm done with questions. You're fun, Gaili of the Grove. You'll stay with me," Cascade said.

Fiona moved to intercede. She wouldn't see Gaili coerced for mere answers. "That's not necessary," Fiona interjected.

Cascade flinched. Without turning, water rose from the corners of the room. From bowls and pots and vases and vials, it flowed toward Fiona. Fiona tried to dodge, but the water wrapped around her limbs, restraining her. Some tendrils were cold, some warm, their grips not unlike the feel of her old whip.

The nymph whispered a melodic song that started to calm Fiona down. She was finding it hard to stay upset. The longer she stared at Cascade, the more her skin shimmered, wet like droplets against the sun.

Fiona struggled to remain in control. "Release me this instant."

Cascade shook her head. "This is between the faun and me."

Gaili looked from Cascade to Fiona, eyes wide. "Oh no, this is my fault."

Fiona worked to push away from the wall. "It's not, just stay back." Fiona closed her eyes, aggravated at the nymph, and said, "I wasn't going to touch you."

"Why should I trust you?" Cascade said, moving closer to Fiona.

"Because I'm here to solve a crime, not meddle with you."

"Are you sure it's a crime you want to solve? Perhaps it would be better to stay with me where it's fun." Cascade smiled enticingly.

Fiona stared at the nymph for a brief second, drawn into the depth of her welling eyes. But she saw Gaili shift, heard the pounding of her own heart in her ears, and shook her head. "If you don't let me go, then we'll be here like this forever. How quickly that will become boring after a while."

Cascade stared at Fiona as if trying to read her. "I don't like boring." The nymph sighed, flowing away toward the desk over the sand in the room.

The melodic song playing in Fiona's mind grew quiet. The water pushing her against the wall swirled back into its containers, leaving her free. She pushed herself off the wall, breathing heavily as heat flushed through her body. She took a deep breath before saying, "That was uncalled for and intrusive."

Cascade tilted her head. "You are an outsider here. Some would say the same about you." She turned, seemingly dismissing them, her skirts rustling over sand, and stuck her hand back into the pot. "I've had my fun. When you talk to Olea, ask her about the key. She got the chest, she unlocked the chest, but how? People often overlook her words and what she says. Do not. We're more alike than it seems." For a brief moment, she seemed almost translucent before shimmering back to a solid form. "But don't believe all her words either."

Fiona didn't wait to see if there was anything more proper to say. She opened the door to the office and stormed out and straight to Jacopo. "Cascade can be prickly, hmm? You could've warned us."

"I did try to keep you in the dry. She gets upset when she can't have the elements of surprise on her side."

Yes, because otherwise no one would have anything to do with her probably. "I thought nymphs were tied to their location?" Fiona said to Gaili.

Gaili shook her head taut face. "They learned to manipulate that after the Inking. Something about the opening of the pages helped them there."

"The necklace around her throat?"

"Yes, water from her sea."

It seemed awfully unsecure to have one's whole lifeline dangling from their neck. Fiona rubbed her wrists where the tendril of water had wrapped itself around her. Maybe not completely unsecure. She sighed, thrusting the episode as far back from her mind as she could. "Well, let's keep at it then." She looked back to Cascade's closed door. If staying in line meant not dealing with her, she'd try her best. "Is Olea in?"

"Perhaps I should wait out here," Gaili said apologetically. "You'll be quicker, and I won't distract anyone."

"Absolutely not. That wasn't your fault." Fiona motioned toward Cascade's door. She smiled to put Gaili at ease. "Just follow my lead and everything will be fine."

Voices drifted from behind the door Jacopo led them to, this one decorated with thick bushes surrounded by trees. After a knock, Fiona was surprised to see Dorin open it. The room was crowded with books, loose papers, crates, and chests. Along the walls hung strips of gray, green, and brown wood marking an organization of the piles that Fiona could see but not understand. A large desk took up the middle space among these things with a couple of wooden chairs off to the side as an afterthought of company seating.

"Oh, you're already making the rounds this morning. Good. I hope you've been able to make some progress." He nodded to Jacopo in dismissal. The latter turned without saying a word and walked back to the first floor.

"Yes, although we've come to talk with Olea next."

The short woman who sat down before them was quite the opposite of Cascade. Her skin was ash gray with black grooves that twisted like ribbons caught mid breeze. Her silvery-green hair was piled in small braids that looped around her head. Wrapped bands of leather in the shape of oblong leaves clung to her arms like sleeves. The leaf motif carried throughout on her practical layered woolen dress. She could just make out the chain of a necklace beneath her dress. This was perhaps one of the only people in power who eschewed the fashion of those around them. It endeared Fiona to her immediately.

Inclining her head from the doorway, Fiona said, "How do you do?"

Olea rose and took Fiona's hand in her own warm and rough ones. "It's a pleasure to meet you. I've heard so much about you. Quite enchanting, much of it."

Fiona was taken aback. "Well, of what Dorin has been saying about me, I assure you only most of it is true."

Olea raised an eyebrow but said nothing further. She turned to greet Gaili in the same manner.

Gaili blushed and bowed her head. "I've heard much about your work in Thicket. You're quite the archivist."

"Thank you. I do love finding new bits of history and lore. I'm glad my passion benefits others as much as me."

"I heard you found the chest the crowns came from," said Fiona. "Can you tell me more about that?"

Olea sat down again stiffly. "Of course. Artifacts from the Circle of Seasons are as scarce as details about their final whereabouts. It took some time and spelunking, as your people say, but finally I unearthed this chest in our neighboring region."

"Oh," Gaili said, delighted. To Fiona she murmured, "The Garden region was rumored to be the last place anyone saw them."

"It was. It most definitely was," said Olea. "Of course, the chest wasn't easy to get to. The area was in ruins."

"Yes, and there was a cipher on the chest that took some time," Dorin interjected excitedly. "Solving it is an achievement none can boast of except our dear scholar. She figured it out all on her own."

Olea said haltingly, "It was more luck than study."

Fiona noted that she looked away every time the cipher was mentioned. Was she hiding how she figured it out, or was there something else? She thought of Cascade's words. "I'd love to know how you went about finding the chest. In my line of work, tracing the happenings of the past comes up more often than you would guess. It's difficult alone."

"Truly, it was a team of people going through the ruins. Not only myself. I have no special secret."

"Don't be so shy about your talent. You deserve the accolades," Dorin said as if it wasn't the first time.

Olea looked as still as a tree, blinking slowly. She certainly seemed to be hiding something.

Fiona turned away in thought. "May I?" She motioned to the chest.

"It's empty now, of course, but feel free," said Dorin.

Fiona bent to look at the small wooden chest. It was preserved very well. The lid and the chest had several clasps with an inlaid copper rod running through it. She could just make out in the light several small holes in the rod, like a flute without a mouthpiece. "This was all that was keeping the chest closed?"

"Yes. But it was a specific secret that needed solving. And the cipher key was beneficial in other ways," said Dorin.

"Or would've been," Olea said quietly.

"The cipher solution went missing too?" Fiona said. This was new evidence.

"Yes, along with the journals. They were semi-unintelligible to read..." Olea trailed.

"What could you pick up in them?"

"Blueprints. Outlines, notes of thoughts, concepts of various inventions and experiments conducted by all the Circle of Seasons," Olea said, rummaging around on her stacked desk. "I have a list here if it'll help. Of course, it doesn't have near as much detail as the journals." She handed over several sheets of paper in a neat list with cramped writing.

Fiona gave them to Gaili, not wanting to pull out her scarf again in front of Dorin. "Did anyone else know about the chest and items?"

"Everyone who knew they existed," Olea said slowly.

She seemed hesitant to say more even after Dorin glanced at her. He spoke up: "Of course. When Olea found the chests, we discussed internally about the lead-up. We wanted to gather some interest in the updated Pavilion displays. Then a few days later we unveiled them privately within the Seven."

"Did anyone take an unusual interest in anything?"

Olea glanced at Dorin. "Well, Dragomir was very interested in the crowns, but her and Bardo immediately got into a fight when she asked if she could study them first. Of course, the stewards were fascinated as well, but none of them more than the others." Olea said.

"So Orsa was there?"

"Yes. It was a big moment for all of us," Dorin said.

Fiona nodded. "Olea, what is your opinion of Orsa?"

Olea frowned. "Well, she's very closed off. Not impolite by any means, but she seems more cautious and dutiful than others. I'm not even sure I know what her field of study was. It seems odd that someone so thoughtful would steal from us."

Or was she so thoughtful as to learn exactly how to steal from them? Fiona wondered. "What was found that made you suspect Orsa?"

"A bracelet. She wore it every day. It was small and made of beads of amber with a silver plate attached. I think it had her name engraved on it." Olea looked through her desk. "Ah, I believe Clara still has it."

"And when Orsa was confronted with the evidence?"

"She said it wasn't hers," said Dorin. "But she couldn't show us hers nor tell us how she lost it. I wanted to believe her, but how else did it get in Olea's locked office if she wasn't the thief?"

"When you hired Orsa did you bring her on to the staff yourself or was it an open call?"

Dorin scratched his chin. "Actually Clara hired Orsa. I needed someone new when Taliana left, as her wife was my previous steward. One's retirement from Keeper life triggered the other's. So we asked around, then Clara found her and brought her on board."

"But she works for you and not Clara?" It seemed odd, that.

"Yes, Clara had to let her steward go. Some issue with his demeanor toward her. But she doesn't see the need to replace him. Says she is perfectly capable of running her own office. It's her self-reliant mentality, I think," Dorin said, bright eyed, clearly in admiration. "She wouldn't hear of Orsa working for anyone else but me, and she has been—*was* the perfect steward."

"She really liked Orsa though. I think she feels bad to be swindled," Olea added, stiffly pulling the subject back. "As bad as Clara can feel either way."

"It just seems odd that Orsa would take the contents of the chest but not the chest itself. It's rather small. Seems that would've been easier to heist," murmured Gaili.

"But that's not all that was taken," Olea broke in.

"It wasn't?" Gaili said with some surprise.

Fiona felt the same way but schooled her features. "What else is missing?"

"Besides the chest's contents, some of the old display items are gone too. Bardo's bell and Clara's watch. We replaced those so the guides wouldn't notice."

That did seem odd, but comparatively everything in the page did to an outsider. "So there's more here than just a theft of crowns." Fiona raised a questioning glance at Dorin. "Why didn't you mention this yesterday?"

"The Summer Crowns had to be the main target. They are the most valuable and unable to be replicated," Olea said.

Fiona could sense the same unease as before in them. Before she could say anything, however, Dorin frowned. "Actually that's what Olea and I were talking about before you came in. Dragomir was interested in them, and she hasn't arrived yet."

"No one knows where she is?" said Gaili.

"Afraid not," said Dorin, clutching his cape. "She hasn't been seen since she left yesterday. Her steward said she wasn't at home last night. It could be nothing. Everyone has autonomy here, and we're not due to assemble for any judgments for another week." He shifted, glancing away. "Hopefully."

"Her administrator doesn't have any plans for her on the books. He seems just as surprised as we are. It's unlike her," said Olea.

"Well, that puts Dragomir a bit higher on the list of suspects if she has indeed disappeared," said Fiona. "As you say, it may be nothing. Let me know if anything changes or you don't hear from her soon." She wouldn't go running after the first people to not check in without understanding more about them. It was alarming what the Seven thought was important information and what wasn't. She couldn't take her leads from them alone.

Olea nodded. "If you'll excuse me, I want to get some scribing done before talking to Thicket visitors. It was nice meeting you both. If you have any other questions, my door is open to you."

The ladies made their murmurs of appreciation and followed Dorin out of Olea's office. "I wondered if you'd be willing to stay in the area until you're forced to go back to Spine. Of course, not up till the moment of sickness, but..." He trailed off, looking uncomfortable at the mention of the page turner weakness that forced them to live on Spine and not be away from it for too long, lest they become ill. While it was widely known, it was impolite for non-turners to ask too many questions about it. "We could set you and your assistant up in the Trussadary Inn, where some of our visiting guests stay, paid for of course."

"Is there a reason we need to be here around the clock?" Fiona said, trying to mask the annoyance in her voice.

"It would make the leaders feel easier if they knew they could find you without having to schedule a turner or travel to Spine, or elsewhere," he said, looking chagrin. "Some think if we're paying you to investigate you should be within arm's reach. I know it's an inconvenience, but it would keep the tension to a tepid level."

And make it easier for whomever was most interested in her investigation to keep tabs on her. No doubt the Order of Seven commanded more spies in this page than in Spine, what with the Travel Guild influence there. She glanced at Gaili. "I'll talk it and the terms of our payment over with my partner and get back to you."

Dorin took a step back, bowing to Gaili. "Apologies. I thought you were assistant to Investigator Thorne. Please excuse my mistake."

He was being so gracious that Fiona could see Gaili's wheels turning of how best to correct him without seeming rude. Before Fiona could interject, however, Gaili said softly, "No need to apologize. I thank you for including me in your invitation."

He opened the door to his chamber, a small fruit tree decorating the cover. "I believe Clara has stepped out for a meeting about the new theater, but she should be back later this afternoon."

"How long have you known Clara?" Fiona asked. She glanced at Gaili, but the faun was studying her dress intently. Probably to hide any facial expression about her old mentor.

"Oh, a few years now. She's been a large contributor of knowledge to the various academies in Copper over time. I got to know her in my previous role, when I was overseeing much of the academies in the Glade region. She's donated many clever items like her original pocket watch, a scope letting you observe things in the distance, and the like."

"Did you suggest she come on board when Taliana announced retirement?"

"Er, no." Dorin scratched his nose. "Taliana actually suggested Clara as her replacement. Assignment to the Order of Seven is usually through applications, and previous Order members choose the upcoming Seven for the next term. Faekin from all over apply from the main institute studies: geography, alchemy, astronomy, mathematics, anatomy, and engineering. We try to have a diverse group and cover each study, each region, and each level of society. Clara fit quite well in Taliana's role."

"So Clara has been on board for about six months." The same amount of time since Gaili was inked, Fiona noted. *Interesting.*

"Yes, and she's already given much to the Order of Seven and governing of Copper. She's stubborn and sometimes temperamental, but what genius isn't?" Dorin said.

Fiona glanced at Gaili, who was nodding along in agreement. She stifled a groan. Some people could get away with murder if they talked well enough. It only took a few times of being duped to see through the false veneer. Fiona felt like she was the only one who saw through Clara's. All well. That wasn't the case to solve.

"Besides her, Dragomir, and Bardo you've talked to all of the Seven. What do you think so far?" Dorin said after a short silence.

Fiona answered quickly lest Dorin get his hopes up: "That I know far too little to make a pronouncement of anything yet." *And that each member of the Seven is happy to hand over another member as a person of interest.* "We've gotten much information this morning, but besides the Seven I'll still want to talk to the staff and of course Orsa herself."

"You'll find Orsa at the Towers of Calistino. It is within the city but on the water's edge and furthest away from our pagemark here. And of course, we use turn stoppers, as barbaric as that sounds. Although she is no turner, we placed her there in case one might want to assist her. The Summer Crowns are too valuable to let our only lead get away."

Turning the page from a building or unsecured location like that was inviting turning into the gutter and possible death. Pagemarks were large, secured areas for a reason. But they always had to line up with somewhere safe; otherwise, you were asking to be in a bind. Breaking someone from a prison to another page had been tried over the last few centuries. It was a risk only those who needed to escape bad enough would take.

"If you don't believe she did the crime, is there a need to be so cautious?" Fiona asked.

Dorin hurriedly closed the door behind them and sighed. "I can't think just of my wishes for Orsa on this. Not until we retrieve the curiosities. If she does know where they are and another page turner could abscond with her, there's no telling if we'll ever see them again. We need to recover them as soon as we can. It's one of the reasons I insisted we bring you on to help."

If a page turner had them, they could be anywhere in the Book. Fiona could see why they wanted her to work quickly. They said their goodbyes and set off toward the Towers of Calistino.

AS SOON AS THEY stepped away from the Pavilion and walked down the well-worn path, Fiona remarked casually, "So you're amenable to staying here a few days? I thought I'd have to bribe you."

Gaili laughed. "Perhaps you still should. But I thought about how much ground we could cover if we didn't have to pop back home all the time or at least had a place to lay our lace..."

"And?"

"And I thought how nice it would be to continue visiting with Matteo. When I left, I was Clara's star pupil. Now she's a Keeper and I've returned as a shop owner without a proper—well, anything."

"Surely your friends and family are proud of you. You've started your own business, Gaili, and struck out to do something with your talents."

"I-I haven't told them about the shop actually."

"You haven't what?"

"In my letters I...don't mention it. I talk about the research I've done, the studies. Things that I would've kept doing under

Clara. I don't want them to worry about me not having enough to eat or a roof over my head."

Fiona often forgot, to her embarrassment, that not all page turners were treated the same by their pages. She rarely moved in circles outside of her miniscule one until recently with meeting Soots and Rockcruncher. She had been traveling along, turning page after page, without really learning anything. "I didn't…" She paused, looking for a way to support her friend without making it about herself. "They'll love to hear about you, in any situation." She smirked. "But a visiting dignitary's house isn't a bad way to show off. Tell Matteo what you're really up to. Let your family know all the creative things you're accomplishing that are keeping you afloat."

Gaili fiddled with the ribbon of her sleeve. There was silence as they walked over the stone footbridge into a deeper part of the city, the only sound the rushing water of the canal beneath them. Then with a small sigh, Gaili said, "I do hope it'll make them happy. It would comfort me to know they aren't disappointed about Keeper Clara."

"No one who has any sense could be disappointed in you." Fiona grinned at the faun and then quirked an eyebrow. "Now Clara is another story. Who wouldn't be disappointed in that woman? She's dreadful." Fiona put up her hand, laughing. "I know what you're going to say, but let me have my snide comments where I may. I'll need to be on my best behavior while we're here."

Gaili inclined her head but kept her own counsel. They walked in companionable silence through the towering homes that edged the path toward their destination. More and more faekin traveling to and fro around them, gradually eclipsing them as they mingled in with the life of the city. Though some looked at the two, they acknowledged Gaili as a guide and carried on. All the while Fiona chewed on the information they had gathered. She only had basic knowledge of the Court of Copper from training and gossip. She'd need to understand much more if she was going to figure out who had the most motive to steal from the Order of Seven. Including if it truly was Orsa.

"Now that we're away from the fray, tell me, what should I know about the Circle of Seasons? I feel like there's more there than I can rightfully understand as an *outsider*," she said, mimicking Cascade's voice.

Pulling down a browning leaf from a passing tree, Gaili twirled it in her fingers. "The Seasons were, are, fae inheritors of the spring, summer, autumn, and winter spirits. You know, like how nymphs are inheritors of nature elements and fauns of the woodlands and forests."

"You're a spirit?"

"In an essence, yes. It is our belief that the spirit continues reincarnating itself lifetime after lifetime to experience all it can."

Fiona had never heard Gaili talk with such wistful tones before. Though spirits meant quite a different thing to her human mind, she set the comparison aside and urged her on. "And so the Seasons are always the four?"

"Yes, they were. I think. I mean, there could only ever be four at a time. And as the fae were the inheritors and our creators, they ruled over the entire world as deities."

Fiona stopped again. "Fae created you?"

"Well, not created me directly, Fi," Gaili said, as if it was rather obvious. "Our species. Each born by the ruling fae from the beginning of time." She laughed lightly. "What did you think *faekin* meant?"

"But"—Fiona looked around at the diverse groups, including fae among them—"they don't seem to be the sort."

"I'm getting to that bit," Gaili said, laughter bubbling out of her.

Fiona imagined Gaili liked pressing her impatient buttons when she could. It made her slow down to linger in her friend's enjoyment, but only a little. "Okay, so then legend has it the Seasons disappeared at the start of the Inking?"

"Oh yes. It's not legend really. There have been no more Seasons since they went away and Larrakane pronounced herself. For some faekin it was deity replaced by deity."

Resisting the urge to get into the curious philosophical debate about the chicken or egg, Fiona said, "Your seasons, your actual weather, continued?"

Gaili nodded. "Archives show that after the first year, when nothing much changed but the rulers and the ruling class, the Order of Seven was formed."

"Remarkable. Were they good rulers? These Seasons?"

"I think that depends upon our definition of *good*. The first few Circles and the fae in general bore more power than the rest of the world combined with the season spirits. And some fought against them, like the nymphs and fairies. After that the next few Circles seemed to usher in some peace, although history shows it ranged from forced peace to barely contained turmoil. So were they good leaders? I don't know. I'm sure some of them tried."

"You're right. I guess it can't always be as clear cut as one would like." Fiona couldn't help thinking of her own responsibilities to her Queen and power therein. "Which Circle of Seasons made the Summer Crowns?"

"The lost one. After the hag eradication—"

"Hag eradication?" Fiona exclaimed. "I thought those were myths! Shape-changing witches who stole children and cooked them, as my mother liked to scare me with. Saying they'd turn from Copper to Rise, pretend to be her just to get me since I was such a bad child. Kept me up almost half the night on more than one occasion. They existed?"

"Your mother used to tell you that?" Gaili said, frowning. "That's awful."

Fiona's cheeks burned, thankful with her brown skin her feelings on the matter were nearly invisible, and kept on: "They were actually real though? And then eradicated?"

"Yes, but no stolen or cooked children. But many were advisors to the Seasons and ruling fae. Fairly small in number compared to the other species. Anyways, they were unfortunately...removed. Or sent off to the Wilds. Not a bright spot in our history. But we were punished for it with the plague."

"Now the plague I know about," Fiona said. It was the only thing in Copper history that was also taught to children on Rise. The plague happened before the inking in Copper. With thorough study, the Copper page eradicated it before the Book opened up. Once it was discovered that, consequently, it was the same plague happening in Rise, Copper shared the treatments, as part of negotiations between the pages. Rise would always be in debt for that, though humans tended to forget quickly.

"So many had died that the willingness to open minds with everyone, determine how to stop the plague, and more united all the faekin with the final Circle of Seasons. The Seasons, to push forward the goodwill, created many things for the various regions. The Summer Crowns may have been one of those items. Old families, local governments, and the like still have artifacts from that goodwill push, but they stopped working after a fashion. What was in that chest are the only things I've heard of that still had any power left from the Seasons."

"So they would be valuable to any number of people for a variety of reasons."

"Yes, inside and outside the page. I can imagine alchemists and inventors from across the Book looking to distill what the crowns can do or replicate them, as Sofia is already trying to do. It's so rare we come across items that don't work here because it's from another page."

"For you maybe," Fiona said as they walked over another half-wall foot bridge, "but even what Cascade can do naturally is more than any human is able to imagine. I'm finding the Book more fantastical every day. And as long as that fantastical isn't attacking me, I'm loving every minute of it."

"I'm glad. For me, every new discovery is something to be excited about, and when you find the Summer Crowns, my only hope is to get to touch them just once."

Fiona smiled. "When we find them, it'll be a priority."

Gaili blushed and nodded her head. They entered a large open square with several buildings that surrounded it in a semicircle. Little snaking paths darted between the buildings leading farther away and deeper into another residential area. In the center of the square was a sizeable pale-pink marble well decorated with laurel leaves, like a central talking piece. Indeed there were many faekin around it, filling pails and pots underneath the iron spigots that shot water directly from the cistern beneath. Chatter in the faekin language crowded around them as Fiona and Gaili continued on past the working people and to the towers situated on each side of the square.

The towers seemed to touch the sky. Open slitted windows marked each level of the buildings, and a linked bridge high up sat in between them. It was shockingly well lit within the tower. Soft glowing lamps and rays of amber sunlight streamed through the window slits. Though the stone walls were cracked and dark, they seemed quite cleaner than Fiona had expected. The prisons of Rise were already dank but fell even further into dreadfulness in comparison to this.

Scents of warmed linen and soap wafted down the hall as a warden strutted toward them, alerted by some unseen signal. Keys jangled on one side of a blue cloth belt tied around her waist while a small book swayed back and forth on the other. "Hello. Do you need assistance?"

"We're here to speak to Orsa? She arrived last week."

"Oh, yes. Poor thing. And who are you? For the record." The warden pulled up her attached book, its chain wrapping around her tattooed arm as she consulted it.

Fiona chewed on her lip, briefly hesitating. If she gave a false name here it could be confusing should the Seven check. "Fiona Thorne."

Gaili gave her name, and the warden jotted it down. She tutted, closing her book. "I don't know if she'll be up for a visit, but we can see."

"Did something happen?" said Gaili.

"Well, it's not my place to talk about others." The warden glanced around as if remembering herself. "You can ask her yourself. Just...be gentle with her. She's been fairly quiet since she came here. Very polite and whatnot." She crooked her finger and led them back through the narrow halls and up a wide ramp that circled round the tower.

They passed several levels of small landings, each with a short row of three or four doors. Not many people were kept in the tower, it seemed. The landing floors were covered in exquisite rugs of geometric patterns and deep colors. The halls illuminated as below with soft candles.

"Who maintains this tower?" Fiona asked.

"Why, the prisoners of course. Mind you, this tower houses more political criminals than murderers or thieves. They have plenty of paper to spend on their expenses here, if their fortune wasn't taken from them."

"So they pay for the upkeep?"

"And the servants who clean it. Better than some homes in the country, if I say so myself." Her voice sounded warm with pride. "I'm sure most country folk wouldn't mind a bed in one of my rooms."

"But they are still prisoners, yes? No matter how nice the accommodations are," Fiona said.

The warden sniffed. "We do the best we can to blend the distinction."

Fiona thought that no amount of paper in the Book would make her forget she was caught in one place for any length of time.

They finally stopped after a while. Fiona glanced out the window, resting from the walk up. She could see a good portion of the square, the road back to Calistino, the canals buffeting each of its side. There was the tip of the massive domed temple to Larrakane at the city center, and even in the far distance she could make out the outline of mountains. They were high up indeed.

The warden put a key in the lock and twisted it for the wooden door to pop open. Inside Fiona could see a small sitting area with a settee, table, and throw rug. Light came in from another narrow window. Toward the back of the half-moon room was an iron door.

"If you'll make yourself comfortable, I'll check on Orsa and let her know she has visitors."

"Thank you." Gaili inclined her head in a show of appreciation.

The warden smiled at her, ignored Fiona, and sauntered to the iron door, unlocking it. She darted inside quicker than her looks indicated she could and shut the door.

"I think we've gotten off on the wrong foot," Fiona said, motioning to the warden.

"She takes pride in her work," Gaili said quietly. "I'm sure she has to deal with quite a few upper-echelon people visiting here. Whether they want to or not. That's no easy task to balance."

"True," Fiona said.

"Besides, I do agree with you. A gussied-up prison is still a prison. Some turners say that's how they feel in Spine. Cursed to go everywhere and yet stay nowhere."

Often turners fell into the two camps: those who saw it as a blessing, or as a curse. But Fiona couldn't see how the freedom to move about the Book could ever be outweighed by the supposed burden of having to come back to Spine.

"Would you rather not be inked?"

Gaili shook her head. "I will always prefer it. But getting so sick you can hardly stand just for being someplace else too long—I'll never understand why it's part of the package."

Fiona nodded. "Nor I. Perhaps we'll have the frightful luck to ask Larrakane ourselves one day." She winked at Gaili. "Although I doubt she'd be ecstatic that's our first question."

The iron door opened, shifting Fiona's thoughts, and they turned at once to the sound. A faun, almost as tall as the doorframe with large dark eyes like mud puddles, shuffled out, her furry hooves and pale golden hands bound by the manacles known as turn stoppers. They were often used to keep skips and rippers, errant page turners, from being able to move between pages. Though they were in use, there weren't very many that existed.

While Orsa glanced at Fiona and Gaili quizzically, she said nothing as she made her way to the settee and sat down. The warden uncuffed her hands and stood in the corner of the room.

Fiona moved her skirts, sitting down opposite Orsa, and said, "I'm Investigator Thorne and this is my partner, Gaili. We're here on behalf of your sister."

Orsa's eyes widened slightly, but she looked down at her hands. "Is she well?"

"She is, although saddened by what's happened here, of course. Can you tell us about it?"

Although there was no draft in the room, Orsa shivered slightly. "I don't know what there is to say. I took the paperwork from the Order of Seven's office."

There was a small gasp from the warden in the corner. Fiona turned around just in time to see her holding her mouth in surprise. The warden composed herself. "Apologies."

Tucking away her reaction for later examination, Fiona turned back to Orsa and continued, "You freely admit you took the paperwork?"

"Yes. I did it."

"Why have you previously been saying you hadn't?"

"I was simply trying to lie my way out of any punishments."

Fiona tapped her finger on the table, thinking. She glanced at Gaili, whose brows were furrowed staring at Orsa. Something wasn't adding up with the sudden confession.

"How much paperwork was there?"

Orsa's head snapped up, her eyes finding Fiona's. Where Fiona thought she'd find misery, she instead saw frustration. "Quite a bit of it. There were more than three journals' worth." That was in line with what Olea said earlier, but she could just be going off what she saw when they opened the chest.

"How did your bracelet get trapped in Olea's office?"

Orsa pinched her lips together. "I snagged it on the corner of her desk. I didn't realize I had lost it."

This was contrary to everything she had been saying before, as far as Fiona knew. Fiona tested the waters. "You wear this bracelet all the time and yet you didn't realize you had lost it before you left Olea's office?"

"I was in the heat of the moment."

"What was in the journals?"

"Private information that may be best left that way," Orsa said, motioning her head to the guard in the corner.

Fiona frowned. There was cagey and then deliberately vague. "Where did you hide the journals?"

"I'm not ready to admit that information yet," Orsa said through gritted teeth. Her fingers were wrapped around each other tightly. The golden skin stretched over her bones as if she hadn't eaten in quite a while. In a place like this, Fiona doubted very highly food was being kept from her.

"But surely you would if it would get you out of here," Gaili said pleadingly.

Orsa shook her head.

She might not admit it, because she didn't know it. Fiona wondered what was at play here. She glanced back at the guard and then ventured another question quietly: "What about the other items? Did you take those as well?" The Seven went through quite a bit of trouble hiding the total extent of the theft, and she didn't want to let it slip.

"I took it all."

"What about the spyglass?" said Fiona, mentioning a display item not on the list. There was nothing she could ask about that Orsa couldn't have an answer for unless it wasn't part of the chest or the theft.

"Why won't you stop asking me questions?" Orsa slapped her hand loudly against the table and jumped up as well as she could with her legs shackled together. "Tell Dorin I did it. I'll give the location of the contents when I'm sure he and the Seven can meet my request. That's all that needs to happen here."

The warden bolted forward, but Fiona held up a hand. "I promise, I'm not trying to upset you. I just want to understand. So I can make sure I tell them properly." Fiona moved toward Orsa, looking up at her. Closer, she could see the woman was stretched thin. She dropped her voice to a whisper. "We aren't here for the items or the Seven. We're here for you. We want to help you and your sister."

"Please just tell us what is going on," Gaili said.

Orsa looked down at her hands again and then at Gaili and Fiona. She jutted out her chin and said sharply, "I took *everything* that was in the chests and I want—I need exoneration. People like me need exoneration. We deserve it. Tell *Dorin* that. If he agrees and makes it happen, then he'll get everything back." She sighed heavily and then shook her head, swallowing words she was clearly holding back. She turned away from them and shuffled back to the iron door.

The warden, somewhat slow to realize that the visit was over, stared before jumping in to unlock the door for her.

Fiona called out, "And what should we say to Elinor?"

After a pause, her voice was thick as Orsa said, "That I thank her for the care in sending you two. And I'm sorry I didn't listen to her."

The iron door finally opened, and Orsa ducked, making her way back inside her cell. The warden locked the door slowly and then hung the keys back on her belt, not really looking at what she was doing.

Fiona ushered Gaili out the door and down the ramp, her slippers slapping against the rough stone. The guard jingled close behind them. Once descended, the warden continued toward the outer door, anxious.

Fiona stopped just before exiting, watching the warden, and said, "You seemed surprised by her confession."

"She's been so adamant against it before. And I believed her." The warden shook her head sadly. "The few that have visited her certainly said as much. People who've worked with Orsa day in and day out. Just a bit shocking, that's all."

"Perhaps it's best to give her time before I mention this to the Seven. She could be overwrought." Curious, Fiona asked, "What happened earlier today with her? You said you weren't sure she'd be up for a visit."

"A visitor this morning. When I came back in the room, poor Orsa was as far as she could be from that woman. She's been dainty ever since she got here. I didn't have any concerns leaving her alone with such an important guest. I should've had concerns about that vile woman though. She was yelling fierce at Orsa, but I couldn't understand it. I have to imagine there's something there," the warden ended, more to herself than the ladies. She shook her head and took a breath. "Ignore what I said. I shouldn't speak of other people's business."

"Who was she?" Fiona asked. There were only a couple of people Fiona could think of who even knew Orsa was here, yet alone cause a scene with her.

"Oh no. No, I can't answer any more questions. I've already said more than I should." She busied herself tidying up the desk area.

"Would you mind giving us her name?" Fiona asked. "I'd like to know what she had to yell at Orsa about and do something about it."

The warden shook her head again, adamant. "I think it's best you two leave."

"We could give a donation..." Fiona started.

The warden raised her chin and crossed her arms. "You think I'd throw away my job, my calling here, for a bit of paper? You aren't the first person to come here and bribe me, and you won't be the last," the guard said. She waved her hands. "Leave before I charge you on interference of Copper business."

Fiona threw up her hands, stalling for time. It had been the wrong thing to say, clearly. She assessed the guard, remembering what Gaili had said earlier about her. Perhaps if she came at it from a softer angle, she could convince her. "Wait, I didn't mean any ill intent. I simply hate to watch someone suffer in confinement like this. We know you do your best here. We're just trying to pull at any string to unravel the mystery and find the real criminal. Please believe us."

The warden hesitated.

Fiona, feeling a tinge of guilt, pressed, "For Orsa?"

There was a moment where she felt like she may need to be more duplicitous before the warden's shoulders drooped and she nodded. "If it will help Orsa. But you didn't get anything from me, and if anyone asks—"

"I stole your sign-in book. People would believe you without a doubt." It had been her backup plan, after all.

Nodding, the warden opened up the notebook and showed it to them while looking away. Listed were several names, including Dorin, but the last one was of Keeper Clara.

Gaili started, "But why would Keeper Clara—"

"Thank you for your time," Fiona said, cutting Gaili off. "We appreciate your willingness to help our investigation, and we won't stay a moment longer." She tugged on Gaili's arm. "Shall we?"

Gaili nodded, confused, but let Fiona lead her out and away from the guard back into the square.

When they got farther away, Fiona said, "Sorry, I didn't want to cause any more worry or give information to that warden."

"Oh, I'm sorry, Fi. I almost ruined it."

"No, never you mind. Without you, we wouldn't have gotten the name anyways. You read her much better than I did," Fiona said, consoling her friend, "and we learned quite a bit. Clara visited Orsa, riling her up. No wonder the guard look troubled about saying too much."

"But Clara isn't a blotter. Yelling at Orsa seems foolish," Gaili said, frowning. "Why cause a scene?"

Fiona noted that Gaili didn't say it seemed out of character for the Keeper. "I don't know. But without pleading, we never would've gotten the name. Perhaps she didn't think anyone would find out." Fiona was certain that was the case but sprinkled doubt for Gaili's feelings. "I wonder what she said to upset Orsa enough she was willing to admit to the crime."

"There was something off about Orsa. Not just what she was saying to you. But her appearance as well."

"What do you mean?"

"Well, typically, faun siblings all look quite alike. We have a defining trait that carries through each of us from our parents. For example, all my cousins have bright white ears. Elinor and Orsa look nothing alike."

"Hmm, and I suppose it's not often you have non-kinship family. People you call family along the way?"

"It's not abnormal, but we're fairly clear on family delineation, especially among the upper sets."

"What makes you think Orsa and Elinor are among the upper set?" Fiona asked.

"Well, the expensive accommodations for one thing. Elinor said she was good for the paper and would cover all expenses no questions asked."

"And the tower Orsa is in is paid for by the prisoners. Conceivably, whoever owns that tower prefers less prisoners who have more money."

Gaili nodded. "There's also light faekin tattoos on both their faces."

"I didn't see a thing. Are you sure?"

Gaili hesitated. "I think so, at least. I should've pointed that out to you earlier I suppose. I thought you noticed."

"Hmm, if Orsa could afford better treatment and nice accommodations, why work as an administrator to the Seven? Or steal from them for that matter? Money is clearly not the reason, so I suppose she isn't selling the information."

"No, no it is not." Gaili sighed. "I know we learned a little, but I feel like it's not much at all. We don't know why Clara would come and publicly accost Orsa. She's already in jail for the crime. And we don't know why that would make Orsa have the sudden change of heart."

"True," Fiona said slowly. She was worried about saying too much to Gaili with how she felt about Clara. It would take a little work managing, but she suspected she could at least talk to Clara. And save Gaili from having to deal with the woman at the same time. "Do you think we should stop by Spine before we go to stay at the inn? Gather some supplies and such?"

"Oh, that makes sense. I didn't even think of that." Gaili perked up at the change of subject.

"Perhaps you can go on ahead and I'll meet you there. I want to pop back to the Pavilion and see if Dragomir or Bardo have arrived."

"Oh, okay." Gaili's brow furrowed. "I suppose that will give me time to pick up items from my shop as well."

"Perfect!" Fiona said, a little too jubilantly. She didn't want Gaili to suspect her true intentions and felt a little guilty for pushing her off. But it was for her own good. "I'll meet you at our office, and then we'll turn back here where we can hold analysis over a nice served supper paid for by the tight-fisted Seven." She winked.

Gaili laughed, pulled into the moment Fiona created, and they hugged and parted ways.

Fiona knocked on the flower-etched door with Clara's name and waited, checking her pocket watch. It was well after noon, when Dorin said Clara would be back. She glanced around and realized it was quite empty on the floor. Perhaps they made themselves scarce on purpose when skimmers came through.

Fiona knocked one more time, listened for any sounds of movement within the room, then jiggled the handle, but the door was locked.

While she hadn't intended on breaking into the woman's office, she wouldn't pass up an opportunity to look. People didn't often lead with their secrets during an interview. There might be something to give Fiona an upper hand when dealing with her. Hearing the familiar deep voice of the tour guide, Fiona slipped down to the administrative hall. Distant voices told her this area wasn't completely empty but they were opposite Clara's office.

She stopped at the administrator door to Clara's office and listened in. Silence. She tried the handle slowly, but it was also locked. Looking around once more to make sure she was alone, she reached into her multipocketed scarf, feeling for the leather pocket where her lock picking tools lived. In one motion she slipped them out and inserted a pick into the lock. Working quickly, she heard the click she desired and smoothly opened the door, then shut it tight behind her.

It was dark in the room. She moved gingerly, noted a small skylight curtain that could shine some light in the room, and drew the long rope pulling the curtain up. The office was much more ordinary than Cascade or Olea's had been. It was lushly carpeted with a large oaken desk and matching chair. Tables sat on either side of the room holding scant materials. A large clock ticked away on the wall. There was practically nothing here. Clara must have been fastidious about cleaning.

Darting to the clock, she took it off the wall to glance behind it and on it, but there was nothing. Fiona opened the drawers of the desk gently. The bottom ones held small, unopened crates with the Order of Seven symbol, and within them, paper with the same insignia, envelopes, and quill pens; the top, stacks of papers arranged neatly inside. Glancing through them quickly, lists of shopping items greeted her. It seemed Clara was planning a trip to the Depths soon. She had receipts for rented gear and letters to some of the academies in the Garden region asking for old maps and records to study. It was all so benign.

Tucking the papers back in, Fiona sighed. Perhaps she just wanted something to be here. Something she could use to show Gaili and the others that Clara wasn't such a genius. It oddly made her annoyed at the nothingness. She didn't believe anyone with that terrible of a personality had nothing to hide. She moved the chair and looked under the desk, feeling around for a secret compartment.

"I'm still doing drop-offs," Jacopo's voice came from beyond the door.

Fiona resisted the urge to freeze and looked for a hiding spot. She could fit under the tables, but they were short skirted. She ducked under the desk and pulled the chair close to her, knocking it into her shin. Pressing her lips to keep from yelping at the pain, she made herself as small as she could. Thank Larrakane that fauns were tall creatures.

The door opened just as she pulled her legs toward her. Huffing and puffing came into the room as if Jacopo was carrying something large. She heard a thud of a crate hitting the desk and then sliding onto top.

"Thank you for the help, good man. Almost done?" Jacopo asked.

"Last tour's finishing up now. Drink after?" the centaur guide said.

"On the Seven, of course." Jacopo laughed.

"Of course," the guide replied. "Wait, does she always leave the skylight open?"

"Daft woman," Jacopo muttered under his breath. "What's the cord stuck on?"

Fiona watched helplessly as the chair pulled. She frantically tugged it free on her end and pressed herself against the inside wall of the desk, holding her breath. She would be extra nice to Jacopo if he stayed focused on leaving the office.

"Oh. If it had been a snake, it would've bit me," Jacopo said. The light cut out and the room returned to darkness.

"Maybe you need that drink now."

"Dealing with that firecracker, always."

There was a sound like a slap on the back, and then the door shut. Once the lock clicked, Fiona let out her breath. If the Seven were worried about spies, there would be few avenues to explain herself in this predicament. She pushed the chair and crawled from under the desk. Her slipper caught, and she yanked up a fold of the lush carpet as she pulled it free. She smiled as it uncovered a small door in the floor. Running her fingers around the edge, she found no wires or any indication of a trap. Opening it up revealed several bound books stacked neatly on top of each other.

At first delighted to think they were the missing journals, she scanned them looking for the information that Olea had given her earlier. But it was clear these were published books and all in the Copper language she could only somewhat read. Not wanting to take too much more time, she opened them up and turned them over to empty them out, but nothing came. She jotted down the names, authors, and any unique descriptions she could make out while quickly squinting in the darkness. She would head to the library and find what could be so noteworthy in these books to hide them. Placing them back gently in the box, she closed it up and replaced the carpet. While not the telling sign of a thief she had been looking for, it was something. She slipped out of the office and away from the Pavilion to hurry home to Spine.

7

AFTER A BRIEF STOP to see if any letters had arrived from Henrietta and to pen a note updating her on their temporary move to Copper, Fiona headed to the temple district. It was an area of Spine entirely devoted to the Blessed Larrakane. Lush green expanses of lawn with small buildings and shrines for visitors and locals to pay her tribute, enjoy teachings, or just have a bit of lunch in the quiet open air surrounded the investigator. Pages held temples to Larrakane cobbled from the deities they'd worshipped before her appearance; each was unique and slightly apologetic for praising false gods when they discovered there was one true one. But the temple on Spine had no such history.

The square stone streets gave way to lush grass with a circular building rising atop a small hill in the middle. Fiona strode through the grass, ignoring the actual temple to make her way to the other side of the hill and the small library. This singular brick-and-terracotta building was also circular, a symbol of Larrakane, but smaller. Fiona entered the door to see various people—faekin, humans, and more—sitting at the tables pouring over books or talking quietly. All were welcome here, unlike the Travel Guild library, and as such it was one of Fiona's favorite places to be.

Looking around for her normal sage-robed helper, she saw a different familiar face. Deep-gray wrinkled elephas face, trunk stacking books on a table. Her new friend Fali. Well, a tentative friend, nonetheless.

"Fali," Fiona said simply as she strode to his table. "It's nice to see you. How goes things?"

The elephas stopped mid-packing. "Fiona, well met." He patted her shoulder with his trunk. "And here I thought you'd be lying low. Out in the public without a care in the world. Good for you."

Fiona stared blankly. "What do you mean?"

"Have you not seen the latest *Card*?" His trunk pulled it from a nearby table.

Beyond the information about the upcoming nuptials of the Queen's son in Rise and an advertisement for the Waterfall Palace in the Depths was a statement that caught Fiona's eye:

> FIONA THORNE: "The Guild didn't save Blaze. I saved Blaze!" The brusque investigator exclaimed to this scribe that the Guild had nothing to do with solving the sputtering of Blaze. But which party is telling the truth, and what else are they hiding? Pick up the *Card* for an exclusive transcript of my interview with the burgeoning detective.

Next to the pronouncement was a small sketch of Fiona, or what Fiona would look like if she were taller and fuller figured.

A facsimile of her scarf was wrapped around her neck and her slippers had been exchanged for Kerus sandals, but there was a good semblance in the face. This must've been what Dorin was talking about. Her little moment of fame was starting to get out of control.

Fiona groaned and let the paper slip from her fingers. She noticed that the room had gotten somewhat quiet and that a few people were looking at her. "Excellent. I wanted to note that Blaze fixed their own problem, and now I'm front page against the Guild. Honestly!" She rubbed her forehead. "Is there somewhere private we can talk?"

"Oh yes, yes." Fali led the way with his trunk. Through a buffering of tables and around a corner they went. There were small rooms here for private study, and with the curtain drawn, Fali motioned to the chair for Fiona while he leaned against the wall. "Did you come to see me directly?"

"No, but now that I've found you, I'd love to know how you've gotten on. Were you able to talk to Gilded Evenhell about the Painted Edge?" Fiona had suggested he connect with the regulation leader of the Travel Guild and exchange information. Although she didn't trust the Travel Guild well enough to rely on them for information, Fali didn't share her view. She didn't know if that was his own guidance or the logic of his order within the Church of Larrakane, the Followers. But if they could parley, she'd benefit from any valuable information that came his way.

"Actually, no. The couple of times I've gone to visit in the last couple of weeks, she hasn't been available. The little elephas told me she had gone on a short leave of absence."

"Oh," Fiona said, shoulders dropping. She had hoped some movement had been made in the Painted Edge case while she had been running from scribes and recovering from injuries of the previous case. "Well, please don't give up. Dodger may be able to share information with you as well. Not as much as his leader, but if she's out, you can turn to him. Tell him I sent you. I think it would behoove us all to know the whereabouts of the Painted Edge at once." The Painted Edge were known to have stolen an airship from Rise, but no one knew where their mobile headquarters was in the thick, unending forest of Spine. That they had to stay on Spine was certain, as the group was made up of page turners. But if they could move it between Rise and Spine, they could move it between Rise and Mistral. The druids searched on Spine and the jackets in Mistral. So far nothing had turned up.

"We are agreed." He nodded. "If you didn't come to see me, is there something I can help you find?"

Fiona smiled wide, perking up at the forthcoming research. "Yes, actually. Otherwise it would take me hours I don't have. I'm looking for some books. I'm hoping there are copies here so I don't have to deal with the Travel Guild library." She handed him the scribbled note. "Sorry. It was a bit dark when I was making it out."

"It's alright. Let's see here." Fali grabbed the note and glanced at it. He closed one eye and held it closer. "Yes, this one looks familiar. These are most likely in the history area. The Order of Seven's generosity is well known."

"What do you mean?"

Fali moved off and toward another room deeper into the temple library. "The Order of Seven was very eager in the years directly preceding the Inking to show support of Larrakane and anything that graced her name. So they donated quite a few newly minted books about their page and work to the temple. As a show of faith. Quite a few covered subjects on the past monarchs, and they made sure to notate them as 'historical texts.' I think it's quite obvious what they were doing, but I'm sure at the time the Church was pleased."

"So these books are about the Circle of Seasons?"

"Quite right." He scanned shelves, pulled down a tome similar in looks but much less taken care of, and gave it to Fiona. "You should find the rest in here, I would think. If not, I'm happy to assist further, should you need me."

"Thank you, Fali. I do appreciate your help."

He nodded, raised his trunk, and lumbered back to the main room.

The first hour of research passed by rather slowly. Fiona loved books. She loved learning new things and discovering secrets. But much of it was an account of history that more or less matched what Gaili had told her about the various Circle of Seasons and the history of faekin. There were records of each Circle, what they accomplished and, in more fascinating detail than what she thought would be allowed if those monarchs existed now, ways in which they erred. A thin volume, dated several decades after the Inking, was an exploration on the reincarnation of the seasonal spirit and if it was truly a blessing or a curse to the chosen few. Interesting, but why was it worth hiding? It clearly showed that Clara had an interest in the Circle of Seasons. Perhaps she worried having the books would suggest, or alert, that she stole the crowns?

One book was slightly different, and more records logs than anything. There were quite a few pages with lists of the Circles, and Fiona noted that none of the names matched each other. So that meant the seasons weren't blood relatives.

She thought, rather exasperatingly, that the older generation certainly had a penchant for long names. Some were three or four words each making the pages run quite long. With each grouping came points of accomplishments, including items created. She pulled out the list of the Summer Monarch chest items Olea had given her and cross-checked it with the book. While several were there, the majority on Olea's list weren't. If they had been gifts given, as Gaili had said, wouldn't they be included here as well?

Those that matched were initialed to indicate who the original creator was, and they also included a record number to learn more information about them. Fiona scanned the listings, thinking to pick one invention on both lists and dive into it, when her hand stilled at the repeating lines. One set of initials called out to her. She flipped back to the other book with the full names. *Circle of Seasons 1372: Marcela Aurica Caragiale, Summer Monarch.*

She stacked the books as quickly as she could, mentally apologizing to Fali for not putting them back. Slipping the list back into her scarf, she threw back the velvet curtain and strode out of the library and to the turner district with haste. There she knew she'd find a heavily tattooed old friend to interrogate.

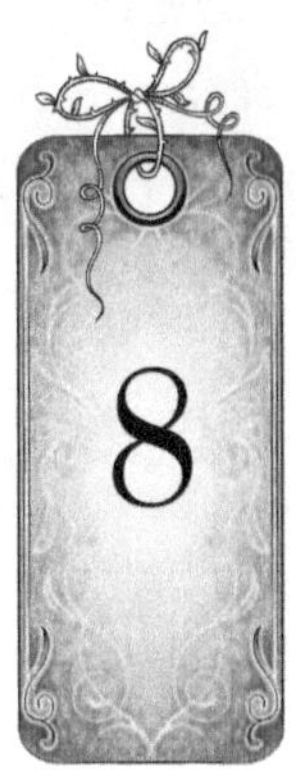

FIONA SAUNTERED INTO THE Thread and made a beeline for Mac. The proprietress was in her customary gauzy flowing azure robe. Her sunglow-gold hair was multiple buns today, like sun clouds that shadowed her face. Fiona could see how she would mistake Mac's coloring for fae shenanigans. How she had taken her sunny disposition for a naturally charming personality. And the tattoos on her hands as a secret history as an experimentalist of cocktails and concoctions. She felt two parts delighted in her discovery and two parts terrified that Mac would deny her any information. Case-related or otherwise.

Seeming to sense her friend's focused approach, Mac turned away from a patron at the bar and said slowly, "Fi, you look like you've just found Larrakane on your doorstep. Are you alright?"

Fiona, feeling for once like she should try to be patient, just nodded. Instead of taking her customary place at the bar, she inclined her head to the stairs that led to the Thread's upper floors and kept going. She ignored the heads turning her way and the way chatter stopped as she walked by. Gossip ran faster than water through the aqueducts high above the city. *Blasted Card and their sketch.* Here in the Thread it seemed all turners read the pamphlet. Pity, she had thought that page turners would be a more discerning bunch with one of their own.

Sighing, she headed up the stairs, trying not to take two at a time in her haste.

"Go all the way to the fourth floor," Mac said, not far behind her. "I don't know what bee has stung you, but if we're going to talk about it, might as well be in private chambers."

Fiona had never been to the fourth floor of the Thread. It was Mac's personal quarters, and though she suspected it would suit her proposed conversation nicely, Fiona was nervous. If her conjecture was right and Mac was the Summer Monarch, would she hate Fiona knowing? Would she deny it and stall her out? Shaking her head to dislodge such dramatic thoughts, she stopped on the landing when she met locked double wooden doors.

Mac breezed by her and placed a hand on the door. She stilled her hand for a second and then swung the wooden door open. "After you."

Fiona walked into the large room but stopped, mesmerized by the trickery of light in play in here. Where outside the Thread the eaves and roof decorations made it seem as if lily-white lace had been draped on the robin's-egg blue building, inside the lace broke up the warm light of the day and cascaded colors across the walls and a few doors that led off it to places unknown. Like a kaleidoscope. "It's quite beautiful."

"Yes, and all mine," Mac said, smiling. "One of the first things I had built when I got to Spine." Mac went to a long settee, plumping a pillow before laying on it. There wasn't a hint of stale, dusty air in here or bubbling noises like downstairs. It was very much a cocoon of sorts away from the wider world.

Fiona felt as if Mac was opening a door, or at least a generous window, and she jumped right out of it. "Were you the Summer Monarch in the Circle of Seasons?"

Mac's smile dropped. Whatever she had been expecting, it wasn't that, by the look on her face. "Whatever gave you that impression?" Mac turned away and brushed invisible crumbs from her robe.

"I've taken a case that has pushed some research my way and…" Fiona eased back and opened her arms. "Look, Mac, you've known me since I was a gangly fourteen-year-old with too big a mouth and not enough smarts. I'm no unread turner. You know that I would only ask if I already found something linking you. And you also know that no matter what you say, I won't repeat your secrets to anyone. My word as your friend, or the dark edge swallow me whole."

Mac sat up and pursed her lips. She debated for a moment, somewhat uncharacteristic of the forward person Fiona had come to know and love. "You must promise me that you will not reveal to anyone what I've said in this room today." She took a deep breath and held out the palm of her hand. "Place your hand on mine. It'll bind you to your word and me."

Fiona jumped up. "I already gave my word."

"But this will ensure it. I won't have anyone suffer because of who I am again." Mac stood holding her hand out to Fiona. "Please, Fi. I don't ask this lightly."

Fiona didn't want to be beholden to any power lest they command her to do something that wasn't right. But Mac wasn't a power. She was a friend and had always taken care of her. If she had been a ruler before, that didn't make her a ruler now. It didn't change who she was. Fiona placed her palm on Mac's warm, worn hand.

Lines from Mac's tattoos spread themselves out, searching, then trailed down Fiona's fingers. It felt like dipping into a cool lake on a hot day and was quite soothing, if not a bit startling as well. Fiona watched as the tattoos spread across her hand, wrapping lines of crisscrossing indigo like basket weave, and then fade. At once there was a strong, taut feeling in her stomach, as if she was being tugged once hard toward Mac. She glanced up to ask about it but stilled looking at Mac. Her face had changed. The amber coloring was more pronounced on her high cheekbones and faded down to her throat. And swirls of inky tattoos now lay near her ear and by her eye, fresh lines Fiona had never seen before. Where Mac had looked perhaps a bit older with wrinkles was new smooth. The feeling washed away and was gone before she knew it.

Mac withdrew her hand. "There, that binding will hold until we perish, it's broken, or I release you."

Fiona rubbed her hand a little shakily. "Let's hope it's the latter then."

Mac nodded, all business now, and moved over to a small work desk. "I am the Summer Monarch of the last Circle of Seasons." She leaned on the desk and crossed her arms, looking more her normal no-nonsense self. "You have to understand, Fi. I've taken pains to mask myself here in the Thread. Though my power isn't what it once was, it's enough to be a difficulty. I'm not worried about myself, but if others knew about me or knew someone who could get to me, it would cause a fair bind in the Court of Copper. Trouble I don't want to start. I like being free."

Fiona raised an eyebrow. "Were you ever not?" Ruling classes were typically the beginning of power, not the end of it.

"I had a certain amount of freedom, yes," Mac said, grimacing, "but I was never free to be myself. To do what I wished or even to give power over to someone who would make better use of it. I had no say in being a seasonal spirit. It was a blessing Larrakane yanked us away when she did."

Of course, it made sense that the Seasons didn't just disappear but became page turners. To know that Mac was over eight times her age confused her though. Typical fae were longer lived than humans, but only by a hundred years or so. "That would mean that you're over two hundred years old."

Mac shrugged. "I was young, and we were some of the first." She turned, fussing with papers on her desk.

But there was no evidence of them returning or resurfacing in the whole history she knew of the Copper page. No doubt someone would've noticed them. "And did you never go back?"

Mac stopped, face clouding over, "We're getting off topic. I don't know what good it'll do you to know however. I don't know where the artifacts and curiosities you're looking for are any more than you do."

"You already knew they are missing?" Fiona took a step back, flustered. Was there any faekin who knew how to give information correctly. "But how?"

"Olea and I have been friends for a few years now. She was infatuated with the Circle of Seasons once she started her archivist training. It took her a while, but she tracked me down after picking up clues and details and piecing them together. I befriended her in exchange for information of life in the Court, and she got to ask me details about the Seasons. It was a fair trade." She smiled wistfully. "It has been a good relationship, if strained at times. She's the only one who truly knows me. Her appointment to the Order of Seven has been great for her, but..." Mac seemed reluctant to finish the thought. "In any case, she wanted to donate something from the Seasons to the museum for the public to benefit from. I thought it fine as long as it was clear that she found it and it wasn't anything I made after I left. I thought it would be easy to spot that it wasn't pre-Inking. So I told her about the vaults. I had long forgotten what we had there."

Fiona's mind was a whirl, taking in the information as Mac spoke. She tried to pull together a coherent thought. "You had hinted you told someone about me. And Olea had heard good things about me. I confess I would've never guessed it was you two together. You both have such differing personalities."

"Yes, she's quite patient with my audacious behavior." Mac cracked a smile but turned away. "But yes, she sent a letter when everything went missing."

Fiona pulled out her list. "These items you journaled about, can you tell me more about them?"

Mac pulled out her glasses, perched them on her nose, and scanned the paper. "Everything I created, even my journals, had bits of information I thought too important to lay out in a common hand. Some things I don't wish to talk about unless more detailed is needed. But, the air bladder—that was one of the first of its kind and able to contain an object so that it could be submerged under water safely. I actually created a version to be used in the Depths fifty years or so ago. It's used by a cruise company now. The bottled bridge I created to try and build a crossing from the main continent of Stream to the island of Dew. Of course, some alchemy doesn't last forever. I've tried to get it to work still but…" She waved a hand, azure robe moving gently. "And the crowns you know can control a facsimile of summer, winter, autumn, and spring."

Fiona stopped pacing. "Wait, they don't simply control summer?"

"No, they were meant to be a representation of the whole Circle, not just me. The others would never have liked that. We only wore them on special occasions as it was."

Fiona sat on the settee rubbing her temples. The guide had said that they were the embodiment of summer. But that season alone. And everyone called them the Summer Crowns. "Drat." Fiona tugged her scarf out of her dress and started pacing. She liked having it in her hands when she needed to think.

"What is it?"

"Everyone knows of the crowns as Summer Crowns."

"They do?" Mac asked. "I hadn't gotten a visit from Olea since I gave her the solution to the chests. Her letter just mentions crowns. Does it matter?"

"If everyone sees them as Summer Crowns, and everyone only talks about the crowns' proprieties to mimic summer, that means that the real crowns were never seen. That they never made it out of the chest in front of the Order of Seven. They only ever pulled out crowns that acted as summer, not as all the seasons."

"Someone replaced my crowns before Olea ever got to the chest?"

"Or Olea replaced them and stole them herself." Fiona quieted, gripping her scarf. She felt awful saying it like that, but it was a theory.

"She would never do that," Mac said. "She would have nothing to gain. I would let her study them without any obligation, and we planned to do just that after the Order of Seven had gotten their fill of them."

Though Mac seemed adamant, the timing was shaky. "Do you think anyone would've had an easy time getting into the chests?"

"Doubtful. Olea is extremely fastidious about securing her finds. Only those she trusts would have access to it. She wasn't storing it at the Pavilion until a couple of days before the unveiling."

So someone wouldn't have gained entrance to the chest until days before it was opened in front of everyone. But then how would any of them have gotten into the chest without breaking the cipher locking it? "When did you give Olea the solution to the cipher?"

"A couple of days before the unveiling was supposed to happen."

A couple of days were more than enough time to pull off a theft. Fiona began pacing the large room again. "That means two days to get into the chests, replace the contents, and close up the chest. Thus, changing the Seasonal Crowns for summer. They wanted to hide the theft to buy them time, so they replaced them with false items. But clearly there was some sort of issue, because the items were stolen again two days *after* the unveiling. That's when Orsa's bracelet was found and the display items disappeared as well."

Mac rubbed her face. "I'm not following."

"Orsa may have very well stolen the old display items, like the bell and watch and the crowns. She may have also stolen the journals and solution to your cipher. She gave no proof she did, but she confessed to me and Gaili today." She left her immediate doubt to herself. Fiona stopped pacing. "But someone else stole the original chest contents before they were even unveiled. Looking at the doors and skylights of the Pavilion, gaining entry would be trivial. Getting into Olea's office is much harder. It all depends on who had access to your solution or who else knew how to break your ciphers."

"No one but I could know that key."

"What about the other seasons?" It was possible that Mac wasn't as secretive as she thought. If the other seasons were alive, they may know precisely what to do.

"I'm the only person in the Book who knows my work, Fi."

"I don't know, Mac." Fiona perched on the desk. "You've been gone from the Court a long time. It's possible someone else found the chests before you gave them up and had a chance to study them but couldn't get into them. Clara was studying all the old seasons and their accomplishments. She could've done it."

"She's probably researching for a new invention or because she's joined the Seven. You'd have to know my mind, the way I think, which key was even needed. It would take decades to work out a key," Mac said, "*if* it can be done."

"Some people have that time." If Mac could be over two hundred years old there was no real accounting for faekin ages. Perhaps they all had more flux in their age than they let on. "I don't think it's too much of a stretch."

Mac sighed, looking a bit older than even her usual self. "Time, sure, but not my knowledge. But if someone took all the crowns, you need to be looking for someone with an interest in elemental chaos. That's not even Clara's field of study. The crowns are facsimiles, yes, but all together they could create unprecedented cyclones or push the seasons out of alignment. Copper could be in real danger." Mac covered her face with her hands and shook her head slowly. "I shouldn't have been so careless. Foolish of me to have left everything in others' hands."

"You thought they'd be under the watchful eye of Olea. You couldn't have known anyone else would get to them first."

"No. But I should've," Mac said. "The only ones in the Seven I know are interested in elemental chaos are Dragomir and Sofia. You should ask them about it."

Fiona sat up. "Dragomir hasn't reported in today."

"Well then, that draws the line directly to her, right?"

"Perhaps," Fiona admitted, "but what is the motive? That I haven't directly figured out. But I suppose it's time to find out where she's gone."

"If you need anything," Mac said, pushing away from her desk, "I am only a turn away. I wish I had something to offer you."

"This is enough," Fiona said. She had always thought of Mac as somewhat like family, having known her so long, but now she felt as if that sentiment was actually true. "I should get back to Gaili and finish up things in the city before nightfall. The Order of Seven has requested we house in Copper for as long as we can so they have access to us."

Mac nodded. "Some ways of power never change. Do be careful out there. Dorin has been shifty to Olea for months. He's hiding something, even if its inconsequential."

Fiona was surprised to hear Dorin's name in the context of a warning but nodded in turn. "We'll speak again before this is done. I'm sure of it."

"Good luck, Fi."

Fiona closed the door with a click. She noticed then that the wood felt warm to the touch, like a bench in the sun too long. What else might she notice of the world now that she was bound to a seasonal spirit?

Back on the main floor of the Thread, the patrons barely seemed to have missed Mac. The system of canisters and pipes Mac had created were pouring from the walls into mugs. A small smilodon was running a few orders from the kitchen out to tables. Fiona had never lingered on the fact that Mac never employed faekin folk, but now she could guess why. And why so much of the cleverness behind the system was so that it could be automated to a degree. How alone and hidden must she have felt?

"You look contemplative this evening." Dodger waved his orange-and-black spotted paw and grinned. He was in full Travel Guild uniform: long black jacket and a dark-blue tunic that cinched with a tight belt. A bandolier of vials crossed his chest and a large pouch hung from his side. "I suppose you didn't hear me say hello. Or are you ignoring me again?"

Fiona broke out into a wide grin. "Never would I ever, friend. I haven't time for a drink, but I would like to know how you're getting on."

"To be talked to by the famous investigator Fiona Thorne is an honor in itself," Dodger said. His tail twitched behind him, belying the anxiousness hidden behind his teasing tone. "I'm happy to walk and talk if you have places to be." He held up a wrapped box. "I have a drop-off to do as well."

"That would be lovely."

They exited from the Thread into the winding streets of Spine. The light was fading in the sky and darkness quickly approaching. Although the day and night cycles were similar to all the mortal pages in the Book, they weren't quite exact. There was never a shining beacon of sun or a stalking emblem of moons. Just light for a time and then dark for another. Fiona did sometimes miss the moon of Rise and staring up at it for reasons she couldn't even fathom.

"So," she began, turning to Dodger, "how are you? I wanted to call on you this week, but I took a case…" She trailed off, trying to say something less awkward. After the fight they had recently about Fiona being an unsupportive and somewhat distant friend, she wanted to put in real effort the way Dodger always did.

"A zebra doesn't grow their stripes overnight, Fi." Dodger laughed. "Call on me when you can. And as to how I'm doing, quite well actually. The Binder has thought very highly of me after the dealings with Blaze and Petronia. In fact, he's promoted me right below Gilded." The Gilded were the highest leaders in the Travel Guild and ran each department of the organization. The coordinated manner in which the entire Guild worked helped it spread from page to page easier than others, like the Followers, who tried to compete with it.

Fiona stopped, clapping Dodger on the back. "That's excellent. Very well deserved. You're the best jacket there is, as far as I'm concerned. It's time someone else thought the same."

"Yes, well, I don't know about all that." His furry cheeks deepened in color. "But I will get to handle some larger casework and even leave headquarters now and again."

"Good. You don't travel the Book often enough."

"I'm still waiting on your invitation to the next case." He grinned. "I believe you mentioned the words *travel the Book and pick up clever things.*"

She chuckled. "I think you added some words in there, but you're quite right. After this case, friend, and you've got it. In fact, this may be the only one you can't touch."

"Court of Copper, is it?" Dodger nodded knowingly. "Sometimes being Guild has its perks." The Court of Copper blocking the Travel Guild from interfering in their matters did leave jackets out in the gutter. Unless they traveled in on holiday of course.

Fiona rolled her eyes. "Faekin aren't all that bad, you know. Just a bit different than the other mortal pages."

"Chaotic. You mean a bit more chaotic than the other mortal pages." He grimaced. "But no, I know. There are only a few in the Guild. The Binder for one, if you can believe it." He looked chagrined. "Though that's not well known. Keep that in your scarf like other secrets."

Fiona smiled at the new information, tucking it away. She didn't know a lot about all the leaders of the Spine, but she wanted to understand her home and how the power worked. She wanted to make changes for page turners, and you can't make changes without understanding the layout. "You have my word. But how is it you know and others don't? I had assumed his appearance was common knowledge to Guild people. Surely those who practically live at the Hinge see him come and go."

"I know the Gilded have private councils with him, but not jackets. The only reason I know the Binder at all is he helped educate me."

"What?" Fiona frowned. She had never heard this bit before. "I thought you came to turner training same as me?" With family left behind but excitement and eagerness to learn how to survive as a page turner.

"I did, but only because the Binder found me when I came to Spine the first time. Or was thrust here. Without parents I wasn't really watched on Kerus. That's nothing new though. There were quite a few of us on the streets then. Less now, I'm happy to say. But one day I was stealing bread in the dusty desert, then sick as a blotter. The next thing I know I'm pulled to this place. Strange and confusing with no real knowledge of where I was."

This was quite different than Fiona had known. Dodger had spoken of his time in Kerus as a rough upbringing, but when she had met him in turner training many years ago, he fit in so well. She thought he had always been here. She was reminded once again of how poorly she had faired at really getting to know Dodger. Thank Larrakane she had been given a chance to be better at it. "And so, because you had no family, you had no one to support you after leaving training?"

"Correct. But I did, in the Binder. He got me into training. I was unread, as any new turner would be. I stayed with him afterward, and long story short, he's made me the smilodon I am today." He smiled. "But that's neither here nor there."

"I find it fascinating. I'd love to hear more about it," Fiona said earnestly. "If I can survive the Court, I'll pop 'round for drinks and a proper questioning." They had gotten to Fiona's door. Fiona invited Dodger in, but he waved her off.

"I know that gleam in your eye, and I don't mind it. You've got things to work out for your case. So have I. Petronia still isn't talking, but I think we're narrowing down on how the Painted Edge managed to get the airship out of Rise."

"I would like to know of it when it can be told," Fiona said. "Actually there's another party who may contact you. They could be of assistance there as well. I told him to drop my name to you since your boss—old boss—Evenhell is out on leave. Fali is his name. He's an elephas with the Followers."

"And you suppose he should be told about the Painted Edge?"

"Actually, the other way around. He has a wealth of information, and between the two of you, you may sort it out. I have no doubt about that. I had told him to talk to Evenhell after my interview with her, but with your promotion"—she smiled—"you'll be an even better connection."

Dodger nodded. "I'll seek him out then." He held up the bag again. "Although I'm on my way to her now actually. She's taken ill and been homebound for the last week. I'll see if she has anything pertinent to tell him."

Fiona frowned at the discrepancy. Fali had said vacation. "Well, no matter what the case, I'm glad he can work with someone I trust."

"She isn't all that bad, Fiona." Dodger laughed, starting down the lane away from her house. "A might stubborn and chaotic, but she's persistent and loyal. Two things I know you to value."

Fiona waved him on, shaking her head, and closed the door. Or tried to anyways. Opening it had dislodged the stack of letters that had arrived since she had been gone. There was one with a seal far more alarming than the letter from her mother, which she still hadn't opened. It was an official seal of the Queen. She cracked it open, scanned the familiar wording, and gave a deep sigh. Every few years page turners native to Rise were invited to visit with the sitting ruler. *Invited* was what they called it, but a forced reminder of their loyalty was what it was. A stay of several days at the palace, dances, and more awaited her. She had several weeks to prepare, but still, the date had arrived all too soon.

"Oh, Fiona. Is everything alright?" Gaili said behind her, interrupting her thoughts. The faun's arms were laden with packed bags. More were being unloaded from a small carriage at the end of the walkway.

Fiona quirked an eyebrow at the bags but stopped when she noticed that Gaili's golden skin shimmered in a way she'd never seen before. Did it have something to do with Mac's binding? "Er, yes, simply looking over some correspondence. What do you have there?"

"Oh, just some things from the shop. If we're going to be staying in Copper for a few days, I need to complete some orders and perhaps craft a few things."

"Gaili, I..." Fiona started, concerned that Gaili might try to do something to prove her worth to Clara and her family. She struggled with what to say. "Do try not to overwork yourself."

"It's kind of you to be worried about me," Gaili said with a shadowed smile, "but there's so much else for you to be thinking about. Don't spend time on me."

Taking a deep breath and ignoring the desire to tell her friend exactly what to do, she changed the subject instead. "I think we should talk to Elinor and give her an update before we go back."

Gaili nodded, some of the shadow leaving her face. "I'm sure she won't be pleased to hear Orsa admitting to guilt."

"Yes, nor the facts that there are too many suspects, a lack of evidence that Orsa didn't do it, and that she's making demands." Fiona tugged on her scarf. She wondered how Elinor would react to Orsa's message. She hated giving bad news to people, and news about a family member even less so. "Also, that there may have been two thefts instead of one." Fiona recounted what she had deduced with Mac. She left out Olea's involvement and Mac's true nature, linking it more to overheard gossip from Mac.

"Two thefts! Well, I suppose we have our work cut out for us."

"Yes, we do indeed. Let's get to Elinor so we can return to Copper and lay it all out. I want to have a solid plan of action for tomorrow."

A chimney, bricked and smoking, sat atop the red tiled roof of the modernized house they walked up to. Striding up the long stone path nestled between dark gray flowered plants, Fiona felt as if she was being watched at every step. She glanced to the glazed windows but saw no form or figure behind them. Shaking it off and squaring her shoulders, she knocked. Expecting to see a servant for a house this grand, Fiona was surprised when Dodger opened the door.

His face mirroring her own and his whiskers twitching, he said, "Fi. What are you doing here?"

"I'm here to meet a client." She glanced past Dodger to the darkened interior chamber. "How come you to be here?"

Dodger opened the door wider, ushering them in. "This is Gilded Evenhell's home. She has a friend staying to take care of her. She's asleep, though, so I was on my way out." His brow wrinkled. "You didn't tell me she was your new case."

"She isn't," Fiona murmured, glancing at Gaili, "but I'm sure the explanation is clearer than that. Her friend and our client must be one and the same."

"Ah, well then, let me find the house steward and—" He was cut off by a young human woman appearing. The house steward greeted them and showed them to the drawing room silently. Dodger made his goodbyes, casting one more curious glance to Fiona, and took his leave.

They had a moment of silence before Gaili burst out with, "Do you think Dodger's boss would be upset if I took some flower clippings on the way out?"

Startled, Fiona turned from the ornamental sword she had been admiring above the fireplace. "Flower clippings? Whatever for?"

"The ones lining the pathway are somewhat rare and really only native to the Wild region in Copper. It's amazing that they even took here. When I think what I could create with a few petals—" Her sentence broke off as the drawing room doors opened and Elinor came in.

"Any news?" she said, closing the doors behind her gently and leaning against it. Although she looked rather elegant, she lacked the polish of when they'd first met. Her hair was wrapped around her horns at an odd angle. Bags deepened under her eyes. Unlike Gaili's skin, Fiona didn't notice a shimmer or any changed effect. If anything, her skin looked drawn and darker, but the tattoos on her face were prominent.

Though they weren't as intricate as Mac's, they were there as Gaili had said.

"We have some, although I'll start with the worst of it. Your sister has plead guilty to the theft."

"She what?" Elinor took an unconscious step toward Fiona.

"We visited her today," Gaili interjected softly. "It seems she's had a change of heart."

"Yes, although she won't say where the items are or why she took them," Fiona said.

"That can't be. She would never do that." Elinor clenched her hands.

Fiona said slowly, "Do you know what could make her lie?"

"One of the Seven must've made her."

Clara's name was on the visitor board, but it wasn't enough to prove coercion. "Perhaps, but it would be easily discovered if they visited her, and what then? They are the highest power in Copper and are allowed to visit whom they please. What would they have on your sister that she would do as they ask?"

"Nothing. There's nothing."

Fiona pursed her lips. "And then there's the demand she has made for the return of the items as part of her confession."

Elinor's head popped up. "What demand?"

"Exoneration. Of herself and those like her. I'm not sure what she means exactly. If fauns or stewards are unlawfully locked up?" Fiona said, glancing at Gaili. She hadn't wanted to broach the subject with her, but it needed to be asked. Gaili, for her part, looked just as confused as Fiona felt. So perhaps she wasn't on the right path. "We have very little to go on, and the only option is to find where it's all hidden and make a plea on her behalf. The best way to free her is to get her to tell us what she knows, but she seems bound to silence."

Elinor's large faun eyes were unblinking. "She didn't do it and you must prove that. I'll pay you anything you want," she said dismissively, "but the only thing that matters is finding her innocent so she can be released. She can't stay locked up in the tower for long. It won't end well for her."

"What do you mean?" Fiona took a step forward. Something was amiss. She couldn't put her finger on it, but Elinor was holding something back. Perhaps if she saw there was no way out for her sister without giving Fiona something to work with. "Trust me when I say I value my freedom and the freedom of others, but I can't prove innocence where there is none. If there's anything you can tell us about your sister, what she was doing working for the Seven, any secrets—now's the time."

Elinor turned away and began pacing the parlor. "I don't know why she was working for the Seven. I told her she could come live with me, but she turned me down. I tried to convince her not to trust them, but she's always been so stubborn."

"Trust them with what?"

Elinor stopped, jaw stiff. "Just in general. They don't care about all faekin, as they pose. If they did, they would take counsel from the Travel Guild, as other leaders have, or focus on their actual citizens and not their superfluous studies. The only people in the Pavilion who care about the page are the stewards."

"Do you think that's why she wanted to become one?" Gaili asked. "So she could do something for the people. Influence the Seven in some way?"

"Perhaps. This isn't the way to go about it though," Elinor snapped. Rubbing her face, she said, "Apologies."

Fiona felt that Gaili was on target but didn't understand Elinor's reaction. Something she should be proud of her sister doing angered her instead. "Is it because of the Seven she shouldn't be doing it or because the people aren't worth it?"

"The people are worth it. You don't have to be bound to power in order to accomplish your goals. You can go around them if you've got the patience." Elinor sighed. "This is neither here nor there. Please, prove my sister didn't do this. She's the only family I have left. She doesn't deserve to be there." Indicating the conversation was at an end, Elinor opened the door to the drawing room.

Fiona said softly, "And if I can't prove your sister isn't the culprit?"

"I believe you're capable, or else I would've never asked you. I am never wrong in assessments."

A bold statement if Fiona had ever heard one. The look of formability on her face felt familiar. Perhaps it just mirrored her own from time to time. "We'll be in Copper until we have to return to Spine. It may take a long while to clear her name. Much longer if we can't find the items and she's uncooperative."

"I'll be here for as long as it takes." Elinor opened the front door, shooing away the approaching house steward at the same time.

Fiona stopped inside the doorway. "Is the bracelet you wear the same as your sister's?" Fiona pointed to the amber-beaded jewelry on her wrist.

Elinor nodded and wrapped her hand around it. "Our family made us matching ones when we were little. I've taken to wearing it now. Fanciful hope, I guess. Why?"

"Hers was found as part of the evidence against her. Can these be bought anywhere?"

"No, nowhere," Elinor said. "There were only for me and my sisters. They engraved our names in them. Our elder sister passed away not too long ago, so only Orsa and I remain."

Fiona nodded, feeling guilty for bringing up dark memories. "We'll keep you posted." After Elinor closed the door, leaving Fiona and Gaili alone on the sidewalk, Fiona whispered, "I am quite certain that this case is getting out of hand."

EVERYTHING ABOUT COPPER WAS brilliant. This is where Fiona knew that being bonded was actively affecting her senses. The sky, which always held a copper hue, deepened into hundreds of variations of the color across a spectrum of amber, honey, and gilded stars. Calling it Copper seemed so human now. It was clearly more. Much more.

The oak trees that greeted them as they first arrived were taller than she saw before and more alive. They didn't move, or talk but their leaves rustled in a harmony of sound that mixed with the melodious music playing throughout the courtyard from a fairy troubadour and their lute. If they didn't hear the accompaniment from the trees, Fiona wouldn't believe it. Their wings, like drifting blush lily petals, fluttered to the music. She wished she could share all these new sensations with Gaili and ask her thoughts. She wondered if she saw Copper like this all the time. But breaking the bond would mean breaking her promise. So she walked along, barely knowing where she was going, trying to commit to memory the heightened sights and sounds of the page.

The lodgings at the Trussadary Inn were definitely a perk of being a hired investigator she didn't often receive. The inn wasn't too far from the Pavilion, making access to it a quick walk. The garden grounds, wild and lush beneath the shade of evergreen trees, had an almost overgrown quality to them. Their earthy scents were heady and fragrant. A variety of colored rose bushes, yellow, white, and red, dotted the landscape like a paint palette ready for the artist to begin.

Inside the inn was beautiful as well. Stuffed velvet pillows adorned the marble floors and wooden chairs throughout the entryway, and a large sitting room overlooked one side of the garden through an arched window. The pleasant staff, who knew her and Gaili upon sight, made them feel welcome, offering small crystal cut glasses of a peacock-blue drink. Hesitant at first, Fiona watched as Gaili sipped and then took the drink in one gulp.

"I've often heard of this drink. Crystal Bliss. But I've never been anywhere so high up as to be served it," Gaili murmured softly for Fiona's ears in her human language.

Fiona raised an eyebrow, studying the drink through her new eyes. It brightened when she swirled the liquid, and she drank it in a gulp. It was sugary sweet but instantly bolstering. She felt as if she had rested for a solid week. My my, what the rulers of the Court kept to themselves.

Faekin shimmered in various ways, some as bright as Gaili and others more muted or darkened. There was no immediate system Fiona could tell through her sight, so she did her best to note the information to journal down later. She wasn't sure who the varied guests were to be staying in such lavish lodgings, but she felt equal parts blessed and awkward to be among them. Though she had been raised to nobility when she became inked, she had only learned the basics needed to not embarrass herself or her mother when she visited Rise. As her visits became fewer and fewer over the years, all learned habits started to wane under the freeing space of living on her own and doing what she loved best—being far too nosy.

A couple of the guests seemed interested in her after hearing the staff address her with her real name. She should have asked Dorin to use another but was unused to the need. Having taken care to keep her scarf hidden and a less noticeable veil over her hair, she had hoped to blend in next to Gaili.

A young faun who had been dusting the entryway moved closer to her, and the dusting became more of a pretense than real work. Gaili left to catch up on some work and they agreed to meet for the evening meal. Turning to go to her accommodations, Fiona nearly ran into the tall faun.

"Oh, pardon me, mistress." The golden faun bowed. Her skin was a bit taut as if she was tired. "I can help you take your bags to your room." She didn't shimmer like Gaili and seemed to have a grayer, more muted aura, much like Elinor's had been.

Fiona smiled. "That's unnecessary but thank you. I prefer to hold my own." The young faun's face dropped, crestfallen, and Fiona, guilty at putting the faun out, offered, "But if you would direct me to my room, that would be most helpful."

The faun immediately turned, beckoning Fiona on. Once they had gotten upstairs, the girl chirped, "It's so nice to meet someone of your stature. I've read so much about you."

Trying to hide the grimace from her face, Fiona said lightly, "Oh, thank you."

"I've met some of the Seven before, but none of them seemed as approachable as you. They're always a bit hushed together when they come."

Thinking that perhaps she could use her reputation to her advantage to gain information, Fiona ventured, "Do any of the Seven come here often? I'm always curious about the habits of successful leaders."

The faun glanced back the way they came and then moved in conspiratorially. "Between you and me, Keeper Dorin has come here a few times to meet with one of the young stewards. A faun, like myself. And Keeper Clara is forever coming over here and tucking herself away for hours at a time. I'm not sure what she's doing. But of course, it's not my place to question the Seven." The faun bowed her head as if embarrassed to be gossiping.

"I don't think it's at all out of line to be curious what the Order of Seven is doing," Fiona said, trying to ease the girl and prod at the same time. "Clearly, they enjoy the space provided here, and that's probably due to the great work you and the other staff members do. If I was only a walk away as they are, I'd see this grand place as an extension of the Pavilion."

The girl beamed. "They are here so often, it must be for exactly that reason."

"Do you ever see Keeper Clara reading books or talking to that young faun?" Fiona asked, testing the boundaries of what this servant was prepared to tell her.

The girl nodded. "Yes, but she does come to read books a bit. I've never been able to catch a glimpse of them though. You think they're something special? Should I watch out for them?"

Fiona realized the girl was eager to be some sort of help to a detective. She didn't want to get her in a bind, however valuable a little spy like her could be. "No, I think you'll naturally pick up on anything amiss. Don't go out of your way to learn anything. It's not an easy job, being an investigator. And sometimes it comes with little reward."

The faun's brow furrowed, but she inclined her head in deference. They arrived at Fiona's room, where the faun bowed. "Appreciate the talk, mistress. If you need anything, use the pull bell by your bed."

"If you could have evening meal for two sent up here, that would do nicely." Fiona smiled. "What's your name?"

"Sybil, mistress."

Fiona slipped a small sum of paper to the girl. "Thank you, Sybil." It was helpful to know about Dorin and Clara's activities. No doubt the young faun just thought a bit of any old gossip would be nice to pass on before she turned to go.

Fiona placed her bags into the room and was momentarily stunned by the view. The room held plenty of daylight from the copper sun through glass windows. They were patterned with a variety of colors but Fiona couldn't make out the image no matter how she tried.

She couldn't sit still and poured over Orsa's personal appointment book, coinciding the entries within to those of appointments she made for Dorin. There were coinciding entries in Clara's appointments as well, corroborating the maid's gossip. Fiona tucked that away to examine with Gaili in preparation for their next steps.

Shortly after dinner had arrived, Gaili knocked on the door completely redressed as if she was eating with the Seven directly. Though her deep-olive bodice, high golden trimmed collar, and freshly pinned pink curls gave her an air of sophistication and loftiness, a smudge of oil on her neck peaked out where she'd missed it. Her movements seemed laborious and heavy as if she was already exhausted from working.

Sitting next to her friend for dinner, Fiona leaned in and said lightly to ward off any embarrassment, "Seems you've left a bit of work on you."

Gaili's golden cheeks flushed peach and she surreptitiously wiped it off. "So," she began brightly, if a bit forced, "where do we begin? It took me ages to set up a temporary workshop and then I needed to finish a few orders. I'm not sure how long we'll be out here, but I wanted to make sure everything was done so I could run off with you at a moment's notice."

"I do have some method to my madness, but I appreciate the commitment." Fiona took a spoonful of soup, savoring its flavor, before getting to business. "Welcome to the part where I talk myself in circles for a while, make a plan, and inevitably do it all different anyways." She smiled. "I joke, a little. Here's what I'm thinking. There are several fishy things going on with the Order of Seven. The theft or thefts being but one. We know that serval items on display were stolen including the Circle of Seasons items two days after the chest was unveiled to everyone. We know that at that same time Olea's key to the cipher was stolen and that Orsa's bracelet was found in Olea's office. That links her to the theft of the cipher solution and tangentially to the display items at the same time."

"Only tangentially?" Gaili asked.

"I try my best to take each part as it comes. Assumptions make investigators errand boys and false runners. It's better to take each piece and check it carefully."

Gaili nodded her face scrunched in thought.

"Now, according to some new information learned, the Summer Crowns were actually Seasonal Crowns in the chest. Which would indicate that someone removed the crowns from the chest before it was unveiled to everyone. I'm not sure how long before, however. It could've been as soon as Olea got the cipher key, implying it was her or long before Olea ever got the chests."

"But wouldn't that open up the investigation to anyone with a motive?"

"Right. That's too nebulous to focus on until we can tie it into something else, we know. So we look at our other elements." Fiona wiped her hands on her napkin and then fishing into her dress pulled out her scarf. She felt for a linen pocket on one side. Reaching in she thought for a long moment of her traveling writing kit and when she felt it appear beneath her fingers she pulled it out opening it on the table.

Gaili laughed. "I'll never get over how amazing that is. I should dearly like to study it one day. In your presence of course." She stopped, her golden face growing red. "Not that I'm entitled to study it or anything."

Fiona smiled to ease her words. "One day perhaps. At the moment I'm just happy that it exists. I've spent many hours over the years diving into its mysteries. I might want to again one day."

"Well, I did something similar if less amazing." Gaili reached into the side of her dress and made a show of slipping her hand along the curve of it into a hidden pocket. Pulling out journal and pencil with a flourish, she grinned. "It's much more convenient to collect things when no one expects a pocket on your gown."

"Dear Gaili, you are incredibly clever and I am glad to have you on my side. I've never thought of that! We should amend all my gowns as soon as possible. Then it might not be such a burden wearing them."

"As long as you're not jumping in and out of windows, I should think not," Gaili said.

Fiona nodded and finished laying out her tools. Taking a sheet of paper, she wrote as she talked. "Our other elements are the people themselves. Let's start with Dorin. I'll have to tell him tomorrow Orsa confessed and what she asked for. If he hasn't heard by now."

"He seems like such the gentleman and very worried about Orsa," said Gaili, and she took a long drink from her wine glass.

"Yes, he does," Fiona conceded with a nod. "But format has it he's also been *secretly* meeting with Orsa over the last few months, as noted by her appointment book and the inn staff."

Gaili gasped, wobbling the glass. "They told you that?"

"Curiosity and compliments often go hand in hand when gaining information. So they meet here a few times, but what do they talk about and why does Dorin feel he needs to act on Orsa's behalf in secret?" Fiona couldn't mention of course the notion Mac had about Dorin hiding something. "Perhaps it's just a tryst, but it can't be overlooked. Orsa was very adamant about telling Dorin her demand. No one else. And telling him she stole everything in the chests. Which, if that was the case, would mean she did both thefts. Plausible, but why come back and take items she could've taken at any time, like the watch and the bell?"

"The thefts do seem a little unrelated to each other," Gaili said.

"And the only thing connecting them is the crowns. And then there's Olea. She found the chests and she unlocked the chest." Fiona left out that she didn't want to take a reward for figuring out the cipher key. Understandable since it was essentially handed to her from Mac. "The timing throws her into suspicion."

"And I guess by this way, Sofia is also under suspicion, for she seems to be recreating the Summer Crowns already."

"Quite right, with presumably only having one day to study the summer version of the crowns."

"But do you think she could be hiding them to look at them further?"

"Perhaps, but then why would she take the bell and the watch?"

"It doesn't seem...well, the brightest thing to do."

"I agree, but I think a short chat between you and her might cross her off the list."

"Me?" said Gaili.

Fiona nodded. "You can speak her language of craft and that will soften her. Find out if she's just guessing or has a source of hidden knowledge."

"I can do that," Gaili said slowly. "I am quite interested in her work, as it were."

"Then it won't even feel like false prying. That's the best kind of questioning." Fiona smiled. "And so that just leaves Clara, Dragomir, and Bardo. I'm going to talk to Dragomir and Bardo's stewards tomorrow and see what I can learn. I feel that Clara is avoiding me, which throws her into question." *Although her entire personality throws her into question,* she thought to herself.

Gaili said nothing, making her own notes and avoiding Fiona's gaze.

Fiona sensed her demeanor shift but made no comment on it. "The Seasonal Crowns can do quite a bit of damage together and in the wrong hands, according to my information. The sooner we find them, the better for everyone in Copper. Let's hope Henrietta uncovers something quickly to either tie Stoneguard to our case or set her loose. I should like to take attending the theater off my plate if I can." She stared down at her paper covered in lines and names and circles. While it may look a mess to others, to Fiona it was a puzzle beautifully laid out just for her to pull apart and make sense of. She loved unraveling mysteries and satiating her curiosity. Sometimes the path led to tangents, but what was life without something to nibble on at the back of your mind?

Fiona looked up to comment on the nature of curiosity to Gaili but saw her friend's eyes fluttering to sleep. She watched her for a moment, the exhausted faun already overworking herself, and to what end? If she had to prove to Gaili that Clara wasn't worth her time, she would, but she got the sense the faun wouldn't believe anything until she learned it herself. Sometimes the people we wanted most to be proud of us were the ones who were truly inconsequential to making yourself happy.

She got up quietly and put her writing kit back together, removing the evidence of their planning. Gently prodding Gaili who protested that she hadn't fallen asleep, Fiona led her to her bedchambers and said good night. Making her way to her own, she tucked into the oversize bed in the guest wing for an uneasy sleep. Avenues stretched before her as she dreamed, and she found herself going down many of them as oncoming storms of rain, fire, debris, and frost pummeled her from above.

A SHIMMERING-SKINNED JACOPO WELCOMED them with a nod the next morning: "You two are more prompt than half the workers in the Pavilion, except for old firecracker, of course," he said quietly. "She's already in if you're looking to avoid her."

Fiona raised an eyebrow. "Actually quite the opposite. If you don't mind escorting Gaili to Sofia, I'll go to Clara without preamble." If she was quick about it, Clara could be cornered, Gaili would be separated, and she could ask questions as intrusively as she liked.

"Ah, that I can do." He opened the door and motioned them inside, led them to Sofia's chamber, knocked, and showed Gaili in.

Fiona slipped away to Clara's door. She listened through gently to hear quiet humming. Without knocking, she opened it. "Clara, do you have a moment?"

Startled, the shimmering gold-skinned faun dropped her quill, splotching her writing with ink. She stood up quickly, moving papers and ink together. "It's Keeper Clara, mind you. And you should knock before you enter a Seven's office. We deal with highly sensitive information that isn't to be seen by commoners."

Fiona sauntered in, closing the door behind her. She glanced at the documents Clara was trying to shuffle into order, looking for anything familiar, but nothing stood out. "Yes, one can't be too careful about what they leave in their office apparently as well. It seems security is a bit lacking, what with the thefts and all."

Clara shoved the papers into her desk drawer and closed it with a slam, placed the quill in its stopper, and turned to Fiona with an amount of contained disdain that impressed the investigator. "It's not security that's lacking. It's the people who have been hired to do it. Where is Jacopo?"

"He's escorting Gaili to Keeper Sofia so they can chat. I thought it was best to divide and conquer this morning."

"And you couldn't knock?"

"Apologies, it was a momentary lapse in judgment." Fiona feigned innocence. "I thought to speak to you while you were available. You've been *so* busy."

Clara frowned and then ran a hand across her hair, smoothing it away from her horns. "Well, I have a moment now, should you like to update me on how the case is going against Orsa."

"The case to find the missing items is moving forward," she said, subtly correcting her. "Did you suspect Orsa for a thief when you hired her?" Fiona sat down in front of Clara and watched the faun closely.

"Of course not, don't be ridiculous," Clara said. "She seemed nice, if a bit quiet. But now I suspect that was too quiet, if you know what I mean." She leaned forward. "She never really told anyone about herself or her past. Have you talked with her yet?"

"Yes, yesterday actually," Fiona said, looking to see if Clara would comment about her visit. When the faun said nothing, Fiona prompted, "She may be quiet, but her work history was adequate enough to hire her?"

"Yes, yes, it was all in order. I do know how to hire for something as benign as a steward," Clara said and pursed her lips.

"She was a good worker with a good working past, but when you hired her, you didn't bring her on as your personal steward even though yours had left. Why is that?"

Clara shrugged. "I didn't need one. The stewards share duties for all of us."

"But everyone else seems to have a primary. You don't have one? Who keeps your books in order, makes your appointments, manages your letters, that sort of thing?" Orsa's books had been clear in that she worked for Dorin and Clara, managing them both. Why was Clara pretending she wasn't?

"Are there any updates to actually report to me instead of wasting my time?"

"None pressing." It was odd. She would've expected the knowledge that Orsa confessed to come from Clara. Why had she not told anyone of her visit and results? Did she press Orsa to confess without knowing if she would follow through? Orsa told her to tell Dorin specifically, not Clara. Fiona had assumed it's because Clara already knew and secondarily because of Dorin and Orsa's connection.

Clara picked up the watch hanging from the belt of her dress, but before she could say something about the time,

Fiona continued. "Were you interested in the crowns?" She directly left out their type. She didn't want to let loose the only information it seemed the rest of the Seven didn't have just yet.

"I have no interest in the crowns, the bell, or any of that other nonsense. Think for one moment, *Investigator*: Why would I steal my own invention?" Clara raised an eyebrow.

"The journals must've held some valuable information that even in your field of study might have been interesting," Fiona pressed, thinking of the hidden volumes under Clara's desk. "And now you may never retrieve it if whoever stole the items doesn't return them. I believe for everyone it's an insurmountable loss of *history and information*."

Clara's eyes narrowed. "Then they aren't as forward thinking as I am. There will be other breakthroughs. Just because its Olea's discovery doesn't mean the rest of us won't make some of our own." She began gathering her things. "Now if you'll excuse me, I really must be going. Should you have any other questions, don't bother coming to me with them." She smiled, but it was clearly mocking.

"Just one more. Orsa's bracelet? Olea said you still had it, and I wanted to examine it."

Clara furrowed her brow. "Olea is wrong. I don't have the trifling thing. I don't need a reminder of what Orsa did dangling around."

"Were you frightfully upset at Orsa betraying you, knowing that you hired her?"

Clara's head snapped up. "Betray me? How could she betray me?"

Hello, that was a reaction. "By stealing from the Seven, of course. It reflects back on you, does it not? As if you directed her in some way. Perhaps it would be that dotted link between you two that would make you so upset you'd do anything to get the whole debacle over with so you could move on from it."

The faun leaned in, staring at Fiona, unflinching. "Listen to me. I'll talk slowly so you understand. I don't care about Orsa. She stole from us, and she's been captured. That's all that matters. The wardens will find the missing items. I don't need to expend my energy over someone so far beneath me."

The faun's condescension and attitude broke what little reserve Fiona had. "How can you deny—You went to the prison tower yesterday and *yelled* at Orsa." Fiona glared at Clara.

"I most certainly did not." Clara waved her away, huffing. "How dare you! Spread your false, insidious rumors about someone else. I have no attachment to Orsa or this case. There's no reason for me to care." Clara pointed to the door. "Get out of my office this instant. I don't care what Dorin says, you're a waste of my time." She marched to the door and flung it open.

Fiona bit back a retort. Why would Clara deny what could be easily found out? What was she missing? She took a breath and smiled wide to put Clara off with politeness. "Of course. Thank you for your time." She couldn't directly accuse one of the Seven without substantial proof. She needed to figure out what Clara's game was, pretending not to have visited Orsa or coercing her to confess. Where could she turn to find more clues? Could she search the Keeper's home? That would be tricky—people like her had scores of servants. Chewing on what to do next, she decided to at least work on another angle if only to whittle down her list.

Without a backward glance, Fiona took her leave and went to the administrator rooms directly behind Dragomir and Bardo's offices, hoping to cross off two tasks at once. She knocked on the front wall in between. A well-dressed jade-winged fairy and wine-skinned, black-haired centaur looked up at her as she came in between their steward rooms. Though they were separate, as soon as she spoke of her desire to ask questions about the two Seven members, they both came to the hallway.

"I am happy to help you, Investigator," the centaur said. "I have a certain amount of skill others lack that may give you the answers you seek." They pushed back the edge of their dark cape dramatically and threw a glance at the fairy that was clearly meant to make sure the insult targeted directly.

"I don't boast of being able to look up information and read words as if it was a challenge, as some of my colleagues do. But I'm happy to answer your questions and give you the *correct* information." The fairy fluttered to the other side of Fiona.

The intense light glimmering off her jade wings made Fiona wince. She forgot for a moment the fae auras until they all but blinded her. When she opened her eyes, she was surprised to be surrounded so quickly and in between the two clearly tenuous coworkers. Taking a step back into the wall, Fiona said, "That is very kind of both of you. I simply had some questions. I'm sure you've been asked—"

"Yes, yes, about where Keeper Bardo went." The fairy rolled her eyes. "I've told the other members and I'll tell you: Bardo's datebook is booked for the next two weeks. He's away in another page and should only be reached in case of emergencies. I'm more than his personal assistant, you know."

"As if you do any more than others," the centaur muttered.

"I do more than **you**. You may have the back half of a horse, but you have the front half of an a—"

"Wait, wait just a minute please." Fiona broke in, waving her hands. While her experience with faekin was limited, she knew as much as she needed about working with someone you couldn't stand. "Perhaps I can just look at the appointment books myself. Then you could each go back to doing your job. I know it's quite a bit of work to support all the Seven and their duties."

The centaur sniffed, turning around. "I only support Keeper Dragomir. The others each have their own as well."

"And I only support Keeper Bardo. Though I'm sure I could do more for the others if needed." She flew away to her desk.

"How many stewards are there in total?"

"Five," the fairy answered, returning and handing Fiona a diary. "Keeper Cascade won't hire one after the first one quit on her."

"And poor Orsa worked for Keeper Dorin," the centaur said. "I'll suppose he'll have to hire someone else now."

"And Keeper Clara has none? Do you do any work for her?" She suspected Orsa and Clara were very good at hiding their arrangement.

They both shook their heads, though the centaur made a disgruntled face. He also handed Fiona a diary and nodded. "I'm meticulous in my details, unlike some."

Fiona tuned out the fairy's reply as she opened the diaries to see if there was any information to glean. The next couple of weeks were empty for Dragomir starting with the autumn equinox when the items had been stolen. Appointments picked back up after the month ended. She flipped back as far as she could, ignoring dates with people she didn't recognize and noting location names like a vacation to Empearal, in the page of air, and the Great Stairs in Kerus, Dodger's page.

She cross-referenced the dates with Bardo's calendar to see that he too was blocked for almost the same times, but it was always empty. Odd that they would match up. Flipping to today's date, a blocked stretch of time with the initials *SD* starting the day of the autumn equinox till the end of the month were penciled in.

"What is this *SD*?" Fiona asked.

"The Shimmering Depths." The fairy peered over, pointing. "That's when Bardo was supposed to head off for a day study to the Depths. But the scheduling of the unveiling scuttled that trip."

"And it was supposed to be only a day long?"

"Yes. After trips like that to study some part of an elemental page, he usually dives into his findings for a few days after. He does not like to be disturbed."

"Got it. So Keeper Bardo is either in the Shimmering Depths or diving into his findings currently."

"Yes, yes," the fairy said dismissively. "I've said this before. It's not my fault some people can't find their scholars."

"I don't need to find her. She's not on trial here," the centaur said, visibly pouting.

Fiona exhaled, exhausted by the two, and handed them the diaries back. She smiled and moved away quickly, saying, "Thank you both ever so much. You've helped me clear up things tremendously."

"We did?" the centaur said.

"They did?" the fairy said.

Fiona nodded and turned, making her way back down the corridor, hoping the two would go back to their offices instead of standing there arguing. When she didn't hear any bickering behind her, she gave a quick glance and then sighed with relief.

She tapped on Bardo's office door and then let herself in. It was clean and airy with a larger skylight than most of the other offices. A gauzy hammock hung above a desk, and shelves lined the wall with scrolls and books. Blueprints of a domed cathedral were framed and hung in a place of honor in the center.

Going through his desk, his shelves and his work, Fiona could tell Bardo was clearly a scholar of mathematics and architecture. He had more blueprints and sketches than Fiona could make heads or tails of, as well as treatises on bookkeeping, mathematical puzzles, and the like. A variety of books on different historical eras of Copper—the early Circle of Seasons, the hag eradication, subsequent plague—and other tomes about the Book were organized haphazardly on a shelf. Fiona sorted through looking for any new information, but all she found of interest was a variety of mementos nestled among the books: stationery from various extremely upscale inns around the Book, a flimsy wooden fan, and a vial of thin, wisping air. The last one surprised her. This sort of trinket only came from Mistral, a favorite among skimmers who visited Empearal but only during the border retreat where the emperalis air elementals let folks in once a year.

She did the same with Dragomir's office. It was surprisingly similar in a way, clean and airy, although there was a large branch and azure flower candelabra instead of a skylight. There was less furniture here, making the room more spacious. She supposed that made sense for a centaur to want room to move about.

There were many papers on elemental theory and a selection of books describing the elemental chapter of the Books, the categorization of the four elemental pages, in vivid details. Drawings hung on the wall, and there were several of the fire page at the forefront. Fiona raised an eyebrow, reading as much as she could over them. They even chronicled the recent decline of heat and resurgence from the last few weeks in Blaze. Dragomir was quite interested in the page, that much was clear. Enough to steal the secondary crowns though?

She turned her attention to the candelabra. A creation of Dragomir's to be sure. It was quite intricate and the more Fiona stared the more she was sure the flowers were moving, as if a gentle wind was blowing around them. All except one. She reached up on tiptoe and pulled it down. Looking in the silver pipe, she saw stationery paper, blank, but a duplicate of the kind Bardo had tucked away. It was wrapped around a small thin silver chain with a tiny bell on it.

The search confirmed her suspicion about the two working together. Perhaps on this very theft. She needed to get to the Depths and see Bardo for herself. But first she wanted to check in with Dorin, let him know her next step and what she'd learned about Orsa. She found him in his office.

"Come in, come in. I got an earful about you just now." He inclined his head to the administrative door of his office. "You upset Clara quite a bit."

"It wasn't my intention to upset her," Fiona said slowly. "Just to interview her as I've done to everyone else. She has been hard to pin down."

"Well, if you can stick to only talking with her as necessary, I'd appreciate it. She can be a bit sensitive, and I don't want to upset her. The grand opening of our new theater near the sculpture garden is coming up, and she's been working night and day on it. Even having a magnificent statue of Larrakane carved in the new style."

Fiona pushed down her immediate objection to coddling Clara but couldn't conceal her frown so much. She moved on. "I wanted to give you a brief update before going to my next stop. I believe I know where Keeper Bardo may be and am on my way to interview him now."

Dorin's fae ears perked up a bit. "That's an achievement. Do I want to know how you discovered his whereabouts?"

"It's probably best you not know the exact details of how I work. Less to have to apologize to Clara about." Fiona continued on, hoping to not have upset Dorin too much with her pointed jab. "But the other news is less good. While I still think it's worth looking into Keeper Dragomir and others to find the missing items...Orsa confessed to me yesterday."

At this Dorin sat up, all smiling and ease vanished. "Orsa confessed? To stealing the items?"

"She said she stole everything in the chest and to tell you directly."

"I knew it!" A screeching voice came through the administrative door. It flung open and bounced back as Clara stalked into the room. "I knew you were holding something back. Biding your time, gathering as much information as you could. She's a spy, Dorin. She has to be!"

"I'm not here for any secrets except to uncover who stole your missing items and where they are," Fiona said, taken off guard.

"How can that be true when Orsa has confessed? I asked you if there were any updates and you lied to my face. You weren't going to tell us. Orsa might have even told her where the missing items were."

"She did no such thing," Fiona said coldly, feeling like a blotter for letting Clara rattle on without interruption. "She confessed, yes, but I was only told to tell Dorin." Drat. She hadn't meant to say that part. What was it about Clara that drove her to forget herself?

"Why is that?" Clara sneered. "He's not our leader. We're all equal. Why Dorin and not the rest of us?"

Fiona looked at Dorin, whose expression had gone from open and confused to guarded. "We are all equals, yes," he said slowly. He shook his head at Fiona. "It's clear that your intentions weren't what they seemed. I'm sorry to do this, but you leave me no choice. You are fired from this case. If Orsa has confessed, then that settles who stole the items." He took a deep breath, lowering his gaze.

Fired. Her? A sudden headache presented itself and she swallowed her immediate desire to shout at them all for being so exasperating. Dorin had to be hiding something, but what? Fiona weighed her options. Either force a reveal right here, give more information to Dorin but Clara as well, or play the hand as if she had dealt it to herself. She sighed. Direct access to the Seven had been rather nice while it lasted. "I understand."

Dorin's shoulders sagged as he took in her acceptance, but he nodded.

Clara stamped her foot. "Dorin, that is not enough. She should be banned from the page. She's a Guild spy!"

"I assure you, I am no spy for the Guild." Fiona crossed her arms and stared Clara down. For Larrakane's sake at least let her keep her reputation her own.

"There is not enough evidence to suggest that at all, Clara. She's an investigator, and as much as that comes with practices we can't sanction, it would be somewhat ridiculous to think she'd do everything in the way we would."

"You should have her promise you she won't interfere with the Seven again." Clara hissed.

There were small gasps from the crowd that had gathered behind them in the doorway, including Olea, Cascade, Jacopo, and Gaili. Fiona looked pensively at Dorin.

"That is not a light request. I believe you understand that Keeper, and therefore will forgive your moment of frustration that caused the suggestion." Dorin arched an eyebrow betraying the careful façade of a person trying to work within the confines of a modern age. "I will, however, take it upon myself to oversee an investigation into Thorne at once with the help of Olea. If there's anything that shakes out after this that seems unlawful, she will be banned from Copper." He turned to Fiona. "Do I make myself clear?"

Fiona nodded relieved to not be trying to talk her way out of another fac bind or explaining her current one. "Absolutely." As far as she knew, that was an easy line to stay on one side of for now. Unless Clara decided to fabricate something.

Clara looked from Dorin to Fiona and back to Dorin., The small crowd pressed in waiting for her reaction and Clara seemed to sense she'd get no further with everyone having heard Dorin's proclamation. She groaned. "Olea's head has probably been turned. Work with Cascade instead and you have a deal."

Before Dorin could object, Olea piped in, "My head has not been turned, Clara, but your suggestion isn't terrible. Cascade would be best to work with here. My time is claimed currently, and besides I believe it's something she hasn't done yet."

Cascade clapped her coral hands. "Hear! Hear! I'd love to investigate the investigator."

Fiona didn't like the way Cascade stared at her when she said it. Almost like it would be the highlight of everything that had been going on.

"Then it's settled. Jacopo, please see Investigator Thorne and Miss Pannete out," said Clara with glee.

Fiona skirted her way around the crowd and toward the wide eyes of Gaili. Fiona shook her head minutely, and Gaili straightened up and began making her way out with Jacopo leading the way. Clara followed as well to the front steps of the Pavilion.

"I hope your escapade was worth it, Investigator," she said, dropping any polite pretense. "But I do think you probably came up empty handed." She smirked and walked back inside, calling over her shoulder, "Serves you talentless page turners right. You are not the power here. Don't forget that." She disappeared through the door.

Jacopo mouthed, "Sorry," behind her and disappeared as well. The doors to the Pavilion shut with a small snap that felt very final.

After briefly explaining the situation to Gaili as they headed to the inn, Fiona was fuming by the time they walked through the front door. There was a part of all this that felt like a trap, but she couldn't pinpoint when she began to feel that way. And if it was a trap of Clara's making, then she had to hand it to her, it had been done easily and thrown Fiona into a confused shamble.

She almost didn't stop when she heard her name being called. A house steward ran over to them. "Letters for you both, madams," he said, handing them each messages, "and a visitor for you." He motioned for Fiona to follow.

Fiona nodded, barely listening, and was led to a private sitting room. Dorin, a light sheen of sweat over his arched and perfect face, paced in front of the fireplace, velvet cape fluttering behind. "I haven't much time. Clara just left for an appointment, and I don't want to be gone too long. She's been looking to have you off the case since I hired you."

Fiona's brain stuttered as she tried to switch from wonderment at the appearing fae to his words. How had he beaten her here? "Well, mission accomplished. Why did you agree so fast?"

Dorin scratched the back of his neck. "Because I have to do what's best for the Seven as I juggle everything else. I want to trust you but..." He petered off. "What all did Orsa say to you?"

Fiona watched Dorin as she recounted Orsa's message. "She said that they deserve exoneration. People like her. What does she mean?"

He swallowed. "I don't know."

"Or you won't say."

He pulled at the neck of his violet tunic. "This all seems more intricate than I thought. I'm not sure why Orsa is asking for something I don't have the power to give." He sighed and looked at the clock. "I've been here too long. I don't expect you nor advise you to do anything else on this case." He bit his lip and for the first time looked more human than fae. "If Orsa's confessed there's not very much I can do. She'll be sentenced swiftly with or without telling us where the items are."

"You still want to try and save her," Fiona said. It was clear he was in pain. "Are you and Orsa together?"

Dorin stopped halfway to the door. "What? No, not together. I'm sorry I can't tell you more than that but...know that I appreciate your help." He rapped on it twice and it was opened by the house steward who looked not at all surprised to see him. He closed it soundly behind him.

Fiona stood at a loss for what just happened. Inspecting the fireplace, she saw a small circle etched into the brickwork. It was dull and sooty, but there were definitely shoe outlines within. Fiona couldn't make out what it was exactly, but she imagined it was another fae secret. Putting that thought aside for now, she opened the doors and strode off to find Gaili in her room.

The shimmering golden faun was already waiting, pacing the floor, and Fiona relayed in detail what Dorin had done and said. Gaili's eyes were alight as she said, "I've heard of these but only in history books! A fairy ring. Although I don't think they are supposed to be simply anywhere. I'd love to inspect it and find out more."

"When we have more time, I'd love that too. But what do you think of what he said?"

"It's not a lover's tryst then between him and Orsa. But what else could it be?"

"I'm unsure, but either way things have just sped up. Orsa will be sentenced. Dorin has no plans of meeting her demands. We've lost access to the Seven. It's all quite fallen apart. And yet it's even worse."

Gaili crinkled her brow. "What could be worse than all that?"

"Cascade's watching us for fun," Fiona groaned. No doubt the mischievous nymph would put gusto into this indeed. "We'll need to cover our tracks from her if we can, so she doesn't interfere with us."

"Oh, that is worse." Gaili nodded. "There are not a lot of ways to dissuade a nymph like her once she's put her mind to something."

Fiona frowned. "And here I thought you'd have good news to share. What of your letter?"

"Matteo wants to have dinner with us." Gaili smiled shyly. "I can put him off though—"

"No, don't do that. A nice dinner with an amiable man is positive."

"What of your letter?"

Fiona quickly tore it open and read the short note in quick succession. She took a deep breath and let it out. "Henrietta has news she wants to discuss in person. Why couldn't she give an update in the letter? Well, it'll be a nice distraction, I give you that."

She turned, looking out the window at the Pavilion in the distance sitting like a gift in the palm of the trees. A gift, but for who? Gaili patted her on the shoulder. Fiona sighed and grabbed her hand, squeezing it. The day had started off so well too. So sure that she knew exactly how to pin Clara and she had bumbled it. Well, if there was one thing you can say about Fiona Thorne, it was not that she wasn't persistent. For all that was still under Fiona's control, she'd continue on and perhaps, with a little help, clean up this mess.

DECIDING THAT SHE'D HAD enough of trying to fit in, Fiona, with great relish, changed out of her Copper dress and bodice into her normal wool stockings and garter, close-fitting velvet doublet with tunic-length skirting, and comfortingly scratchy, too-many-textures scarf around the neck and shoulders. If she was going to be known, then let her control her image at least. Gaili caught Fiona up on her meeting with Sofia as she changed. Though the two fauns got on easily enough, Gaili didn't suspect Sofia had anything to do with the thefts.

"She had been researching elemental chaos and the very idea of the Summer Crowns gave her ideas. She's been working through them in the wake of the theft, hoping she could replicate what little she was able to. I didn't think you'd want it to be known that there were other crowns, so I just posed theoretically what a winter version would do. For example. It was clearly an idea to chew on. Not one she had waiting in the wings."

"So not our thief for either theft then. Excellent work, Gaili, thinking on your feet like that."

Gaili blushed. "I simply did as you directed."

"I think you did more there. Truly you got answers I wouldn't have been able to. Very valuable to have you work with Sofia," Fiona said, pressing lightly. She had hoped that the last few days had been showing Gaili that she was more than adequate to support Thorne Investigations.

The faun shrugged and asked Fiona what she had learned, changing the subject. Fiona caught Gaili up on what the situation with Bardo and Dragomir.

"Why would they work together?" Gaili said.

"I don't know. I think they might often work together in secret. Perhaps they are both working on something and don't want the prying eyes of the other Seven to know about it? Maybe it wasn't just Dragomir's idea to steal the crowns but both of them? In any case, I think I know where they may be. But do you know a pagemark that's reasonably far from here and leads to the Shimmering Depths? The Waterfall Palace within the Depths to be precise?" Fiona had heard of the palace of the icy elemental water page many times throughout her life but seldom had reason to go near it.

"The Waterfall Palace!" exclaimed Gaili, unfurling her maps of the Book. "I've never been there. Oh, it would be so nice to stay."

"Well, that might not be in order this trip, but perhaps in the future."

"There's a pagemark from here about an hour outside of the city that could take us to the Depths."

"Excellent. We should head over before dinner."

"Well, I'm ready to go whenever you are, although I don't think I'll be much help."

"You will be," Fiona said firmly, "just by being yourself. And perhaps you already have! I have some supplies for the Depths in my scarf, but jelly breaths..." Fiona smiled wide and hopeful. She always kept basic equipment—such as her dark-view glasses or whip, when she had one—within her scarf, but potions expired, so it wasn't practical to keep a constant, expensive supply on hand. If she ever needed to escape a page, it was usually to Spine, or Mistral in a pinch. The Depths took a tad more preparation.

Gaili laughed, her shimmering golden skin somehow radiating in Fiona's fae-bonded vision. "Of course I have some. I brought a sampling of jelly breaths just in case we needed to go to the elemental chapter. What sort of alchemist would you take me for otherwise?"

They quickly got preparations underway, packing everything they would need either in Fiona's scarf or Gaili's bag. They got into a hired carriage outside Calistino. The carriages were horseless, running on alchemical concoctions produced in the Court from the various harvests of the tree nymphs and fairy farmers, making them faster and more efficient than any other page. There was still an attendant to top off the concoctions and direct the carriage, but all in all one couldn't ask for a more comfortable, quick journey through the countryside.

They tucked in loose clothing and slipped on the typical turner wet clothing that would cover them in the water properly. It was made from an algae plant that grew in abundance in the lower half of the Depths. Some of the first turners had the ingenious idea to make clothing out of it, enabling them to be faster through the page and more like the natural creatures that inhabited it. While in the mortal chapter the wet clothing would be considered very revealing, in the Depths it was unlikely to draw an eye except reveal you as an outsider.

Though the Depths was perhaps the second safest page to turn to from anywhere, it was not without its dangers. While Fiona wished she had already replaced her whip, she knew it would be useless underwater. "Do you have anything a bit stabby?"

Gaili frowned. "I left all my metal craft supplies back at the shop. Are you worried we'll encounter something dangerous?"

"I simply like to be on my guard. I miss having a weapon, as finicky as my whip could be. There's only so much sparring one can do with words if a creature is intent on eating you. But we may not be in the water long. We'll make a beeline from the pagemark to the Waterfall Palace."

At the pagemark the ladies got out, covered by their cloaks for modesty, and went to the designated area. Trust that a pagemark in Copper couldn't just be an empty area with a booth. A large cobblestone circle had been set up with a rushing fountain of russet water. Like weak coffee. Fiona could see the water shimmering in the same way that all the faekin had been since she became bonded to Mac. She wanted to run her fingers through it but played with her scarf instead. "Gaili, is that water from Copper? Or the Depths?"

"I'd assume Copper. I don't know of any pages that have a bit of other pages in them the way that Spine does."

"Yes, nor I." Fiona's eyes narrowed watching the water. "Just curious. Probably my mind imagining too much." She hated she couldn't say anything about her bonded sight to Gaili. Sighing, she said, feeling a bit tired, "You know, a sign to which page we're going to would do as well."

"You don't like the fountain?"

"No, it's not that. I'm just being ornery. Forgive me. Shall I lead this one?"

Gaili nodded and held out her hand to Fiona. She grasped it and pulled from her scarf a small fragment of a nautilus shell she had found on her first trip during training. She rubbed her fingers over its smooth, cold exterior and marveled at the way it still felt somewhat wet even after all this time. Focusing on the Depths, she saw the rushing of the icy blue water as it surged past her and the shape of the Waterfall Palace as she had seen before in paintings. She took a step forward as the world of Copper, bright with amber light and quiet in this somewhat emptied pagemark folded away before her to reveal a wall of rippling, glowing blue-green water. The smell of salt and the sound of it filled her senses. She took another step forward, holding tight to Gaili's hand, into the water. As she did, she felt something whip around her ankle, drawing her attention. She fought off the hesitation to pause, for if she did, she didn't know what trouble would happen with the turn. She could be split from Gaili or they could be tumbled somewhere they didn't want to go. Pushing through the distraction, she continued forward until nothing but cool azure water surrounded her and the light of Copper shut off behind them as the world folded back to what it was once more.

She squeezed Gaili's hand in to reassure herself that it was still there and then whipped around, swimming and glancing for what had come with them. For it had to have been something traveling along. There had been no tug to keep her in Copper. But she saw nothing but the shifting currents of the water amid the bioluminescent light from various algae in the page, the darkened shapes of a mountainous structure in the distance, and small creatures who ignored them swimming by.

Fiona took a small inhale, measuring the effect of the jelly breath they had eaten. Though the water filled her mouth and nostrils, it only tickled a little. It was neither hot nor cold, and if it wasn't for the water surrounding them, she could very well believe they were still breathing air. "Did you see anything come with us?"

"Anything? Was someone else there?"

"I don't know. I thought I felt something like a vine wrap around my ankle but it could've been my imagination. Let's be quick about getting to the Palace."

They swam then, lucky to ride along the current among speckled orange and yellow fishes, their luminescent blue light throwing shadows their way. The shadowy shape in the distance began to take form as they went along into a large rocky ledge. *Rock* wasn't the exact term for it. It was a mixture of white and purple shells, orange coral, and attached green anemone dotting it's exterior. A massive reef, an exotic home to the tiny and large who resided within it. How far down it reached, Fiona couldn't tell. The current was swift, forcing the water over the edge of the reef ledge like a horse galloping toward freedom, and where it fell, bubbles and swirling water coalesced into a majestic pool of movement. On the far outside edges, the water stilled, a different current than the one above. It put to Fiona's mind very much of the water cascading over the side of one of the floating islands in Rise. *Waterfall* was apt. Now to see the Palace portion.

She motioned to Gaili to follow her and then swam around the large reef, the suits making the long journey easier for their bodies. Built into the back of the reef was an arched entrance crusted with starfish and a landing area for land-dwellers to stand. A dock floating in the water and anchored to the reef gently swayed on the landing area. The sound of the burbling rushing water filled their ears so that they had to shout to be heard.

They landed at the entrance, Fiona trailing behind Gaili. She had told the faun to go through the motions of inquiring about a room, securing it, and then being taken to it. Fiona would be there as a helper of sorts, but her aim was to gain access to the register and search for Bardo. Luckily it had become Travel Guild law in the Book for inns to start carrying a register, among other rules to ensure no skips—page turners on the run from the law—were staying there or had been. Of course, they could only enforce this in pages that allowed them access, like the elemental water page. It should make what in the past was hard-won information little more than a few minutes of theft.

As they entered the arch, a mermaid floated out to meet them. Her kelp-like hair drifted in the water around her pale lilac shoulders that were covered in small pops of coral. Its lengths hid ample cleavage and curves in a way that accentuated them more than obscured. While it was customary that those who interacted most with skimmers who toured the Book tried to follow the propriety of the culture they were interacting with, some followed the letter if not the law of such gestures. "Greetings, travelers," she said in the halting common tongue. "Welcome to the Waterfall Palace, sparkle within the Depths. How can I help you this visit?"

Fiona nudged Gaili, who startled out of her wonderment. The faun licked her lips quickly and said in Aguan, "I would like a room please. Or to inquire about one?"

The mermaid smiled. "Your pronunciation is quite perfect." She assessed Gaili up and down and then, seemingly pleased at what she saw, swirled in the water, her hair uncovering angles that made Fiona's face grow warm. "Certainly. Right this way, madam." Propelled by her large pearlescent tail, she swam through a smaller arch entrance and into a room with cubbyholes, a small stand, and another no-less-curvaceous mermaid, who smiled in greeting.

Fiona glanced at the cubbyholes to see large shells, starfishes, and other bits of the water page attached to lines of rope. Beneath each cubby was a plaque of some sort and a few words. She frowned. She could speak Aguan fine enough, but she was terrible at reading it.

"Now how large of a room are you looking for? And how long will we have the pleasure of your stay?"

Gaili blinked, eyes wide. "Well, I suppose one night. And a room for two?" She glanced at Fiona.

Fiona dipped her head low. "If it will please you, mistress."

The mermaid nodded and pulled open a large chalkboard, looking at the Aguan writing on it. Fiona tipped upward, treading water slowly, trying to rise above the stand and see what was on it. Drat if she couldn't understand what any of it said. She should've swapped places with Gaili, who could probably read it with no issue.

"Do you think," Fiona said, trying to come up with a way to tell Gaili to look at the ledger without seeming suspicious, "we should stay on the opposite side of the Keeper, mistress? His assistant didn't say what room he was in, but perhaps you know?"

Gaili frowned.

The mermaid behind the stand pursed their lips. "We do not want any issues here, please. If you have conflict with a guest, it would be better that you not stay."

"No, no, I assure you. We do not. I just want to give the mistress her privacy," Fiona said slowly. "Something we are sure you can give to the mistress, of course." Fiona added on, trying to pull their eyes: "She has been through so much this week, we simply want to give her the best vacation money can buy."

The mermaid's eyes lit up. "Well, that can be arranged. We can do the upper floor beneath the roaring river. It is quite opposite from the waterfall suite."

And just like that, they had their information. Fiona spoke up, keeping her head low, "That should work for you, mistress."

Gaili nodded. "Yes, that will be fine."

"Marvelous." The mermaid who greeted them clapped her hands. "If you'll just sign here, we can show you to your room."

Gaili signed the chalkboard after glancing wide eyed at Fiona. She was probably worrying about if they had achieved their mission or not.

The mermaid grabbed a starfish out of a high cubby and gestured for them to follow. A thick curtain of seaweed parted before them, unveiling a large hole that she swam through. Fiona had wondered how they would be getting to their room, as she saw no entrances from the outside. Here now she could see a network of tunnels, natural to her eye at least, were made in the mountainous structure. The mermaid swam slowly, allowing them to follow along as she went up and up within the structure.

"It sounds like Bardo is staying in the waterfall suite," Fiona said, slipping into the language of humans and swimming alongside Gaili.

"Oh good." Gaili sighed with relief. "I was worried that I bungled it."

"Never. But remind me in the future to have you read the information we need instead of me. Now just to get there from here." Fiona looked around. "You keep following. If she asks where I went, say I forgot the luggage and had to return for it. Feel free to make me out to be a simpleton."

"Oh, I could never do that! You're clearly bright."

Fiona smiled at her friend as she started treading water. "Pretend I'm someone you dislike then, like Petronia."

Gaili's eyes widened, but Fiona ducked down before her friend could exclaim about her sense of humor. It was an acquired taste, to be sure. She turned quickly into another tunnel, looking for a sign or some direction as to how to navigate the place. Surely they didn't take guests to rooms and then expect them to never leave. She knew the Waterfall Palace was supposed to have several extremely nice amenities such as a thermal bath, a relaxing grotto, and a diving chamber.

She found what she was looking for and puzzled out the sign—written in Aguan and, luckily, common enough words for Fiona to grasp—that led to a viewing of the waterfall. Hopefully the room wouldn't be too far from the main attraction. She swam there wishing she had time to explore as a guest and indulge her curiosity on the wonder of the place clearly made in the Depths, for the Depths, and then modified for skimmers to visit.

She heard the sound of rushing water and headed toward it, propelling herself up into the hole where the viewing chamber was. She stopped short when she found herself surrounded by a throng of people. Of course it would be a popular spot in the palace. Before she could turn around, she heard a whispered voice in her ear: "Now what are you doing here? This doesn't seem like the kind of place a jobless investigator would head to next."

Fiona whipped around to see nothing but the surrounding water behind her. The voice had been familiar though. She narrowed her gaze. "Who's there?"

Several people glanced back at her, the sound carrying farther than others' voices with the aid of the water-breathing jellies. She smiled and ducked her head, swimming toward the translucent wall that showed the waterfall. She placed her back to the wall and stared out at the room and the other people. Who had been talking to her, and why could she not see them?

"It's not that simple, you see," the voice said on her left ear this time, a melody rising in the words. "I'm in your head. Or I'm everywhere. I'm everywhere and in your head." Cascade. That dratted nymph had found her.

"Do stop being a distraction. This is highly inappropriate."

"As inappropriate as stealing information?" the voice said again but in the other ear.

Fiona shook her head. She didn't know much about nymphs, but she had the sinking suspicion that Cascade was using her element to its fullest. There wasn't much she could do to outrun a water nymph in water. She moved away from the wall. She needed to get rid of the nymph if she was going to find Bardo and interrogate him about Dragomir. "I didn't steal anything. What do you want, Cascade?"

"To have some fun, of course. This is new. I've never been to the Waterfall Palace before."

Fiona raised an eyebrow. "Never? Have you never been to the Depths at all?" There was silence. A first. Fiona got the impression the nymph didn't like the question. "What can I do to get you to go away?"

"Oh, I'm just doing my job. Don't spoil this for me," Cascade said, a pout in her voice.

"And I'm just trying to do mine," Fiona said irritably. "Do you not care about anyone but yourself?"

"Of course I do," Cascade said, a rush of cool water dispersing around Fiona. "Just because I like to have fun doesn't mean I don't care."

"Well, you certainly don't show it. You could at least try to not hinder me proving Orsa's innocence," Fiona said pleadingly. She turned a little, looking for any sign of Cascade. "It may be all fun and games for you, but the rest of her life is at stake. You of all people should know what's like to be tied to something you have no control over or the power to change unless an outside force intervenes. Let me do my work and be that intervention for Orsa. Please."

Again silence. Fiona stared out into the water, ignoring the crowd who was now openly turning and watching her talk to herself. The water shimmered in front of her and she could see the outline of Cascade, though she was fairly translucent. The only difference Fiona could tell was that Cascade was more amber then the blue-green of the Depths.

"Fine. But if Clara asks, I'll say you coerced me. Not that it would be any different. I lie to her all the time."

Fiona smiled despite herself. "Thank you. Why don't you take over our stay here? You might as well enjoy the room since we won't."

Cascade lit up, her true coral coloring fading into view. "Let the record state I never asked for it or about them." She darted up and out with only a small wave cresting toward Fiona.

Fiona suspected Cascade already knew what was going on and where the room was located. Cascade was full of secrets, that much was sure.

She looked around and noticed that the crowd had come closer during her conversation with the invisible Cascade. There was a spattered murmuring. Fiona groaned inwardly. Now there would be evidence that she had been here. She needed to get to Bardo quick before this got out of control. Fiona got away from the intrigued crowd, slipping out. There had to be an entrance to the private waterfall area somewhere. She trailed her fingers along the wall, feeling every nook and cranny for something different. Everything looked the same. As she was speeding along, she passed a patch of seaweed on the wall. She stopped and pressed her hand to the seaweed. There was nothing behind it. She couldn't tell how to get it parted as the mermaid did before. She dived in, struggling through the seaweed till she was on the other side.

She traversed a short passageway before coming to a large clam with a door knocker of shell upon it. It was the only sign in the passageway that it wasn't an immediate dead end. Fiona pulled her drifting curls away from her face as she thought about the best way to approach this. First, she had to get in the room. It wouldn't do any good trying to interview Bardo out here. Then she'd have to wing it from there. She just needed to understand if her suspicions were correct. Were Bardo and

Dragomir here together, and was it with the stolen items or with no knowledge of them?

She knocked on the door, the sound echoing into the chamber that lay beyond it. There was an immediate sound of suction around the door as it opened away from her. A short, bald, golden-skinned fairy, silver opalescent wings flickering behind his back, hovered in the waterless room.

His face scrunched up in confusion. "Where's the tray?"

Fiona swallowed, thinking fast. "Oof, forgotten. Seems we couldn't understand what you wanted so thought I'd come here direct," she said in Aguan.

The fairy frowned, but before he could say anything else, Fiona propelled herself through the opening. There was a barrier, like thin jelly, that she passed through. It seemed to cover her, making her feel slimy for a moment. Just as quickly as she noticed it, it dissolved into nothing. Fiona had heard of specially made material for places that mingled the elements, but she hadn't expected the oily feeling.

The room was a large chamber with doors on either side of its oval shape. Algae-covered rocks lined the wall, like decorative trim, pushing air bubbles that burst. Minute popping noises the only evidence that something was at work to bring in breathable air. The back wall was transparent from floor to ceiling and had a lovely set of oyster shells as chairs seated in front to watch the view. Outside she could see the rush of the waterfall as it passed by. It completely blocked any prying eyes, should they be on the other side.

She turned to the fairy, whom she assumed to be Bardo. "Actually, I'm here with a few questions for you. Do you happen to know where Dragomir is residing at this time?"

Bardo flitted back. "Who are you?" he demanded.

Fiona glanced around the room for anything relevant. "I'm an investigator looking into the theft of the curiosities at the Pavilion. Dragomir hasn't been seen since they were taken and is a prominent suspect." She could try to gain information with mostly honesty or mostly lying. She decided to try both.

"I thought Clara handled that with the wardens." Bardo narrowed his eyes. "Orsa was arrested before I even left."

She slowly moved toward the far side of the room. "Yes, and that arrest is almost certainly incorrect. Dorin and Clara hired me directly. Some additional clues point to Dragomir as a suspect. Where is she?" Fiona turned toward one of the closed doors.

Bardo flung himself in front of her. "Excuse me. You have no right to come in my room and ask questions about myself or Dragomir. I have no idea where she is. Why in the dark edge would I?"

"Well," Fiona said slowly, "I do believe you two are working together."

"I wouldn't work with Dragomir if my life depended on it," Bardo scoffed.

"Really? How do you explain the unexplained absences that you both take at the same time?"

Bardo crossed his arms. "Us being gone at the same time explains nothing. It's not my fault she likes to leave around the times that I do. She's probably just mimicking my behavior for some nefarious purpose."

Fiona nodded. "Oh, that very well could be. But you do seem to both go to the exact same places too. An Empereal trinket here. A stationery keepsake from an expensive inn there. It seems that you two have been conspiring together for some time." She moved away from the door toward the other end of the room, letting her eyes roam the interior. It was a living quarters of sorts with tables, chairs, and other accoutrements for a pleasant stay.

"You've gone through my office! You certainly had no permission to do that, I don't care who hired you." Bardo flew after her and wagged his hand. His face was beet red as he yelled, the sound only slightly muffled from the rushing water. "I'll have you taken away by the palace staff. Coming into my room and accusing me of plotting with Dragomir. And for your information, Dragomir, wherever she may be, wouldn't have stolen the curiosities."

"How can you be so sure if you're not close?"

"We've worked with each other. I don't have to conspire with someone to know that they wouldn't have done what you're accusing."

"Reports say that she was very interested in the Summer Crowns when they were unveiled. I believe you two even had an argument about them."

"The Seven argue all the time. Why don't you ask what we don't argue about?"

Fiona spied what she was looking for and swam toward the waterfall. She picked up two mugs and sniffed both of them. They each had the same aromatic cordial inside. "If you're alone, why have two glasses of the same drink?"

He crossed his arms, then dropped them. "I don't have to answer to you. In fact, I'm done entertaining your questions at all." Bardo flew to the clam door and opened it.

"It's fine. You can tell the palace staff about me. But when I show Dorin and Clara how everything in your trinkets and datebooks line up, you won't be able to ignore their questions."

"No, don't," a feminine voice said from behind Fiona. She whirled around to see a sleek-looking centaur with golden braided hair coming out of the door Bardo had been guarding. "I didn't steal the crowns. We didn't steal anything. We're not scheming together."

Bardo flew to her side and floated next to her. Fiona recognized why they seemed familiar now. She had seen them arguing together as her and Gaili had arrived at the Pavilion that first night. "Well then, what has been going on? Because as far as Clara is concerned, you are a suspect, even if she's already got poor Orsa locked up."

Dragomir looked at Bardo. Bardo shook his head no, but a silent communication passed between them. Bardo sighed.

"We're simply together. No conspiring, no thefts. Simply...together."

Fiona blinked. While she had suspected someone to be having a tryst, it hadn't been these two. "I'm... What? Sorry?"

Dragomir smiled. "Yes, that's sort of the reaction we expect should anyone find out. But regardless. We're not conspiring over stolen curiosities. We thought the matter had been settled with Orsa's arrest and so felt comfortable leaving as we normally did."

"One of us on a work trip and the other on vacation."

Fiona frowned. "But your administrator didn't know where you were, Dragomir."

"Well, I never tell him the exact details. He is among the many people who wouldn't be able to understand Bardo and I. All leaves fall the same direction to many faekin, as the saying goes. No one can understand looking past old scars to something new like Bardo and I can." She smiled up at him. "But I did say I'd be going on vacation."

"Dear, I think your steward may have been too busy arguing with mine," Bardo said, a tender change in his voice as he addressed her. "Remember they were talking back and forth about Orsa and Dorin. It would be just like him not to pay attention when she's got something to say."

"You're right. They are almost as bad as we were." Dragomir smiled, poking Bardo in the side.

"Well, I do believe you two aren't conspiring. About the curiosities at least." Fiona sighed but was thankful to cross them off the list of suspects. She bit her lip. "What did you mean about Orsa and Dorin? What were your assistants saying?"

Bardo and Dragomir glanced at each other uneasily. Bardo started, "There is something it may interest you to know." He crossed his arms again. "But before I tell, you have to promise not to mention anything about us or where you got the information."

"I'm sure she wouldn't tell," Dragomir said.

"All the same. I'd like your assurance that what you know about Dragomir and I will remain a secret. The Order of Seven isn't ready for information like our relationship just yet. And I won't see Dragomir hurt."

"You have my word."

"Yes, but is it worth anything?" Bardo said.

"Bardo!" Dragomir exclaimed.

"No, he's quite right to ask. He would've been a blotter not to. But I can assure you I'm quite good at keeping secrets. If there's a need for what you're about to tell me to be said to anyone else, then perhaps it can just be from Bardo. It's clear from his datebook that he is in the Shimmering Depths. I have no reason to press you for more than that."

Bardo nodded. "Clara and Dorin have been acting suspicious, even before the curiosities went missing. I haven't known Clara a long time. I was much closer with Taliana before she left. But Dorin I've known for years now. Something happened when Orsa came on board." He glanced at Dragomir before going on. "Our assistants think there's a dalliance there. I had some suspicions as well, but they were confirmed when I overheard a conversation between Orsa and Dorin at the Trussadary Inn when they didn't know I was there. I went to meet with Dragomir quickly, but once I found another Seven there, I left. They were talking about the plight of Orsa's people in a strange manner. Her being a faun, I wondered if she meant her family in specific or her town. But as I continued listening, I realized she wasn't talking about fauns. She was talking about hags."

"Hags? Like the mythical wise women who scare children?"

"Hags like the shape-changing faekin who are supposed to be exiled from all proper society."

Dragomir clasped her hand around his, moving forward. "We never said anything of course. I mean, who are we to judge? Orsa has been so nice and easy to work with that I thought Bardo just heard wrong."

"Yes, until I got an itch to prove to myself that I wasn't. I saw her change. Just once. In Dorin's office."

"How on earth did you see that?"

"The skylight looks down from the roof. It was easy enough for me to get up there unnoticed." The fairy smiled. "Once I had proof, I stopped looking though. Like Mir said, who are we to call out someone else trying to go against the growth?"

"So you believe Clara and Dorin knew she was a hag when they hired her?"

They nodded. "If not, then Dorin certainly figured it out at some point," said Dragomir.

This threw everything Orsa said into a whole new light. Fiona felt she needed to connect with Gaili at once. She could use her knowledge to understand what it all could mean and whether it still pointed to Orsa as the real culprit after all.

"Thank you for your time," Fiona said, making her way toward the door.

"Of course," Dragomir said graciously.

"Please don't bother us again," Bardo said with gruffness.

Fiona nodded but turned. "One more thing that you should probably know. Cascade followed me here and is staying in the palace. If I were you, I'd be extremely careful."

Bardo shook his head. "Now that's one person who can keep a secret. Thank you for the warning though."

Fiona raised an eyebrow but swam through the door and away from the private passageway as it closed behind her. Perhaps she had assessed the water nymph poorly. Larrakane help her, she was losing complete control of her intuition. Perhaps it was her. Perhaps it's just what dealing with faekin was like.

FIONA REACHED GAILI AND suggested that they leave posthaste. She gave her a shortened version, unsure of where Cascade was, and vowed to tell her more once they were back at the inn.

They made their way back to the pagemark, this time with no hitchhikers. Although Fiona thought herself an excellent swimmer, she found herself tired from the exercise.

Back in Copper, she was quiet on the gondola ride, leaving the gondolier singing to fill the silence. Fiona had much she wanted to mull over and discuss with Gaili in privacy. Her anxious energy practically made her jingle, but when they approached the inn, she found that her mulling discussion would have to wait. There waiting for them in the sitting room downstairs was Henrietta.

The captain looked finer dressed than Fiona had ever seen her. Instead of her normal pear-green baggy knee-caped trousers and bright blousy shirt, Henrietta wore a fitted black doublet nicely done up with sapphire buttons that sparkled in the candlelight. Her dark hose were silken, clearly expensive, but meant to be seen. And nothing drew the eye better than the brilliant sky-blue cape over her shoulder, throwing contrast befitting the Copper page. Her gray-touched strawberry hair was somewhat tamed under a flat cap, but you couldn't take the captain out of the woman completely.

Gaili had a brief intake of breath before stuttering out, "Hello, Henrietta."

Henrietta grinned and strolled toward her, dipping a low bow. "Miss Gaili, a breath of fresh air doesn't come often to this old heart, but seeing you provides the same enchantment." She nodded to Fiona. "And Mistress Thorne. Well met. I have tidings I know you need to hear. And a treat from home as well." She held up a familiar brown bag. The smell of coffee beans wafted in the air.

"That's very thoughtful. Thank you, Captain." Fiona smiled despite her anxiety. "How do you travel Copper without a guide?"

The captain winked and tapped her nose. "Some ports are more well met than others." Henrietta held out her elbow, and Gaili entwined her arm through. Fiona went to step forward before Henrietta held her other arm out saying, "Don't think me impolite. I have room enough for two."

Fiona laughed and took Henrietta's arm, letting herself be escorted into the lodge. The dining room was quite crowded for the evening meal, but they were able to get a table with a seat to spare for when Matteo arrived. Henrietta's charming demeanor and cutting dress proved quite enchanting for the innkeeper, and before Fiona knew it, they were sat with beautiful cut glass goblets of wine, platters of fruit and cheese, and warm hunks of bread. More food than she had ever been served there before.

Henrietta raised her goblet and her bushy eyebrow. "A toast to our bright futures, eh?"

"And what's so bright about them?" Fiona asked, a tiny bit over being patient.

"Getting records for your mysterious person was extraordinarily easy," Henrietta said and then took a deep long drink. "I found out that your Sadie Stoneguard holds quite the estate in Three Churches."

"So she truly is from Rise?" Well, she could be wrong about one thing without being wrong about everything. It had been known to happen on occasion.

"I'm not sure what her family's fortune is, but they've been known on Rise for half a century at least. Perhaps a page turner was in her family tree and that moved them up," said Henrietta.

"But don't you stop being a noble family once you don't have a turner in the family?" said Gaili.

"Ah yes, but if you had the means to propel yourself into the right social circles, your family could benefit for a long while," Fiona said.

"But forty odd years a generation doesn't make," Henrietta said. She was right. Even if Stoneguard had a page turner in her family one generation from her, her house would be more well known to Fiona and, she suspected, Henrietta as well.

"Do you think it's false nobility?" Fiona said. It had happened before. Doctored papers detailing the page turner ability in a low-born person to raise them to nobility. Long before detailed records were kept by the Rise libraries, it was easy enough to claim the worth of an aristocrat and even take an office of the Queen. Not high enough to get caught, just high enough to have some power over those below the aristocracy.

"Aye, could be." Henrietta nodded. "But if so, it's well done. I talked to servants and had some chat to others who have met or known the woman for years. If it's false, it's been followed through well and she's completely integrated with the higher set."

"Any idea of her interests from those discussions?" said Fiona.

"Not particularly. She does seem to dabble in art pieces, music, sculptures and the like, but what noble doesn't currently? But that's not the most valuable of my information. This black card you found." Henrietta produced it from within her jacket, tore a corner off it, and held it out. "Put it on your tongue."

"What are you doing?" Gaili said, mouth dropping.

"Good authority says this is a sleeping draught made stable. One of the reasons I wanted to see you directly with the information."

"Impossible." Gaili cocked her head. "It would take a strong additive to condense a potion such as that into a card. And one that doesn't work on contact?"

Fiona glanced at Gaili but then took the small corner and placed it on her tongue. It dissolved almost instantly. Her head began to feel heavy, and she shook it, surprised. "I'm feeling a pull on my senses with even that bit."

"The whole card can be dissolved in water or a glass of wine. It would put an elephas to sleep with that amount. You could of course make someone swallow it, but that would take an angry hand."

"And Stoneguard had a stack of these?" Gaili said to Fiona.

"Yes. That's quite a bit to think on." Fiona chewed on the matter. "Do you know how these are made, Gaili?"

"No, but I could experiment and find out."

"Yes, do. She must be an agent for the Queen. Were you able to discover anything there?"

"If she's an agent for the Queen, the lengths to which she's gone to fabricate her life would make sense. But she's not a page turner."

"True. That makes her less valuable when the Queen has so many of us on retainer. Well, it's all helpful information if not entirely clear how it fits into the whole picture yet. I owe you one." Fiona ran her fingers up and down her scarf. If Stoneguard could get people to sleep, she could steal from them. But without knowing who she really was, it was hard to determine motive or opportunity. And why would she come back to the scene of the crime to take a tour?

"Matteo!" Gaili exclaimed, rising from the table. "I'm so glad you wrote. You know Fiona, and this is our friend Captain Henrietta."

Matteo's faun fur was smoothed down and curled to perfection, only showing from the calf down under tight silken hose that left little to the imagination. His top was ruffled, high collared, and deeply violet as to be a bit like looking into the dark edge and feeling oneself drawn in, despite all warnings learned in life. Fiona raised an eyebrow at the clothing that she felt would've looked dreadful on anyone else. But Matteo pulled it off with very little effort.

"It's nice to see you again," Fiona said.

"You as well, Mistress Fleur Oatfallow." He chuckled. "I see that you have many names, but for a friend of Gail's I won't put my guard up."

"The duplicity was necessary for a variety of reasons. Are you still employed by Mistress Stoneguard?"

Matteo's smile fell as he sat down. "No, thankfully. My contract to guide her around Copper ended the night you met us. I saw her safely to the pagemark and dusted my hands of her."

"Was she awful to work with?" Gaili asked.

"Quite rude. So many places around our page she needed to see firsthand. The Calistino gardens, the Lucent Island battlegrounds, the steam forests in the south. Exhausting to travel with her. If it wasn't for the immense amount of paper tossed my way to guide her, and the plush carriages she provided for the long journeys, I would've quit on the first day."

Fiona leaned forward. "She's quite rich then?"

"She may be, but it wasn't direct from her. Another paid me, out of Spine I do believe."

"Spine!" Gaili said. "Why would someone from Spine pay you to take her around Copper?"

Matteo shrugged. "I didn't think it worth asking. But is there more here? You both seem uncommonly interested in her. Even providing a false name."

Fiona shook her head, not ready to divulge information even to a friend of Gaili's. "I like to keep my anonymity."

"Well, if that's the case I would suggest keeping your likeness out of the *Card*," Matteo said, chuckling.

"Or your real name out of people's heads," Henrietta added. She turned to Gaili, "Soon enough you may have to be the front person for her. A job I think could go to no prettier a dove."

Gaili blushed.

Matteo glanced between the faun and the captain with an appraising look. What Fiona thought would've been jealousy was instead clearly admiration. "No one could do it better, I agree."

"Fi could and does." Gaili looked at her hands as she rubbed them together. "She doesn't need me simply because she's becoming more well known."

"Aye, but she'd be a blotter not to consider it."

"It's more than considered," Fiona piped in. Perhaps these were just the two people who could help convince Gaili where she could not. "I've offered employment to Gaili in my investigations already. She provides so much support, it makes practical sense."

"Truly? That's wonderful, Gails. You always wanted to have a reason to travel the Book. Larrakane blessed you with ability and now means." Matteo grabbed her hand and squeezed it. "You can stop your studies for a while, I'm sure. It would be good for you to have a vocation to call your own."

Gaili's rose eyes went wide and she stared at her hands. Fiona pursed her lips, chiding herself. She had forgotten that Gaili made no mention of her shop to her friends and family back home. And she had inadvertently opened the door without making sure she was ready to tell. Fiona tried to manage the situation a bit. "Gaili has such wonderful talent. I could regale you with what I've learned, but perhaps, Gaili, you'd like to tell Matteo of how we met?"

Matteo lifted an eyebrow and smiled encouragingly.

Henrietta, seeming to sense a shift in the mood, laid a reassuring hand on Gaili's shoulder.

Gaili took a small breath. "I helped Fiona when she needed custom clothing for a flame sprite. Well, maybe not clothing. It was a pocket of metal really. That's all."

"And you created this yourself?" Matteo asked with something akin to happiness in his voice.

Gaili nodded, looking relieved at his response. "I have an artisan shop on Spine actually."

"That's splendid! You always were keen to work with your hands." He took a drink from his mug. "I'm delighted for you. I'm glad you're not shutting yourself in books and simply following after Clara. Talk about a rude woman," he said to Fiona.

"Do you know Clara well?" Fiona asked.

"Indeed. That faun would have you believe she didn't grow up in the same place we did. She may be a Seven, but she came from the same roots as all of us. Now she's an absolute nightmare to work with compared to Stoneguard."

"You're working with her now?"

"No, but I was a few days ago. Gathering old maps of the regions from the archives. Taking her to various locations around the region based on some work she was doing. Interesting places, but bah, again, if the paper wasn't flowing, I'd have never done it. But it gave me some time to delve into my own interests too." He took another swig and looked to Henrietta. "I heard her call you Captain before. Where do you ship out of?"

"Mistral, incidentally," Henrietta said, eyes roving the faun. "A beautiful place everyone should find their way to someday."

"Is that an invitation?" Matteo said, smiling. He winked at Gaili and, still holding her hand, caressed it with his thumb. "Any friend of Gails must have quite the creative mind or interesting life. I'd love to hear about your travels."

"And I should like to tell them to delightful ears. I'm glad they have multiplied," Henrietta replied, ending with a booming laugh.

It took Fiona a moment to notice as she chewed on the beats of her case that Gaili was blushing but not moving from either suitor. For a moment Fiona felt lonely in the midst of the crowded dining room. It was an uncomfortable feeling and one she wanted to shake off as soon as possible without spoiling anyone else's fun. She plastered on a smile and said brightly, "I'm going to go upstairs, I think. My head is full of details that must be either puzzled out immediately or slept on."

"Oh, Fi, I can fix you a small tonic if you have a headache," Gaili said, moving to get up.

"No, stay, enjoy the rest of the evening. I shall be perfectly fine with a closed eye and a little quiet."

"If you're sure," Gaili said.

"I am," Fiona said firmly but smiled to soften it and, before there could be further push, got up and went upstairs. If she was going to be lonely, she might as well do it alone without false face.

She dragged the largest chair, piling pillows and blankets within, to the glass stained windows and sat it squarely in front. Copper glass was the best in the Book and the stained glass decorations and patterns within marveled the imagination of the other pages. She removed mortar and kettle implements from a pocket she rarely used toward the end of her scarf—she was always ready to make a cup of coffee when needed—and opened the pouch from home. Fiona settled herself in the chair as the water heated in the fire, and she stared at the window, slowly grinding beans in her mortar.

The amber glow of lamplights outside and in cast shadows and added a foreboding depth to the portrait she didn't think the designer had meant to share.

Fiona felt quite drained. Now that Orsa had confessed, Fiona had only a couple of days at best to understand what had happened and get Orsa out of the situation that she may have put herself in. Or at the very least have something concrete to share with Elinor and put her at ease about where her sister's life had led. What did it mean that Orsa was a hag? What was her goal? While Fiona's mother had done a wonderful job of scaring her as a child with the Copper nightmare, she was a grown woman now and could look at the stories with more reason than fear. If Orsa's goal was to exonerate the hags for whatever part they played in history, why steal to get that? It sounded like she had a working relationship with Dorin, and by Dorin's own confession he wanted things to be well for Orsa.

And if Orsa was a hag, did that mean Elinor, her sister, was as well? They didn't look alike, as Gaili had made note of, but would the same hold in their true form? It certainly explained why through her bond with Mac, Elinor looked so different than Gaili, Matteo, and even Clara. She didn't quite match the other fauns' essence, if that's what she was seeing. Who would tell her the truth if she asked? Elinor already proved resistant and Orsa even more so.

The crackling fire reminded her to remove the kettle, and she poured it over the freshly ground beans. Fiona inhaled deeply the sweet scent of chocolate mingled in the aroma of her favorite coffee. Steam rose from the cup, misting her face. The first sip seemed to take the edge of her tiredness away.

Beyond the idea of hags, there was also the Seasonal Crowns to think of. Mac said together they could do serious damage to the page. Who would want to do that? Of her, thankfully shortened, list of suspects, there still remained Clara, Dorin, and unfortunately Olea. Dorin at the very least didn't seem to want much beyond helping Orsa, but that could be his play. Clara clearly wanted to be in charge but wasn't. But there were easier ways to take over the Seven than create havoc. Olea loved history, lore, and studying those things in great detail. What if she thought she could find more with just a little power? Would she really do that to Mac, someone who seemed genuinely thankful not to be in power anymore?

Fiona took another hot sip, staring at the glazed glass, its triangle patterns glinting in the light. She focused not so much on the specific patterns but the glass as a whole. Gazing at it and trying to empty her whirring mind of all thought, she saw it now for what it was. Larrakane. A representation of her, at least, from the faekin perspective. But it was clear that the visage of a striking woman clad in twilight-blue velvet folds had to be her. Crown of black curly hair mixed among the stars. What Fiona had mistaken for an open palm earlier was a slim open book. Clever. If only letting go to understand the puzzle worked that well in real life.

13

"ORSA'S A HAG?" GAILI exclaimed the next morning over coffee and breakfast. They were seated in the same room, the copper sun rising and cascading light into the room from the window that now looked once more to Fiona like a smattering of colored patterns. Perhaps it was only in twilight that its real picture could be revealed.

"I believe it. Elinor herself said she wouldn't last in the prison, she looked ill when we saw her, and Bardo says he saw her change to her true form with his own eyes." She had filled in Gaili with everything that had happened while they were in the Depths without holding back. She felt she kept her word as Gaili was working the investigation with her, and she didn't want to keep yet another thing from her.

"But that's amazing. She must've lasted all this time hiding away from society. I wonder what drew her back to it. I don't believe anyone has seen a hag in almost a century."

Fiona stifled a yawn, surprised about how tired she felt. "Is there any danger if she's discovered?"

"Certainly, there will be folks who want to keep her locked away forever or banished. The same as if she was found guilty of the theft."

"That would be incredibly cruel."

"I agree, and I doubt the Seven would do something like that in this day and age. But it would cause a panic, no doubt."

"So we shouldn't tell them about it if it can be helped."

"Possibly. If she's scared of being found out, she might not talk either."

"I don't want to frighten her. If she refuses to talk again then we're at another dead end." Fiona sipped her coffee slowly. "We'd need to find someone else we can ask questions of to learn more."

If there was a place to get answers, it was with someone who had access to information the normal populace wouldn't know. Dorin was already a jumpy risk, and they couldn't ask these questions to any of the other Seven. There was only one faekin Fiona felt she had full access to who knew the value of getting to the point. She put her coffee cup down. "Alright, let's get back to Spine. I think I know who we can talk to, but you'll have to follow my lead."

"Of course," Gaili said, getting up immediately.

They packed quickly and made their way to the pagemark. It was odd, the itch to get back to Spine. It started slowly, but after a couple of days of being away, it was a hammering of anxiety and an off feeling until your foot touched the soil of the sprawling city. They turned the page back and in the arches district where they waited for a carriage to take them to the turner area.

"You didn't return last night. I take it you had a good time catching up?" Fiona said, smiling to her friend. In the light of day it was much easier to be less lonely and happier for Gaili.

"I did. Matteo asked loads of questions about my shop and what my life was like. He seemed not to care at all that I wasn't working for Clara."

"See, I told you anyone with brains would think it was good you were out from under her thumb."

Gaili inclined her head. "But chatting with him and Henrietta about my work was nice."

"And then?" Fiona said, nudging her friend in the arm.

"And then we had a lovely evening talking about travel and all sorts of other things."

"In the dining room all night?"

"Well, we did retire to Matteo's room when the staff told us they were heading up for the night."

"I think you have two people very interested in you, my friend. But how will you choose?" Fiona said, linking her arm with Gaili as they rounded the corner to the turner district.

For the first time Fiona saw an impish smile on her friends face as she answered quietly, "Why not both?"

Fiona laughed and pestered her with questions on Matteo's attraction to Henrietta and vice versa until the carriage pulled up to the stop and they made their way to the Thread. It was part interest and part distraction on her part to question Gaili. Though she hadn't had many suitors in her lifetime, she had certainly never had more than one at once. And two who happened to be interested in each other at the same time? Say what you would for faekin chaos, they knew how to live life to the fullest.

The distraction worked, however, and she didn't have to lie to Gaili about why they were going to the Thread. When they got there, she ushered her inside and up to the third-floor wooden doors. Mac had been standing behind the bar chatting to a patron, but Fiona knew she would follow up soon.

"What are we doing up here? I've never been this far before." Gaili glanced over the intricate door that barred off the landing. "Look at the markings on this door. It's from an old faekin forest in the Garden, I think."

"The wood?"

"The door itself. I remember studying these from history. The old Circles had them installed on all their palaces. What would it be doing here?"

Gaili had proved more intuitive than Fiona had prepared for and she stuttered out, "I couldn't think of one reason alone. Perhaps we can ask Mac when—" The door opened and she stopped speaking. Mac hadn't come up the stairs yet, so who had opened the door?" She slipped inside, calling out, "Hello?" to the larger room. Tugging Gaili in, she closed the door behind her. "Mac, is that you?"

"Ah, no," a familiar voice said, pulling themselves from the corner, "it was me actually. I heard you speaking and thought it best to allow you in."

"Olea!" Fiona exclaimed at the familiar face, "What are you doing here?" She had practically blended in with the wooden walls. Fiona wasn't sure if it was the bonded sight that made her more difficult to notice or if she was just distracted.

"I would ask you the same, but I know I hold no power in this house." She smiled timidly. "I just came to visit an old friend."

"The same then," Fiona said. "But you must excuse me. I need to speak with her alone."

"Well, anything you can say to me you can say to Olea, Fi," Mac said, coming through the door behind them. She stopped when she saw Gaili. Her ease dropped and she crossed her arms. "Although I don't know if you should."

"Mac, this is Gaili. I've told you about her."

Mac acknowledged her but didn't drop her stance. "Oh yes, nice to meet you. Fiona says you're quite the inventor."

Gaili bowed her head in greeting. "It's nothing compared to what some have done. Your room here is lovely for example. And the craftsmanship on the door is remarkable. You're quite creative."

Fiona smiled. Gaili wasn't without insight. She was putting two and two together and being remarkably easy about stringing the information out. Perhaps she was rubbing off on her.

Mac tilted her head, appraising Gaili. "I take it you're working with Fi on the Copper case."

"I am supporting her as she sees fit to have me involved," Gaili said quietly, staring at Mac. For a moment no one spoke, but like a current of tension, it broke.

"Very well then," Mac said in a voice more regal than ever Fiona had heard her before. "As I was saying, Fiona, Olea can hear anything you have to say to me, and she may be *bound* to know already."

Fiona raised an eyebrow at Mac, taking in her meaning. "Well, what I say here concerns more than just ourselves. How can I be sure you won't use this information poorly?" Fiona said to Olea, feeling the focused gaze of Mac. She trusted her friend, but that didn't mean Olea hearing about Orsa would end well for the faun-hag.

"I have no desire to hurt anyone. Lying about the cipher these past weeks has made me feel the type of turmoil I try to avoid." She grasped Mac's shoulder. "It's worth it to not hurt Mac though. I can promise you or give you something to prove that that desire extends to you and anyone else necessary."

Mac's face knitted in concern but she remained quiet.

Seeing her friend's reaction, Fiona sighed. "I think that I'm about full on faekin promises. Thank you though." She took the permission to speak somewhat freely in front of Gaili and started up again. "I'm afraid it's more questions than answers. I think we're at an end to figuring out who may have taken *all* your curiosities and hopefully retrieving them. But I have a few thoughts, and you are my best lead."

Mac sat on the couch, tugging Olea along with her. Her azure robes spread out behind her like a queen's gown.

For a moment Fiona wondered if she was making a display of regality, however subtle. Whether for Olea's benefit or Gaili's, she didn't know. "I have information that may determine Orsa to be a hag. The problem is, that gives her less motive for theft unless I can connect the theft with something that would help her. She asked for exoneration for her people. I have to assume she means hags. What do you know that would tie the two together?"

Mac blinked. "That's quite a bit to throw at me all at once. Give me a moment to think."

"She's a hag?" Olea asked quietly.

"I have a witness who saw her change form at one time," Fiona said, looking at Mac. "But I suspect there are other ways to tell if a person's essence is different."

"I knew Dorin was hiding something but not that," Olea said. "I'm not surprised Dorin wouldn't tell others. He's not like the old ones who still think the leaves of the past predict the forest of tomorrow. But Clara…." Olea trailed off, rubbing the chain that tucked into her neckline. "She hired Orsa. I'm surprise she'd risk removal from the Seven for anyone."

"Removal from the Order of Seven? If she's connected?" said Fiona.

"Yes, she would be considered an ally of an exile and subsequently exiled herself."

Fiona raised an eyebrow. That was far nicer than she gave Clara credit for. Her intuition irked at the idea, but she brushed it aside from now. "What can you both tell us that would connect this together?"

"Well, hags were always part of faekin culture until they weren't," said Mac. "They were, as your people say, right hand to the various Circles."

"There are actually a fair bit of records on them," Olea added. "If you know where to look. I've studied some in my time. They were shape-changers, though they couldn't take all forms. Fauns and centaurs seemed to be the easiest from what I remember."

That would explain why Orsa and Elinor were fauns, even mismatched. Why wouldn't they coordinate coloring though? Perhaps the separation led them to not communicating in person and Orsa didn't remember how Elinor looked. "How long can they hold that form?"

"A few days, I believe," said Olea. "Eventually they'd have to change back or else fall ill. But they were powerful and could do it again fairly soon."

"Sort of like how we can't leave Spine too long?" Fiona asked, and Mac nodded in agreement. "Yes, I do believe

Larrakane seems to like that limitation. But surely you would notice them?"

"Well, in the past they only changed for information gathering, spying on enemies of the Circle, that sort of thing," Olea said. "Reasons to not be noticed. I dare say they learned to be covert."

"You said perhaps a way to see if an essence was different," Mac said, sitting up. "How did you—Can you see auras now?"

Fiona sat on the armrest next to the fae. "I can see a color, or an absence of one, from some faekin. Gaili and many other fauns all shimmer with a gold luminescence. In varying degrees though. I haven't discovered a pattern yet."

"You can see auras?" Gaili asked. "When did this happen?"

"When I bonded Fiona to myself," Mac said, studying Fiona like a new project. "I'd never bonded a human before. Perhaps beyond secrecy it has altered you somehow." Her eyes narrowed. "Your essence has changed a bit. How do you feel?"

Fiona thought back across the last few days. Had there been much of a difference? "A bit tired all the time now that you asked."

"You may not be able to withstand the bond. It may be using your energy to maintain it." Mac felt Fiona's pulse. "I'm sorry I didn't think that through. I don't know how else it may affect you."

Gaili looked shocked. "I'm surprised you didn't say anything. I've read Copper was different to season eyes."

"I told her not to tell anything of who I was or how she got her information. I can see you kept your word," Mac said to Fiona, "even if you may have bended the request a little."

Fiona bowed her head. "Time is of the essence now, and I figured if you didn't want Gaili to know, you'd tell her to leave. You've told many people to leave without any timidity before."

"Bar brawls and revealing my heritage are two different things, Fi." Mac sighed. "But if you trust her, I won't worry. Much."

"I assure you I would never speak of you to anyone else." Gaili bowed low to Mac.

"Oh, please don't do that. No one in this establishment is worth bowing to, I assure you." She waved her hand at Gaili to rise up, becoming a bit more like her old self. "Now. The only thing I think could connect my items with hags is the past. Honestly the Seasonal Crowns are powerful all together, but you'd have to have knowledge of seasonal spirits to use them properly. The only ones who may know besides an archivist could be a hag. They are fairly long lived and weren't advisors for nothing. With all my journals and the crowns, yes they could be a force to be reckoned with."

"So they could turn them into weapons and look like other faekin to infiltrate Copper."

"If they wanted."

"What were the parts of the journals you didn't tell me?" Fiona asked. "That would need your code to break?"

Mac looked uneasy. "I did quite a bit of research on several topics, of course. As well as the instructions on how to make the crowns, which I will *not* repeat." She clenched her golden fist and took a deep breath. "But in making the Seasonal Crowns I began to notice that in some parts of Copper, the effect they had was more powerful than others."

"What do you mean?"

"Take the Winter Crown for instance. In some regions it could make a small area chillier. It could freeze a few leaves or even create a few snowflakes. But in one part of the Garden region, it was as if I was getting close to something and siphoning the power from it."

Fiona was confused. "Like a source?"

Mac nodded. "Being closer to it amplified what I could make the crowns do. Of course, I didn't know what it was then. But it was the first time I suspected there was more to the world than just the never-ending copper sky."

"But you detailed this down."

"Oh yes, and other locations where the crowns seemed to work with greater energy. There was a small area not too far from the outskirts of Calistino that grew taller plants with the help of the Spring Crown. And somewhere near the coast where the Summer Crown could make the waves recede and sizzle, drying up the water."

"The Depths pagemark," Fiona said remembering the shimmering fountain from their journey yesterday.

"Perhaps," Mac said, a question on her face. "If you've seen what I mean through our bond, then yes."

"So you could test the presence of other pages before the inking?" said Olea.

"A page directly next to you only though, surely?" said Gaili. "Copper may be the last known page in the Book, but Kerus has its fair share of water and desert to source."

"Or the dark edge perhaps?" Fiona said. There was no telling what lay in the dark edge. Simply getting close to it created terror in stout explorers.

"That's what it seems like now," said Mac. "I've always believed there were more pages than simply the known seven, though I've not been able to prove it. But of course, I was inked before I put any of this together. While interesting, I didn't think it much mattered except to say that Larrakane's Book was always there. It simply hadn't been opened yet."

"But if someone has the crowns, they could wield them as power in various pages, amplified by that page and possibly the ones beside them," said Gaili.

"Or find where the barrier between the pages is weak," murmured Fiona.

"Why would anyone want to do that?" asked Gaili.

"Why would Orsa?" said Olea.

"I think that may be a question she can't ignore," Fiona said. She stood, making for the door.

"Wait," Mac said, grabbing Fiona's hand. "Let me release you now."

"No," Fiona said, "it's been helpful, though I've been too dull to understand it. I propose we wait."

Mac opened her mouth, then paused. She sighed. "Not too long, Fi. If it's using your energy there may come a point where it's depleted. I don't know what will happen then."

"It's a chance I'm willing to take. If I can see faekin essences, I may be able to see more."

"Try to be safe."

"If you need the wardens, tell them I sent you," Olea said. "I'll support you in whatever way I can."

"Thank you. If we do find anything out, we won't hesitate to act."

Though it took longer than Fiona had patience for, they turned the page back to Copper safely and found a gondola directly to the Towers of Calistino prison. Thankful to have Gaili with her to take turns turning the page, Fiona let the tiredness she had been holding at bay set in and closed her eyes for the ride through the canal.

They made their way through the populated square and into the prison's stone archway. The warden walking down the stairs to greet them in the entryway, the same matronly faun as before, raised an eyebrow and nodded in recognition. "Sorry, misses, but Orsa isn't allowed any new visitors." She kept going through a small hallway seeming to hope that would be the end of the conversation.

It would take more than one turned back to stop Fiona. She followed quickly into the guard's office. "But we're not new. We're old. You know us," Fiona said, a little sharply anxious to be up the tower.

The warden sat and moved plate and cups to the side, busying herself. "Yes but I also know that I've been told to not allow you up that tower. I know you're off her case."

"Who said that?" Gaili asked.

"Keeper Clara. And I don't want any trouble from the Seven." She raised her hands toward the sky taking a seat at her desk and muttering, "Already got an earful about the state of Orsa from Keeper Dorin."

"What's wrong with Orsa?"

The warden bit her lip, face softened, before saying, "She's been looking sicker. I told him she eats and I'm doing as much as I can. She won't let me send for a doctor."

Perhaps it was the mention of her refusal, but Fiona had a sinking feeling of why Orsa was refusing. "If we can't go up and see her, fine. But what's the harm in bringing her down to see us? You're still following the request, aren't you?"

The warden shook her head. "No, I can't do that. It would be the same in her eyes. Please go. I can't lose my job." Her face wore a pained expression.

Gaili glanced at Fiona, wide eyed, and Fiona sighed. She gave a short nod of leave and walked out, tugging on her scarf in exasperation. She wasn't going to harm the poor warden, but they had to do something.

"What do we do?" Gaili said, following her.

"I'm thinking," Fiona said, shorter than she meant to. She couldn't very well scale the tower. She paced away from the building, dodging running and giggling children, centaurs ambling through the square, and more. She startled some of the large sleeping birds with her quick movement, and they unceremoniously squawked at her, but she ignored them in her thoughts. What she needed was to get the guard to go away for a bit, so warden didn't know she was there. And her keys. She could wait until it got dark, but that was hours and hours away. She grimaced, staring at the resettling birds as a thought came to her. "Do you have the black square I gave you last night?"

"Yes, it's in my bag."

"I think half of that will do it. She already had a cup in there to drink from."

"Perhaps I can try to add it in?" Gaili said, wringing her hands.

"No, absolutely not. If she caught you, you might end up in the tower yourself." She couldn't let Gaili come to harm like that. "I'll slip in. I've done as much before, but what I need is a big, loud distraction." Fiona looked around the square for something that could fit the bill. There were some small shops but nothing she could buy that would produce the desired effect. She didn't want to create too much of a panic and get the wardens to notice. The faekin children raced toward her, and she moved quickly to get out of the way before inspiration struck. She strode to the group, pulling papers from her scarf. "Anyone want to make a few papers? I need someone to run into that building, quick as you can, and back out again."

A small fairy bounced up and down with an excited flap of her wings. "Like a race?"

Fiona nodded. "Sure. Just until you see a scowling faun with keys that jingle. Then right back out again."

"I'll be the fastest," the small fairy shouted.

"Or me," said a young faun. "I've beat you racing before."

"Well, let's just see then, shall we?" Fiona said. "Gaili, stay at a distance so you're not connected to me. If the wardens come, you get Dorin or Olea."

Gaili nodded, eyes wide. Fiona distributed the diamonnette paper among the children and told them to count to thirty before they started. She strode to the other side of the entrance and stood beneath one of the arched windows to wait.

They could have just taken off with her money, but Fiona knew such a competition among children boasting of winning was just as valuable. Just as she got into position, the children had already started their race. They seemed neck and neck shooting into the building. Fiona took a deep breath, darted in behind them, and turned immediately to the tower stairs. She ran a little way up the tower ramp, waiting for her cue.

The children ran back out into the copper sunshine with the guard on their tail. They all passed by the crouching Fiona. She ran to the warden's desk and tossed the half card into the open glass upon it. The stomping of feet came sooner than she had hoped, however, and she glanced around looking for somewhere to hide. There was only one other door within the chamber, on a tall armoire, and she pounced on it. Into the closet she went, squishing herself between linens and wall. How often she was finding herself hiding in furniture these days!

By the squeaking of a chair on stone tile, Fiona guessed the warden entered the room and sat down. Fiona tried to control her rapid breathing as she listened to the guard mutter under her breath about long days and hopeful holidays. It was quiet for a bit besides the shifting of weight in a chair and the scratching of paper. How long was the draught supposed to take? Unless the woman just wasn't going to drink any more at all. Fiona's legs ached from the quick burst of running and jumping, and she prayed to Larrakane against getting a cramp now. She leaned her head against the interior of the closest, feeling tired. No, it was too dark and warm, lulling her tired body to sleep. She just needed to wait a little longer.

She jumped when a heavy thud sounded outside the closet. Had she fallen asleep for a moment? She shook her head and quietly peeked through the door to see the warden slumped over on the desk. Sighing with relief, Fiona walked out of the closet and to the woman, checking that she was still breathing. With assurance that she was just deeply asleep, she took the woman's keys and walked to the front, listening for anyone else coming through.

Taking the stairs two at a time she made her way up the high tower as quickly as she could. When she was sure she got to Orsa's door, she unlocked it and moved into the small sitting room, locking it back behind her. She went to the interior door and called through it, "Orsa?"

Doubled over, the tattoos on her face were dimmed to match her pallor. Fiona thought that the woman, if she was a hag, would change to her natural form and then back when she was by herself. Perhaps she hadn't the strength, but why? Her essence was diminished and dark like Elinor's had been. They were not fauns, that much was clear.

Orsa didn't even raise her head as she came in. Her bound hands hung limp in front of her.

"Orsa," Fiona started softly, "it's just me. I've come because we have a few more questions, and if you can cooperate, we may be able to get you out of this."

The faun looked up and said weakly, "I don't think you can, although I appreciate the optimism." She coughed. "But I have nothing else to say unless you've come to fulfill my request."

Fiona frowned. Even now she was pushing the exoneration? She seemed barely able to hold herself together. "Dorin feels he can't make your request. He says he doesn't have the power to grant it. If he did, I truly believe he would. He doesn't want to see you, or any other hags, suffer."

Orsa raised an eyebrow. "Did he tell you that?"

She shook her head. "No. I do believe he will keep your secret forever." She paused and then said, fishing, "Clara may as well."

"Clara? What does she know about me being a hag?"

"I assumed she knew when she hired you? And assigned you to Dorin."

"If she did, she never let on. I would think she would try to wield that information for advantage rather than hide it for me." She paused and then said somewhat cryptically,

"Although having access to Dorin's steward might have been that advantage."

Fiona nodded. It was on par with Clara's personality to see only what she wanted to in people. She overlooked Orsa being a hag but not her capabilities to report back on Dorin's activities. "But what is the point of staying here if it still won't help the others?"

"What others?" Orsa said, voice low.

"The other clans that an exoneration would allow back into society," Fiona said, confused.

Orsa stared at her, gaunt face drawn. "There are no other clans. The Wilds were not kind to us before the Inking. We have all but died out."

"Then who is this exoneration for?" Fiona said.

"For history." She paused, coughing. "I suppose."

"Why would Clara want you to do this?"

"Clara? Clara would be against it, of course. What faekin wouldn't be?"

If Clara didn't tell her, *push* on her to make this ultimatum, then who exactly did? Clara visited her, she hired her, she had her spy on Dorin. Surly she had her steal the items and then take the blame as well, right? Fiona pressed her lips together, thinking. She was missing something but not sure what. "Please, what is going on? Elinor doesn't understand why you are doing this."

"She will one day. When she's free," Orsa said in a hopeful voice.

It dawned on Fiona that she thought she was saving her sister. "You're doing this for her, aren't you?"

Orsa's head drooped as she nodded. She needed to be allowed to change. What had been stopping her? Fiona took a step, assessing Orsa. Beyond the tunic, more valuable than Fiona's own outfit, the wool stockings, and slippers, there wasn't much more on poor Orsa. Nothing else but the turn stoppers at her feet. Though they were meant to stop a page turner from turning the page, perhaps they worked on other changing ability as well.

Fiona searched the key ring looking for one that could fit into the lock. Finding it, she placed it in the manacles but then pulled back from a spike of cold that seemed to pierce her warm skin. Nausea overtook her, and she smelled burning as if paper was in flames within her nostrils. She took a deep breath, fighting through it. She had never been in turn stoppers. If just touching them made her feel ill, what would having them on do to her? She shuddered at the thought.

"What are you doing?" said Orsa slowly.

"Giving you a little clarity while you still have the chance." The lock clicked and she pushed them to the side with the key ring, not wanting to touch them again. "Now take a moment and a deep breath. You're connected to the Book again, right?"

Orsa took a deep breath and opened her eyes. Her hands shook.

"I'm not here to frighten you," Fiona said, "but I can only solve this if tell me the truth. Show me the truth."

Orsa's body begin to shift. The faun horns receded. Her muddy-water eyes shifted to a brilliant blue. Her gold flake skin became a deep copper sheen with a light smattering of fur covering her body. Her stature shortened considerably until she was half of Fiona's size. No wonder her body had looked stretched out before. She was much smaller in this manner. Her essence flickered now, no longer dark but a bright azure. The tattoos on her face dappled with gold light color and where they seemed small before were almost as complex as Mac's.

Orsa smiled slowly and stretched her neck and arms, hands still bound. "I didn't realize that's what was preventing me from changing. I thought it was just another punishment from Larrakane."

"Do you think you deserve punishment?"

"Perhaps, but we don't always get what we deserve in life," Orsa said, her blue eyes flickering.

"Tell me what you know."

Orsa stood stumbling but bracing against the wall. "I can't tell you anything directly though. I can stand here. I can speak. But I have given my bond and I cannot break it."

Fiona puzzled over Orsa's meaning for a moment. It was like all other faekin: a certain duplicity in their words. "I suppose if I say all the right things, you wouldn't need to tell me anything out loud."

Orsa smiled. "Now we're getting somewhere."

"Clara gave you an ultimatum: get the Seven to accept your request or she would harm Elinor."

"Who is Elinor to Clara? Who is Clara to Elinor?" Orsa said, waving her words away with a flick of the wrist. She leaned back on the bench, rolling her shoulders.

Fiona frowned. "But it was Clara who told you something that made you confess and demand exoneration."

"For someone who can walk the Book, you certainly seem to only see the words in front of you."

Fiona got up from kneeling and paced the small cell. She only had so much time until someone found the guard. What was she missing? "If not Clara," she began, "then someone who wanted the exoneration. Another hag perhaps?"

Orsa tilted her head questioningly.

She took the silence as a right track. "Someone who could impersonate Clara? A hag, and that's who came to visit you," Fiona said. "Possibly other faekin as well around here."

Orsa repeated, "Faekin, you say."

"Well, yes, but...can you impersonate non-faekin?"

Orsa's form shifted slowly until Fiona was staring at herself. Perhaps she was slightly taller than she imagined herself. It was troubling, and she looked away. "Illustrative. So you can impersonate faekin and humans..." She trailed off. *Stoneguard.* Stoneguard was a human woman who had interest in the theft. Who was false but real. Who carried hidden daggers and ways to knock people out. Possibly so she could take their form unheeded. "Stoneguard gave you the ultimatum."

"Who is Stoneguard?" Orsa said, for the first time truly confused.

"A human out of Rise whom I met," Fiona said. "Another of your kind gave you an ultimatum. Exoneration or harm to Elinor."

Orsa scoffed, "Like anyone could hurt Elinor physically."

"But a reveal would be harmful. Very dangerous too, depending on who she was or where she lived." Fiona knew that Elinor was visiting Spine, but from where? "Does she live on Rise, Copper, or another part of the Book?"

Orsa said nothing. Perhaps her bond was to more than one person.

Fiona pivoted back. "So Stoneguard set you up. Stole the items and planted evidence to link you. But why you specifically?" Fiona paced, exhilaration running through her as the pieces clicked into place. Why hurt one of the only people who would understand what you've gone through? "She dislikes you."

"What's not to dislike?" Orsa-as-Fiona grimaced. "I did what I thought was best with the job I was given."

"You went to work for the Seven. You went to help people but not your own. And she thinks you should focus on your own people and not the rest of Copper?"

Orsa said nothing but inclined her head subtly in agreement.

"But how did she get your bracelet?" Fiona said. They would've needed to be close in order for her to know the bracelet existed. To know it couldn't be replicated.

"It's one of a kind," Orsa said, as if reading her mind. "Just mine and my sister's."

"Yes, your sister said you had matching bracelets your family made. Is Stoneguard also family?"

Orsa again said nothing. They were all from the same clan. This explained the second theft. Stoneguard must've stolen everything, replaced it, and then wanted to plant evidence pointing to Orsa. But what about the first? Why go back?

"None of this will matter if Stoneguard doesn't confess or we don't find the items with her," Fiona said. "And she can be almost anyone, anywhere." Except she would most assuredly be one place tonight. Fiona was meant to go to the theater with her. It was a date she would most assuredly keep. "I believe I know how to find her."

Orsa nodded, her shoulders slumping despite her natural form. "Do what you can. I haven't made this easy, I know. I should've listened to Elinor when she said not to work for the Seven, but I really admired Dorin. I knew working with him, helping him enact change would be worth it."

"It's too bad she wanted to see you fail," Fiona said, looking back at Orsa. "I have a small chance. If can trap her, well...even if I get her to confess, no one will believe simply me. I need proof."

"Or a witness," Orsa said, sitting back down on the bench. "If you go to her home, I'm sure you'll find proof enough."

Fiona pursed her lips. Stoneguard had a large home on Rise, that Fiona knew. But a witness to her finding proof and then questioning Stoneguard would be the harder part. Who could possibly count as important enough to witness but that she could trust? No one would believe simply her and Gaili. Her mind cleared at the obvious answer. "There may be just the right nymph to help with this."

14

"I DON'T WANT TO alarm you, but this could get extremely dangerous," said Fiona to Gaili as they made their way to a pagemark for Rise.

"You think I should stay behind?" Gaili asked.

"No, absolutely not," Fiona said. She struggled with how to encourage Gaili without controlling her actions. "I think you will be instrumental help. But I leave the choice to you."

They got to the pagemark, a tall stone column that overshadowed them, making the approach cooler than the hot page normally was. As Rise was not on the same level as Copper and Kerus, the other mortal pages, pagemarks to it tended to exist a bit higher for convenience. There were quite a few rumors about what lay beyond the dense clouds below the floating islands, but they never ended well.

Like other areas of Copper with some significance, the column couldn't simply be stone straight to the top. There were boxes of small hedges, plants, and flowers on every level. Some were familiar to Fiona, and by the time they arrived at the top, she realized it was a mixture of Copper- and

Rise-native plants. That caught her as odd. "Is it often that plants of another page can grow in yours?"

Gaili frowned, running her finger over a leaf. "No, not that I'm aware. How did the herbalists get this to happen?"

"I think it was more than the herbalists," Fiona said softly. She touched one of the Rise plants, its soil much warmer than expected. It shimmered in the same way as all faekin creatures that she could see since she had become bonded to Mac, but it was more translucent than the others. Could this be one of the places Mac had noted in her journal where the boundaries between one page and the next were weaker?

She felt a tap on her shoulder and jumped, startled as a tendril of water waved at her.

Cascade laughed. "You looked so focused I had to mess with you."

"Well, see to it that you keep your humor to yourself. I asked you to come because we're going to visit a suspect's home where the items may be. Having them and confronting her where I know her to be later will help us free Orsa. I figured since you're investigating us you might like to be a witness. But of course, I'm not telling you to do anything."

Cascade tilted her head. "Good, because I never do what I'm told." She placed her warm arm around Fiona's waist.

"I suspected as much," Fiona murmured. She pulled out her bookmark to Rise, a dry wooden spoon from her pre-turner days. Grasping on to Gaili's hand, she focused first on the chapter that they were in and then Rise itself. Rubbing her finger over the spoon, she relaxed and let the tug within her pull her forward one step across the open-air platform. A corner of the world pulled back before them, revealing gray sky. She bound the thrum of the spoon, herself, and the others to their destination, and when it connected, she planted her foot on green grass, completing the step. Copper flipped closed behind them. It all took but a second.

A light drizzle brushed their shoulders and hair. Though it was not supposed to be the season for rain, it still found them. A lone crumbled tower sat far into the distance. Fiona glanced around and saw the typical Travel Guild post, banners decorated with their open book insignia and floating island for Rise hanging overhead.

Fiona pulled out her egg-shaped watch to look at the time. "We have a few hours before it's dark and the play starts in Copper. Let's get on with it." After an hour or so of signing in, embarking, and then disembarking on the passenger airship routinely traveling the pagemarks found on the various floating isles in Rise, they found themselves on the Plateau and in Three Churches. The streets were choked with people going about their daily life and then some streaming in and out of small shops and markets. A few skimmers, smilodon cats direct from Kerus by the cut of their togas, traipsed through the district, but no one else seemed out of place but them. Fiona stopped at few carts and bought supplies for her infiltration.

"Stoneguard should still be in Copper, especially as I'm to meet her tonight for the play. I'll dress up like a servant and gain entrance to the house. Cascade...well, I guess, is there any way you can get inside without anyone noticing?"

"I have my gifts." Cascade pulled her necklace from around her neck and placed it around Fiona's. With a giggle, a tendril of amber water seeped out and twined around Cascade's finger. She turned translucent and then faded into the necklace. It sat heavy on Fiona's chest as the rain begin to pick up around them.

"That is quite a talent," Fiona acknowledged. She pushed down the anxiety of having the impractical nymph literally around her throat and started walking.

Fiona shot down an alleyway and had Gaili keep a look out while she changed into a simple brown wool gown, apron, and a flat bonnet to cover her hair. Once done she made the fringes of her hair a little less put together and exchanged slippers for brogue boots typical of the working class. Assured by Gaili she didn't look like Fiona Thorne or too put together, they continued on to Stoneguard's town home.

"There are a few ways to approach this before we have to give up and try again. After I leave, wait five or so minutes and then get someone to knock on the door. You should pay someone." Fiona handed Gaili some paper. "You can usually convince a child to do things like that for fun, but if you see someone selling anything, you can pay them for it and have it delivered to the house."

"I could go up there myself," Gaili started.

"No, I think it best that you stay back. While there are faekin who travel to Rise, it's rarely on foot or selling things." Fiona held back the notion that it was safer for Gaili to be at a distance. She couldn't get her out of danger if she needed to be in it herself. "I'll need to improvise a way out. That may mean running through the front door. If that happens, don't follow me. The less you're connected, the better."

Gaili nodded slowly. "As you say. I'll watch for someone to ask."

Fiona squeezed her hand in encouragement, and they parted, Gaili across the street where she could see the entrance while Fiona carried on to the back steps. There was a small window in the door, and she could see through that the kitchen was empty. Serendipitous, but she didn't want to run into a servant until she had a layout of the house. She examined the lock on the servant's door, its shape reminiscent of a stalking fox with a keyhole in its side. She knocked with a matching heavy vulpine door knocker and waited, counting the seconds until someone arrived.

A petite woman, younger than Fiona, came through a swinging door and across the kitchen. She opened the door, wiping hands on an apron about her cranberry-and-black dress. "Yes?"

"Delivery for Mistress Stoneguard from Lord Henry Hawkport, Earl of Shade," Fiona said, dropping the name of a noteworthy noble in Rise. "Special for her Mistress."

The girl started to take the basket, but Fiona shied away, lowering her head as she did so. "No offending you, but I'm supposed to deliver directly to the mistress or a house steward. Don't want anything missing. Not that you would." She smiled half a smile.

The woman looked about to say something when a large drop of rain hit her face, surprising her.

"It's starting to come down, you see. Mind if I wait inside?"

The maid looked over Fiona, but seeming to see nothing worrisome, she beckoned her in. "I suppose you can wait by the fire, and I'll get the house steward."

Fiona murmured thanks, and stepped into the house. Now for the harder part. She held on to the basket, glancing around the interior to assess the best way to move about the house. Within the kitchen was the woman but no other servants. A house this size typically had at least three or four in the kitchen. "Light workday, eh?" Fiona said, motioning about. "Everyone else have the afternoon off?"

The woman shook her head, closing the door. "It's a small staff. Mistress doesn't need much unless she's entertaining, thankfully."

"That's nice, that's nice." With less people came an easier time of hiding somewhere in the house. Fiona moved near the fire and rubbed her hands to start warming herself.

"I'll go find him and be back in a moment."

"Take your time, dear. I'm not looking to run back into the rain so quickly."

The young woman nodded sympathetically and left up the stairs.

Fiona placed the basket on the table and assessed. There were servant stairs that led up behind a sliver of a door from this entry kitchen and other stairs that led down. The room was sparse with only enough trenchers, cups, and bowls on display to perhaps feed six. So, the house and all the records were for show more than anything. Could she not afford a full staff, or, like Fiona thought, was it easier to hide secrets with a sparse set? She wondered if the neighbors gossiped about it and if she could call on them to get more information about Stoneguard's comings and goings.

The young woman came back with the house steward, a tall human male dressed in the same colors as the young maid. His livery, however, included a small insignia of a fox on the arm. The same visage that had adorned the outer door. "Thank you for delivering this to my hands," he said, smiling tautly. "I can take it from here."

Fiona nodded. "As you like." And handed it to him. She rubbed her hands again, making as if to keep warming them to give herself a few moments. If she could wait until she heard Gaili's distraction, then she could slip away.

"You've been very helpful," the house steward said, ushering her toward the back door, his tone suggesting that she had been very annoying. He opened the door and inclined his head. So, lingering inside until she could distract them to the front wasn't going to work.

Thinking quickly, she said, "Thank you, kind sir. This may be forward, but can I trouble you for a cloak? The rain is much quicker than expected."

He stopped with a grimace, but her words were not false. The rain pounded against the tiles of the roof and splashed into the stone path that led off into the garden. He sighed. "Hold for a moment." And closed the door.

Fiona paused, rocking back on her heels and smiling at the young woman. She turned as if to peer out the small window in the door for a second before running a finger over the lock, examining it. It was hinged to shut and lock on the interior side of the door and thin enough to fit between the doorframe and the door. "Rain like this is so unusual this time of year," she said, turning back to the young woman.

"It is," said the young maid, standing next to the fire. It was clear her job was to watch Fiona. "Hate that it's been like this for weeks. Every time it stops, I think we'll get back to our usual sunny summer weather, but then it starts up again."

The house steward came back and thrust a dusty too-large cloak at her. With no further reason to delay, she took it and made a show of throwing it on as she nodded her thanks to them both before exiting without a backward glance. She stopped in the narrow alley, listening. The sound of the city surrounded her, but she strained to hear a bell within the house. Surely it had been at least five minutes or so. She didn't want to go too far lest she miss the timing. She pulled her lock-picking tools out of her pocket in preparation as something to calm her nerves.

The cold chain of Cascade's necklace around her throat felt like an icy collar. She hoped the nymph wouldn't get impatient herself and complicate things. If she was caught by Rise officers or Travel Guild jackets lurking about the alleyways, the questioning alone would take precious minutes away between now and when she had to meet Stoneguard at the theatre in Copper.

It seemed many minutes before Fiona picked up a frantic banging on the door and the ringing of a pull bell. She pushed down the curiosity to see just who Gaili had gotten to be so energetic and instead quickly made her way back around. Peeking through the kitchen window, she saw that the room was empty once again. She tried the handle and groaned when it wouldn't turn. She adjusted the cloak higher over her head to block the ensuing rain and slipped the pick into the fox lock. Expecting to hear the usual tumblers acquiescing to her bidding, she instead found a solid wall. What in the dark edge could stop her pick? It had looked a simple lock before. She withdrew her tools and hurriedly ran her fingers over the fox and the hinge of the door. There was no sign of anything amiss.

Shouting from the front of the house, a deep voice, broke through the patter of the rain. He seemed quite angry. Perhaps it had been luck and not Gaili who had called the servants away.

Returning her attention to the lock, she coaxed the hind leg of the fox to jiggle. Pressing it, the fox pulled away from the door and revealed a secondary keyhole. With an eyebrow raised at the cleverly hidden space, she worked her tools within it and heard her preferred sound. She replaced the fox and silently opened the door, slinking into the house.

Fiona removed her boots and loaned cloak, bundling them together to not leave wet tracks. She lightly made her way across the room and up the servant stairs, one ear trained on the sounds of the house. The house steward's voice was calm as he talked to the enraged voice. So he could be accounted for there. Now where was the maid?

Fiona bypassed the half stair that led to the first floor and continued up till she got to the second. Cold tile nearly froze her feet in place, but she pushed on, promising herself a hot foot soak with coffee in hand when this was all over. Here were bedrooms and typically a study. She headed that way, padding down the hallway on tiptoe. A rustle of fabric pricked her ears and she stopped. Footsteps approached down the hall. Opening the nearest door, Fiona dashed inside. It was dark and cold, no fire lit within it. Closing the door as softly as, she could she knelt by the side of it. The footsteps passed her hurriedly, and she let out a breath. She supposed she'd start with this room instead.

Pulling out her beloved dark-view goggles, she slipped them on to let the small crack of light from the drawn window brighten the room. Useful in the fire page as well as skulking about in unlit areas, Fiona said a small prayer of thanks to Larrakane as she assessed the room. It was fairly standard guest room, and it smelled a bit dusty, as if it wasn't much used. Well, that made sense. If Stoneguard was a hag, how often did she really have overnight guests?

Fiona searched the furniture and ran her hand about the room, looking for hidden nooks or the missing objects or really anything of note. When she had searched all the possibilities, she noticed it was silent once again in the house. Whatever predicament that had happened in the front was done. Fiona thought it best to move on. She made her way like a ghost into the hallway.

The light that had been streaming through the window was gone. It was closer to night and two more hours before the play started. If she couldn't find anything here, she would have to go to Stoneguard and test her. After talking with Orsa, Fiona wasn't sure if she was the best to tackle the shape-changing, dagger-wielding hag, but perhaps in a crowded theater the odds were even.

She pressed on the double doors at the end of the hallway and was thankful they were unlocked. She slid them apart and squeezed through before shutting them back. If there was any room to check it would be this one. She locked it out of precaution. If the door rattled, it would at least buy her some time to escape.

Fiona began to move toward the desk before a lantern lit in the chamber, blinding her goggled eyes. She winced, pulling off the goggles and backing into the door.

Fiona squinted to see the blonde woman lounging against the desk holding the lantern and a dagger. Her hair was curled and braided to perfection. Her gown fashionable and perfect. Fiona realized how easily it must be to look put together all the time when one could shift their appearance at will. She rubbed her face with one hand while slowly reaching toward her scarf with the other. She stopped, remembering she still didn't have her whip, or anything that would be useful as a weapon. Drat.

Stoneguard set the lantern down and smiled. "Mistress *Oakfellow*. How delightful to see you. I never expected a visit so soon."

Fiona smiled, not rising to the bait as her eyes adjusted to the light. "Indeed, I thought of our meeting when visiting the Plateau and felt perhaps you wouldn't mind a visit. Did you enjoy your time in Copper?" If she could keep her talking, she could think of an escape or, at the very least, move toward a confession. It was a long shot, but it was what she had.

"I did," Stoneguard said. She moved toward Fiona slow and catlike. "It was a productive trip, if not perfect." She stopped in the middle of the thick grass-green carpet covering the floor.

Fiona glanced down and back at Stoneguard, evaluating her. It looked as if she was surrounded by a small pattern pulled into the colors of the carpet. It looked vaguely familiar. Fiona couldn't make out what it was exactly, but she didn't like the gloating look of on Stoneguard's face as she stood in the center of it.

Focus. Fiona needed to get information out of Stoneguard that Cascade could overhear. Needed to not reveal that she learned anything from Orsa. She didn't know how their bond might work or what danger it could place Orsa or Elinor in if she was connected like herself to Mac. "I suppose if I ask you anything, you'll just lie to me," Fiona said, testing the waters.

"I have no reason to lie. I could get the constables on you anytime I want to. If I wanted to let someone else deal with you, that is." Stoneguard beamed. "It depends on what you have to give me."

"It depends on what you want."

"Information." Stoneguard shifted in the small circle. "Always information. I'm willing to be honest if you are, Mistress *Oakfellow*."

"I think you know by now who I am. Let's not waste time pretending anymore between us, Sadie." Fiona raised an eyebrow. "If that even is your real name."

Sadie tutted. "You won't get that, *Investigator*, but I do so love alliteration." Stoneguard arched an eyebrow in return. "So, what will you give me if I answer your questions?"

Fiona tried to think like a faekin: chaotic and a little double-edged. "I can answer a question truthfully for every question I ask you."

Sadie regarded her coolly, but she nodded. "Three questions for three answers." She held out her hand.

Fiona shook her head, guard up. "I think I've learned enough not to shake hands with someone holding a dagger toward me."

A flash of frustration crossed Sadie's features before she shrugged again. "Suit yourself. I was being polite. First question."

"Who hired you to steal the fake crowns, watch, and gem-studded bell from the Pavilion?" She needed to be specific and targeted if she was going to get anything, and she already knew Sadie did that theft.

Stoneguard smiled and clasped her hands together. For a moment she looked less human and more unknown. "That's a thorough question. I see you have played this game before. The answer will bore you though. No one hired me to steal those things."

Fiona frowned. She was certain Stoneguard wasn't acting completely alone. How else could she have gotten in undetected? But if no one hired her, that means she either didn't steal them or decided to steal those things herself. But why?

"My turn," Sadie said, clapping for attention. "Now, which Circle of Seasons member hired you to retrieve the crowns?"

Fiona swallowed her surprise. Of all the questions the woman could ask, that was wholly new. Why would Mac hire her to retrieve the crowns? Unless she meant someone else?

"Remember you have to answer truthfully. Tick tock, tick tock."

"None," Fiona said. Even if someone was a hidden member, she didn't know of it.

It was Stoneguard's turn to frown. She studied Fiona and nodded. "Okay, next question."

"What is your end goal with the Seasonal Crowns?" Fiona hoped that saying *seasons* instead of *summer* would prove that both thefts were by the same person or not once and for all.

"You do know more than any other humans I've met," murmured Stoneguard. She paused, watching Fiona, and then said, "I have yet to achieve my end goal with the Seasonal Crowns."

Fiona frowned. Did that mean she still had them? "But that's not what I asked. What is your end goal with them?"

"But it hasn't happened, so it is not in the past. It's in the future."

"Surely one who knows so much about the past can see that it affects the future. If this question was two weeks ago or two years from now, the answer would still be the same."

"I grant you that." Sadie smiled, seeming to enjoy herself. "My end goal with the Seasonal Crowns is to give them to those who asked me to steal them."

"But you said no one hired you to steal them."

"That was a different answer to a different question."

Of course. Because the Seasonal Crowns were part of the first theft. The one Sadie was asked to do. The second theft was of Stoneguard's own choosing in order to plant evidence of Orsa. Would this be enough to free Orsa?

"Do any of the pockets of your scarf go to the dark edge?"

"What?" Fiona blurted out. "Why would they do that?" Sadie started to answer, but Fiona put a hand up. "No, no, that's not my last question." She sighed. Why were her questions so...off topic? "Not that I know of, but I can't account for where all the pockets go either. I always assumed it was various parts of the pages no one had discovered yet." But the dark edge? Now that was an intriguing thought.

She shook her head. These questions were a distraction. She was more focused on what Sadie was asking her instead of what she needed to ask the hag. Fiona rubbed the edges of her scarf between her fingers trying to think of a question that would force Sadie to reveal something solid she could use to free Orsa. She needed to be specific and ask the right question. She couldn't just ask who hired her, because it sounded like it was a group and she might not even know their name. Or Sadie could give her the nickname or alias of one person. Who got the most value from this entire endeavor?

"Who do I know benefits from everything that was stolen?"

Sadie frowned, thinking. She paced the little circle, arms crossed. "When I give you this name, who will you tell?"

"Do you want me to answer that as your final question?"

She paused but then nodded.

"I'll tell no one," Fiona said truthfully. Cascade would hear everything, and that wasn't telling.

Sadie looked taken aback. She seemed to be trying to puzzle out Fiona's words.

"Remember you must answer truthfully. Tick tock, tick tock," Fiona said with a smile. Goading did usually work to make people forget themselves.

Sadie shrugged, seeming to make up her mind. "Keeper Clara." She pursed her lips. "But I grant you won't be able to stop her grandiose scheme in time."

"What do you mean?" Fiona said.

"I believe you're out of questions." Sadie dusted her hands. "And I have an evening at the theater to prepare for." She twirled once, a pearlescent glint shining off the candlelight as she danced. The essence of the carpet shimmered once again like a flare. Fiona winced at the brightness of shifting auras. The pattern clicked in her memory however and she dived at Sadie. Thin air. The light dimmed around her as she fell hard to the plush carpet.

Sadie was gone.

Fiona pounded her fist on the carpet. Another fairy ring. But where did it go? She pulled back the carpet to reveal nothing underneath, but a pearl-handled dagger clattered to the ground.

"Cascade, I need your help." Fiona tugged the nymph's necklace from underneath her scarf.

Appearing as thin droplets of water that coalesced into a humanoid form, Cascade said, "Here I thought hags learned from the past."

"Sadie disappeared through the carpet. A fairy ring?" Fiona said, kicking it.

"Fairy rings are meant to be on sacred ground. Not simply anywhere. The ones in the Court barely work anymore for travel. Why'd you let her stand in it?" Cascade said with a pout.

"How was I supposed to know? How far does it go?"" Fiona huffed out a sigh.

"Only short distances. And you'd need a key."

Fiona picked up the dagger. "She must've used this. She might be somewhere in the house." Fiona glanced around, on edge again. She could be anywhere. "We can either keep searching in here for the items she took but be ambushed at any time, or…" Fiona stopped. What had Sadie meant about Clara? "Sadie said we wouldn't be able to stop Clara in time. In time for what?"

"If Clara hired Sadie, then Clara has the crowns," Cascade said.

"And with the crowns she could manifest quite a bit of destructiveness." And control the Seven. It was clear Clara wanted to be the leader, but would she risk a catastrophe to do it? "We must get back to Copper." Fiona tucked the dagger into a loop on her doublet. She tugged open the drawing room door and darted down the hallway, careless of the household staff hearing her.

The young maid shrieked as Fiona ran by, but Cascade giggled. There was a splashing sound behind Fiona, but she wasted no time to see what was going on. "Don't hurt anyone," she shouted to Cascade. Out the back door and into the street, she ran directly to an obviously hiding Gaili. "We have to go."

"Did you get the items?"

Fiona shook her head and began running down the crowded street away from the house. She needed a place to turn the page to Copper. No time to get to an official pagemark, but she didn't want to turn into a gutter. This is when the months and years of training as page turners truly mattered.

"Gaili, we traveled south for two hours from the pagemark. I know there's another one to Copper, but it's over an hour away. Think you can sort where we are above Copper?"

Gaili, unused to fits of physical activity like this, gasped out, "Beyond Calistino. Definitely. I would say, oh, the start of the Wilds."

Fiona slowed down now that they were away from the house and ducked into an alley. She motioned to a spot where they could check maps. After a few minutes they had a plan. They would turn the page to Copper from here and, with the bubble brew Gaili had made for Fiona's trips to the fire page, they would float in the air. Cascade, of course, would have to help them get down to the ground. Cascade called the plan a disaster.

Fiona turned to the nymph and held out her hand. "How often is it that a plan hinges on you being responsible? I think it's about time."

The nymph sighed, rolling her eyes dramatically, but placed her warm hand in Fiona's. She drifted once again into a deluge of liquid swirling around Fiona's arm and back into her necklace. Fiona grabbed Gaili's hand and hailed a carriage. She offered the driver double his fare if he got them to their destination with utmost haste.

After Fiona paid the driver his exorbitant sum, they disembarked. The ruins of the First Temple were little more than a skimmer destination at this point for Rise and it was early night now. Empty except for them.

"Are you sure about this?" Gaili said, pulling a dimly lit bottle from her bag.

"Ultimately, no. But I have faith in your concoctions. And that Cascade doesn't actually want to see us plummet."

They held hands in the dim light of the moon. Fiona stared up at it, said a small prayer to Larrakane, and then took a swig from the bottle Gaili handed her. They waited only a moment before their feet started to leave the ground. The world folded away as Gaili turned the page from Rise to Copper. Where currently it was inky sky with a bright crescent moon around them, the fold gave way to its dark-amber silent sister. Rain pummeled them as they stepped from one page to the next.

15

THEY FLOATED IN THE air as Rise closed behind them. The scent of people and wet earth snapped closed as the Court of Copper surrounded them once more. Looking down, Fiona could see they were high above a swath of forest and trees. She was so thankful they weren't crashing down into them she almost cried with relief.

"It's good to know that bubble brew can keep for days," Gaili said, recorking the bottle and putting it back into her bag.

"Yes, and now if Cascade will get out here, we can be off."

Upon hearing her name, Cascade drifted out of the necklace partway and looked around. "You said help you to the ground. You're too far from it."

"You can't stretch from here?" Fiona said. It seemed there was no end to what Cascade could do before.

"I've never stretched myself that far from my necklace. I could fall to pieces."

For the first time since meeting the nymph, Fiona detected a tremor in her voice. "Okay, we'll see if we can..." Why was she suddenly a head higher than Gaili? "Am I floating?"

"Did you take a sip like I said?" Gaili asked, grabbing on to her.

"Yes, a sip!" Fiona shouted. She was starting to feel a bit dizzy, which seemed odd. Heights were not a thing she feared.

Gaili tugged on her, bringing her back down. "We only have a short time before this wears off. If I don't hold you, you may float too far away from me. But if we don't get down safely soon, we'll be getting down in less desirable way. We can take more and go up, but I don't see how that helps us."

Fiona sighed. If it wasn't one thing, it was another. "Alright, ideas. We can sip, float, and wait till someone sees us."

"We could," Cascade said, "but unless it's a fairy, I'm not sure how it'll help."

"Any tree nymphs in this forest?" Gaili asked, looking around.

"Not any civilized ones," Cascade said dismissively.

"It doesn't have to be that complicated." Fiona rubbed her temple. "We'll make a rope out of ourselves. Cascade can be the heavy end and pull us down. Like a lowering airship."

"It's not the silliest plan you've had today," Cascade said.

"Yes, thank you, that's so very helpful." Fiona took off her scarf, making a mental to note to replace the things she needed inside a bit quicker after a case. If only she still had her grappling hook! "Since I'm floating, Gaili, you grab on to my ankles. Tie yourself with my scarf. And you, Cascade, hold on to Gaili. That's it. Now come out of the necklace completely."

"I don't want to," Cascade said in a small voice.

"It's alright. If we start going too fast, I'll take a sip of this while you move back into your necklace." She said it as confidently as she could, ignoring the myriad of risks. "If it helps, I'll take a swig now."

"Sip," Gaili said.

"Yes, yes."

Cascade agreed, and after another small sip from Fiona, the nymph poured down her and Gaili's body to Gaili's feet. Fiona realized that she was quite dry by the time Cascade had completed her journey. Had the nymph been pulling moisture from the rain in Rise all along? They begin to descend slowly, the lightened weight of Fiona and Gaili balancing that of Cascade.

While they drifted, Fiona bandied about ideas on how to get to Clara. She suspected she was at the theater. She had to be. It was no coincidence that Stoneguard and Clara had bookings there on the same night. Why the theater, she didn't know, but if Stoneguard was going to meet Clara and warn her, then Clara would know they were on the way.

"Perhaps we can rally the rest of the Seven?" said Cascade. "Olea is fairly strong of might. Don't tell her I said so though."

"There's no time," Fiona said as she flailed to make contact with the ground. She held on to a limb to keep herself from floating again. "The play will start soon, and it will take us hours to get there from here."

"Not if we travel with the waves," Cascade said.

"Where are we going to find waves in the middle of a forest?" Fiona asked brusquely.

Cascade rolled her eyes. "You truly don't know a lot about Copper." The nymph began to sing, the beautiful voice this time coming from her mouth directly. The song was low and melodic and no less hypnotizing than before.

Fiona raised an eyebrow but said nothing, knowing she was out of her depth. Beyond the wind rustling through the branches of the tree, she saw nothing. There was a prevailing smell of muddy earth, but perhaps that was in her mind. It began to grow stronger though, masking the heavy smells of decaying leaves and earthy wood. The ground trembled as water burst forth from the ground, mud and dirt clinging to shifting forms. Two earthen horses, almost as tall as the trees, stood before them. Cascade dripped down to the ground from their flanks. Their hooves melded with the puddles beneath them, obscuring where one began and the other ended.

Cascade pulled herself taller. "We must be taken to Calistino at once. By order of the Order of Seven."

The muddy horses dropped to the ground in a swift, smooth motion. "Of course, Keeper."

Without a word Gaili lifted her hand to help Cascade onto the back of the horse, falling into a long-forgotten role. She then strode to the other and gently swung her leg over her. "Fi, with me," she directed.

Fiona pulled herself together and let Gaili assist her onto the creature.

"Hold on to each other and stay low," the horse said over her shoulder to them both.

Not one to be told twice, Fiona held on to Gaili tight as they took off through the forest. It was good that she'd been given the warning, for there were several branches and trees crowding the way that might have whipped them of their mount. They were nothing for the horses, who flowed among them, moving swifter than wind or bird.

Fiona had so many questions, but the blur of trees and sky made her feel nauseous and she closed her eyes. She would need what little strength she had left once they reached the theater. Being back in Copper immediately made her feel as if she hadn't slept in days. The bond was pulling on her stronger now. She felt strung with tension but pushed it down. There were more important matters at hand.

Sooner than expected they were among the people of Calistino. The metallic smell of the water and sound of light talking made Fiona open her eyes. The horses did not stop, seemingly invigorated from the canal water that crashed into their path. People parted and watched as they surged through the stone streets going deeper and deeper into the city. A grand theater building with several arches towered within sight. Banners for the city and the Seven hung from it. The horses slowed to a ripple and then stopped. The creature swayed, its fluid body shifting as only some stood still. "I hope that wasn't too rough of a ride."

Gaili shook her head and thanked them. Fiona followed suit but began moving to the outskirts of the building. If Clara was going to make a move here, where most of the Seven and quite a few other prominent people would be, Fiona needed to find her first.

"I'm going to find Dorin and Olea," Cascade said. She removed her necklace from Fiona and settled it back on herself. "I'm not sure if the others will be here, but I want alert them so they can be on their guard."

"May Larrakane give you wings," Fiona said. "If Clara is going to use the crowns here, she'll be putting a lot of people in danger."

Cascade rushed for the front of the theater. Gaili and Fiona went behind the building.

"What do you suspect her to be doing?" Gaili asked.

"I was told together the four crowns could cause a cyclone. With the amount of water in the lagoon she could create a tsunami. Both of those things put everyone in immediate danger."

"It would destroy everyone and everything."

Fiona nodded grimly. "But would those deaths secure Clara power? It makes little sense to me." And to a place Clara had built. That held her name. She was selfish, to be sure, but someone who wanted power like that typically needed people to lord it over.

Around the back of the theater, they saw some actors talking in whispers.

"Let's see if we can integrate ourselves." Fiona walked through the sparse crowd, making for the back door. One of the actors was talking the loudest to garner the attention of the others. As if paying her acknowledgment, Fiona gave a small half bow to the prominent actor. They inclined their head in acceptance and Fiona continued through the open door.

Gaili followed suit. "Should we go to the front to see if she's here yet?"

"The best way to get a view of everything is from above," Fiona said. She glanced around, looking for the door to the costume room. Finding it, she walked inside and pulled Gaili in with her. Pulling items off a half-hidden rack, she tossed one to Gaili and began to slip another on.

Before Gaili could ask questions, the door opened.

"Aye, what are you two doing in here?," said an older human woman.

A younger man stepped in beside her. "You're supposed to get dressed in the dressing room."

"We were late," Fiona said quickly. "Back from supper."

"Manager will have your head if you're not quick. Most of the Seven is in the house…" He stopped and eyed them. "I haven't seen you two before. Which parts are you playing?"

"Standbys," Fiona said quickly. What was this play about again? She cast a glance at Gaili, hoping she would illuminate. "Some of the others got a bit ill. So…we're the servants."

Gaili nodded. "From Act One. The ones in the palace before the king and queen are turned into birds."

The man looked them over. "Those aren't even the right costumes."

Fiona glanced down to see the velvet gown she had been putting on. "Right, well—"

"Actors," the woman muttered, shaking her head at him. "Don't you worry I've got them. You tell the others to hurry up and grab their costumes."

He nodded slowly and walked back out the door.

"You'd be lost without old Sabs. Here." She handed them two servant outfits, still more elaborate than expected. "The action won't last forever once the show starts."

Relieved, Fiona nodded and took the clothes the woman offered. They hurriedly put them on, Fiona stuffing her scarf underneath. She had to grab Gaili's hand to keep her from running out of the room. People paid less attention to those who walked calmly to their places. They went in the opposite direction of the actors streaming into the back and toward the stage instead. "There should be a ladder to get us up to the top floor of the theater where they light the candles and drop setting pieces to the stage."

In the wings they milled until they could get closer to the curtain. The stagehands ignored them dressed as they were. Looking out toward the audience, Fiona acted nervous as she glanced out. She could see seats up front where people were making themselves comfortable. Others stood in the back, but it was hard to see anything beyond that.

"I didn't see any of the Seven. Did you, Gaili?"

Gaili shook her head. "No, perhaps they've gone to look for Clara."

"Then we better get up top." Fiona climbed the ladder with Gaili behind her. They moved along the scaffolding setup to the opposite end. Luckily no one was up here yet, the lights already being lit.

Elaborate wooden trees and castle stone wall facades hung with ropes at various angles. They dodged them getting to the center to see better. From this vantage they could see the whole of the theater and the wings. There in the middle was a large balcony for fourteen. No doubt reserved for the Seven and their stewards or esteemed guests. She could see Bardo and Dragomir there now, sitting on opposite sides. She frowned that they separated themselves even when no one else was around. Dorin, Olea, and even Jacopo was there seated. She paced on the scaffolding, searching for a sign of Clara among the crowd. What was she missing?

"Fi," Gaili whispered and tugged at her sleeve. "Clara would be early. She wouldn't wait until the last minute like this to take her seat. If she's not here, she's not going to be here."

Fiona swung around. "What was the point of her putting together this whole night, being so fastidious about it that Dorin overlooked every overwrought thing she did, if it wasn't going to be the venue for her plan?"

"Perhaps she wanted to be here but not with the Seven?" said Gaili. "I can't believe she'd do something to harm all these people."

Fiona sighed at her friend's doubt. Clara clearly didn't care about people as much as people wanted her to. A full theater or an empty one, she probably didn't need people at all. Of course, if it wasn't people she came here for, then it was probably the place. "Gaili, was one of the places Matteo mentioned at dinner near the theater? The places he said he took Stoneguard? Exceptionally close?"

Gaili began wringing her hands. "Well, yes. I think so. There's the Calistino sculpture garden. The theater connects to it."

"That's where she'll be then." Fiona set back off the scaffolding and down the ladder.

"Why there?"

"Because she's been looking for places around Copper. Old places." Fiona pushed through the crowded backstage area to the door they entered. A few actors yelled at them, but she paid them no mind. "And Stoneguard has been with her. Oh, they did it separately, but Matteo took them both." Out past the theater were stone pathways leading in a variety of directions. "Have you been in this garden before?"

"No, but Matteo was telling me about it. It's a bit of a maze apparently. This way." Gaili pointed out the path.

Fiona quickened her steps into a jog as they passed by theater-goers and then strolling couples toward a tall bush maze. It was almost as high as the illustrious theater and blocked out their view of all but the darkened sky.

"Let's see how quickly we can find the way." Fiona took a deep breath, slowing down her heart from the jaunt as they entered the maze. She was feeling low on energy and didn't want to push herself until she had to. They turned left, following the thick, bushy wall. Occasional cutouts and stained glass gave a depth to the place. Looking through some of the glass, you could see the other side of the bush even if you couldn't see exactly how to get there. It would've been a beautiful place to figure out if Fiona wasn't worried about missing Clara.

They got to a dead end, turned around, and tried again in the other direction. Fiona noticed that even in the warm night air there was a chill emanating from this path. She rubbed her arms as they turned a corner to face a wall of ice. It was solid, cold air springing off it toward them and the frost-covered bushes.

Fiona backed up quickly away from the cold thorns. "I would say we're going in the right direction."

"How did this happen?" Gaili said.

"Winter Crown, I would suspect. Do you have anything to melt this?"

Gaili shook her head. "No, but we can try and backtrack. Find another way."

They ran back and turned down another corridor. This time they got a bit farther before dead-ending again into a bush. "This will take all day at this rate." Fiona grabbed a thin limb and tried to hoist herself up. Her arms shook holding her weight and the limb snapped. Falling to the ground, she grunted.

"She's blocked off the only real path forward. Going up will be too hard. These bushes weren't made for climbing."

"Perhaps," Gaili said, staring at the bush. She bit her lip. "But what if we could cut our way through it?"

Fiona nodded, then pulled Sadie's dagger and hacked at the bush. It cut through the plant swiftly, but to her surprise she saw a flash, like a memory made picture, of herself walking in the maze, and then it was gone. "What in the dark edge material is this blade?"

"It looks antiquated." Gaili ran her finger against it.

"Well, you can look at it to your heart's content later," Fiona said, rubbing her temples at whatever she had been remembering. "If it gets us moving forward, that's all that matters." She cut another line into the bush but then dropped the dagger.

"What's wrong, Fi?"

More flashes this time, her walking the maze, her tossed like a rag doll in the air, feeling cold ice encasing her. She felt them all at once and the same time as forgotten memories. She cursed. "I think when I use, it's hurting me."

"Let me see if I can—"

"No!" Fiona said, grabbing Gaili's hand. "I'd rather not have you take on the pain. We'll only use it as necessary." She squeezed Gaili's shoulder and continued on. Feeling herself lost, the air whipping her face as she remembered being tossed in the air—it almost took her breath away. Why was she remembering things that never happened?

They ran through the next loop of the maze, Fiona swiftly making another exit when they ran into a dead end. The memories compounded again, adding on an image of fire erupting around her. Without protection she could feel the heat on her skin and shied away. She grabbed on to the bush as she lost her balance. She blinked and it was gone.

"We have to keep going," she said and pushed off from the bush, not glancing back. Before long, they ran into another wall of ice. Fiona could see a figure on the other side, murky through the ice. There was a shimmer of light around them, but she couldn't' see anything else. It had to be Clara. She pulled a step back.

"It's her," Fiona said.

"What are you going to do?"

"With the crowns she's more than capable of dealing with us. If they can create hurricanes, they can certainly make short work of us." Fiona pulled the turn stoppers, wrapped in a handkerchief, from her bag. At the very least they would make it harder for Clara to run if they could be slipped around her ankles.

The physical effect from the dagger and the draining bond with Mac had tired her. She needed to be quick if she was going to get the manacles around Clara, stop her, and keep them both alive. If she waited for help, Clara could finish what she was planning. If she failed there was no reason for Clara to not remove her as an obstacle. And then she'd deal with Gaili next. She muttered to herself, "Think Fiona, think."

"I can go first, be a distraction," Gaili said quietly.

"No, Gaili, I—"

Gaili grabbed Fiona's shoulders, leaning in. "No, Fi, you listen. I know Clara. I've worked beneath her my whole life. If she's truly endangering us, the city, Copper... I've been in danger before. This is your best chance. I know how to handle her."

Fiona bit her lip, shoulders hunched. "It's not—"

"Safe. I know. It was never going to be safe. But I knew that every moment I decided to come along." Gaili's brow was set and she stared pointedly at Fiona. "I'm more than capable, remember."

Hearing her own words fired back at her, Fiona slowly nodded. Gaili was more than capable. Committed too. Fiona sighed and flipped the dagger, handing it to the faun. "Well then, make your entrance. I won't tarry too long behind you."

Gaili squeezed her shoulder and stood up. She took a deep breath and then cut a doorway into the ice. Whatever Gaili saw using the dagger set her face in a more determined scowl. The ice swayed in front of her. She pushed it away. "Clara," she called out quietly.

Clara turned around, her skirts rustling against the dried leaves on the stone floor. Three crowns bedecked her body, like misplaced jewelry on her high-collared dress. The tallest adorned her head in pure white spires of silver metal with bright cherry beads at all of its tips. The next crown hung from her forearm, a thin band of bronze with branching vines and lush green leaves made of feathers. A duplicate of the Summer Crowns, circular band of interwoven copper filigree with lemon and rose-gold drop-shaped gems, hung from the other arm. Where was the fourth? "Gaili? What in the world are you doing here?"

"I-I've come to ask you to let me help you," Gaili said moving a step closer. Her arms slackened to her sides but she gripped the dagger tightly.

"Help me?" Clara laughed. "You think I need your help?"

Gaili took a few steps back. "No, I would never dream that you did. I—Seeing you again made me think about how much you taught me. How brilliant you were—"

"Were?"

"Are. I want to help you with whatever you're doing here. Please. I want to show you how much I can benefit you."

Clara's eyes swept Gaili from head to toe but came back to her hand. She leaned forward, her nose wrinkling. "Where did you get that knife?"

"I made it."

Gaili moved closer to Clara, her head bowed. Clara was in the midst of what looked like an impromptu workshop. There were worktables, tools, and more centered around a large fountain in the shape of a tall faun.

Fiona squinted in the light of the candles—no, the statue wasn't of just any faun; it was of Clara. It was beautifully worked in marble. But there was something about it… It shimmered. It was a new fountain, so it shouldn't have an aura. Unless Clara had built it to hide the weak spot. She waited for her chance to run in.

"Give it to me," Clara said, holding out her hand.

Without hesitation Gaili handed it over and then took a step back. Fiona winced. Clara would recognize it belonged to her hired help, Sadie, and Gaili would be found out. Fiona would have to run in and intercede.

"This is well made," said Clara, surprised.

"Candlelight doesn't bounce off the blade. And fire doesn't seem to hurt it."

"Impossible." Clara tutted, turning and holding it to a candle tucked into the statue.

Fiona didn't know if it was true or a lie, but now was her chance. She slipped through the door in the ice and behind a bush. She stopped, focusing on slowing her loud breathing as she peered through the bush.

"I suppose everyone can do something right once. Perhaps there's a small place for you, far down the list, in my retinue." She turned back to Gaili but slipped the knife in her robe. "I'll be keeping this for now."

"Thank you, Clara," Gaili said, bowing her head again. She flinched as Clara moved past her.

The scholar raised her hands toward the ice wall where the hole was. She gritted her teeth and then waved at the wall. Frost rose from the ground up and over the hole covering it. In a moment it was as if no door had been made. A wide grin stretched on Clara's face as she took a deep breath. Shoulders back and head high, she spun around. "Queen Clara, Gaili. Mind your betters."

"Yes, my Queen," Gaili said without missing a beat.

Fiona shifted so she could better see. If Clara blocked this part of the maze, that meant she needed time here. Otherwise, she didn't need so many things and hours, of which the play would take, to concoct her plan. What was she doing?

On the same wavelength Gaili moved forward. "Can I help you with anything now, my Queen?"

"You can stop asking questions, for one. You're a terrible distraction." Clara sauntered back to the statue. "But you do solve a minor problem. Grab those two rods."

"What are they?" Blinking rapidly, Gaili grabbed the two rods of blackened metal from the table. "They look like watch hands."

"That's because they are. Two hands attuned to Book time in our page. A watch is still a watch, no matter how it's presented. Now hold them, one on either side of the statue, exactly perpendicular to each other." Clara took a step back, taking out a small pocket watch similar to Fiona's. She glanced at it and nodded. "There you go. Now touch them together at the ends. Whatever you do, don't drop them."

Gaili nodded but her rose eyes were wide, fearful. She positioned herself as directed, though around the back of the statue farther from Clara.

Clara placed her hands on the watch hands, gripping them above Gaili's. "Now, to align my own time." A mixture of orange, brown, white, and green auras shimmered and spiraled from the gap between the hands as Clara started to pull them apart, straining against some unseen force.

The ground trembled as the shimmer began to sway, spiraling larger. Whatever was happening, one thing was clear: it needed to not finish. Fiona took a step but faltered as the auras grew. It was as if what Clara did was pulling her energy the way that Mac's bond had. She took another step, but her already tired body protested, forcing her to slip on the wet pavement. Gritting her teeth, she pushed forward, trying to remain quiet and take advantage of Clara's preoccupation as long as she could.

Clara laughed, delighted. "Oh, this is more power than I could've dreamed. Those selfish Seasons had this *and* more?" The crowns glowed in their various hues. She pulled her hands apart, straining but moving the rods farther from each other. A resounding ripping sound broke through the center. The world shook as if it was a die in someone's hand, the statue wobbling, the bushes moving, the amber sky and its red moon swaying. It wasn't a quake. It was a shattering.

16

THROUGH THE GAP INSTEAD of the statue was a swiftly shifting current of crystal blue water pouring through to the Copper page. Dark-green algae pressed itself against the edges of some unseen barrier, trying to float through the gap among the wave of rushing cool water. The page had been torn straight through to the Depths.

Fiona took another step, and another, until she felt as if she would fall exhausted where she was. She moved away the handkerchief, feeling the piercing metal of the turn stoppers. It forced her to forget the exhaustion as a spike of nausea and prickling sensation took over. But it didn't force her body to forget. She fell to the ground, all dexterity diminished.

"Time, intellect, and a little willpower can do anything. Bear witness to my newest discovery." Clara shifted the rods so that the hour hand moved closer to the minute. There was a fizzle, like a spark that seemed to jump from the crowns and across the clock hands.

Another ripping sound, this time above the hour hand, sounded through the center courtyard. That it could be heard above the bubbling Depths was alarming. A new gap opened up, smaller and dark. Muted cap-like shapes dotted the distant area. There was bioluminescent blue light coming from somewhere, but it was far off and cast shadows on large objects that seemed to loom.

Clara pulled the rods farther, shouting at a terrified Gaili to keep her arms up. She pushed once more.

A frosty wind whipped around from her ice cascading across the ground where water had been.

A flame sparked to life above them, a ball of fire that drifted, seemingly looking for direction.

Flowers burst into bloom and the bushes grew rapidly, cutting them off from the stars in the sky.

And Gaili's hand started to brown and shrink, a pungent smell mingling into the air. She screamed with pain trying to pull back from Clara. Clara gripped her hands, holding them taut against the rod. "You can bear it for the reward. This is how I get what I *deserve*. Not only complete control of Copper but anywhere I want in the Book. People will bow before my genius. They always do."

Fiona crawled toward Clara among the dirty, slippery ground. The hard edges of pebbles sunk into her skin. A mixture of briny water and earthy fungus was all she could breathe as she got to the faun's legs. She reached out with the manacles but was met with a hoof to the face. Arcing pain tore through her head as burning wetness trickled into her eye.

"No, this is mine," Clara screamed tearing away from her hands a brief second.

Fiona saw pinpricks of copper light start to gather in front of her. She would not lose consciousness. She would not lose like this. She clicked one end of the turn stopper around her wrist, its cold metal shuttering her access to the book with an icy snap. Nausea threatened to overtake her, but the bond and the energy Clara was draining from it ceased. With the last shred of energy, no longer fighting herself, she threw herself forward, closing the other manacle around Clara's ankle.

The world stopped moving. Fire fizzled and ice melted. The arcing wave of water collapsed, flooding the maze and its inhabitants. With a reverberating snap the tears closed.

Gaili cried out in pain, backing away from the statue and holding her hand as the clock hands dropped with a clatter to the ground.

Thrown off balance by the cresting water, Clara fell backward into Fiona, who wasted no time pinning her to the ground. With a knee pressed on her gut and a hand on her wrists, she wrenched the Winter Crown off the faun's shaking head.

"How dare you! This is my power. *My* turn to be blessed."

Fiona ignored her, tugging the Summer Crown off as fast as she could while wrestling with Clara, glad to find her weakened. She hollered to Gaili, "Grab them."

"You little nobody. You are nothing. You are useless just like the other ones. I am a genius. I—"

Gaili thrust her hand over Clara's mouth, shoving a torn black square within. She pressed her jaw closed and covered it, forcing Clara quiet.

Fiona got the last crown off, but it wasn't a struggle. Clara was deeply asleep and no longer fighting her. She looked at Gaili with a raised eyebrow but said nothing. Sometimes people needed to fight back in their own way.

"How did she do all this?" Gaili said. "I've seen what she can do, and this...this is far beyond even her talents."

"With time," Fiona said, getting off Clara and trudging to the worktables. Across them were scattered tools, open books, and old journals. Fiona picked one up to confirm it as Mac's handwriting. "And stolen knowledge." The dagger had fallen out of Clara's gown, and Fiona handed it to Gaili.

"What do we do now?" Gaili said, wincing.

Dorin came running through the melting hole with Cascade and Jacopo close behind. "Everything shook. We thought the whole theater would collapse. But then we saw a copper flare from here. What happened?"

"Clara happened," Fiona said, leaning on the worktable for strength. "We found her. In the middle of the maze. Ripping the world apart. She had all the crowns and journals."

"I don't understand. Why would she do this?"

"For more power," Gaili said quietly. "Running a page wasn't enough for her. She wanted total control."

"You've done a great service for us," Dorin gave her a small bow. "We won't soon forget it."

Fiona pushed the items on the table toward him. "You should put those in a safe place. They are more powerful than they look."

Olea showed up with wardens, who cuffed Clara with fresh turn stoppers, untethered her from Fiona, and took her away.

"I think this should prove that Orsa didn't have anything to do with the thefts. That and what Cascade heard."

Cascade nodded. "It's true. It was all Clara and another person, Sadie Stoneguard."

"If that don't beat all," Jacopo said, shaking his head. "Never thought Keeper Clara would cause so much trouble. Well, I can see these things back and get a cleanup crew here."

"Thank you, Jacopo," Dorin said, handing him the crowns and Mac's journals. "I'd appreciate if you put these in the vault directly. I don't trust handing them off to anyone else."

Jacopo nodded and gave a sad smile to Fiona. He left, following the wardens with Clara.

Fiona sighed, something feeling off but she couldn't tell what. There were so many things odd about the whole event. She picked up the clock hands from the ground. They were surprisingly light and attached at one end. She looked at them, not understanding how they had done what they did with the crowns. There was an edge to one, and she picked at it, removing an unseen cap. A sweet sickly smell invaded her nose. The clock hand seemed to be stuffed with almond-colored lace dusted with a yellow powder. But not simply lace. Bits of broken bronze intermingled within. Was this the fourth crown? She stuffed it back, keeping it close to her vest and slipping it into her scarf, unwilling to give it up until she was sure. Whatever it was, it had opened the page with the others. Opened it to someplace, somewhere, new in the Book. She looked around for Gaili and found her holding her hand to her dress protectively and talking to Dorin.

"Does it still hurt?" Fiona took her hand timidly to see that it was still dark, though not as black as before. It looked cracked and felt rough.

Gaili nodded, tears in the corner of her eyes. "It does, but I can still feel everything with it. It was like she was draining the life out of me."

"It might have been one of the crowns. We should...talk to our authority on them. Perhaps she can do something." Fiona let go gingerly. "I'm so sorry, Gaili."

"Fi, you didn't make her do this. This was all her and no one else."

"I'm not so sure. Stoneguard at least *seemed* to be a willing accomplice." It was the missing confirmation that worried her. Clara didn't recognize the dagger and there had been no time to ask her. What was the niggling feeling still lingering in her mind about?

"We should alert Rise and every other authority to her immediately."

Fiona rubbed her temple. "Yes, in the haste to get here I should've seen to that. She could be anyone by now."

"Well, you know her aura. You can pinpoint her again."

Fiona stared at Gaili and then the faekin around her in turn. "Actually, I don't. Not anymore. Perhaps that...tear, was using my bond as well." She sighed and tugged her scarf tighter about her. "I don't know. I just know putting on these stopped it." She held up the turn stoppers with the edge of her sleeve.

Gaili put her unblemished hand on Fiona's shoulder. "We can talk to someone who does."

Dorin approached hesitantly. "Did you say Clara's accomplice can be anyone?"

"More or less," Fiona said slowly. "I think you know how. Do be careful about who you allow in your inner circle for a while. I'm not sure there's a way to tell false friend from true. Watch people's behaviors and if something seems off..." Fiona petered off. People acted consistently enough. They would have to be stalked quite a bit for someone to get to know their patterns and sayings. "Did...did Jacopo say 'Clara' or 'firecracker' before?"

Gaili shook her head. "I'm not sure."

"I believe 'Keeper Clara.' Why?" said Dorin.

Fiona took off toward where Jacopo and the wardens departed. She ran through the maze, avoiding oncoming people until she got to the entrance. The wardens were placing Clara in a boat and preparing to leave, but Jacopo was nowhere to be seen.

Fiona sat in the drawing room waiting for Elinor. The faun entered, looking somewhat anxious.

"What did you find?"

"The real culprit. Orsa should be free soon."

"I'll be sure to see her at once," Elinor said. "Thank you for finding a way to show her innocence."

"Yes, well it might've been quicker if you had told me from the beginning who you were, Marcia."

Elinor raised an eyebrow. Her visage changed and she shrunk a bit into a human form that was a tad more familiar to Fiona. Marcia Evenhall, Gilded leader in the Travel Guild, stood before her. "You are quicker than most. I think you can understand I was worried you wouldn't take the case if it was coming from me like this."

"I understand why you'd think that. You don't know me well enough to know it wouldn't have changed my answer."

Marcia assessed her and then nodded. "I suppose I've misjudged you twice now. It won't happen a third time, I assure you. I appreciate what you've done for my family."

"Even your other sister?" Fiona said. "Did you know Sadie was living on Rise?"

Marcia flinched slightly. "My sister is dead."

"She most certainly is not," Fiona said, but then softened her voice. No matter Marcia's tricks, she had lied out of what she probably felt was necessity. "Sadie is the reason Orsa was blamed. The reason Orsa couldn't tell you or I what was going on. She bound her to silence. And to protect you."

Marcia sat down. "You can prove that?"

"Barely, but Orsa can. One way or another." Fiona stopped, but then pressed on, curious: "What happened between you three?"

The Gilded leader watched Fiona for a moment before looking away. "Before my sister…passed, we had a rift. They wanted to leave the cold Wilds, fight to regain our place in society. Some of the others did not. I was inked and taken away from Copper before our clan ever settled it. I turned the page back as soon as I could, but they had abandoned the area by then. It wasn't as if I could ask the Seven to track them down. I didn't even work at the Guild yet. It took me a long time to find them, but once I did it was as if no time had passed. Stella wanted to use my ability to somehow take back our place in Copper. Orsa thought the Inking brought change and wanted to work through it to create a new place for us in the page. Neither wanted to leave."

Stella! A name to be tucked away for later. Fiona nodded. "And you were stuck here."

"Stuck?" Marcia frowned. "That's not how I feel. I feel bound to the only place that has ever truly wanted me. I'm around people who care for *me*, not just the wisdom and intelligence I can give them. Being a page turner is the only thing that has truly ever made me feel free."

Fiona could understand that feeling. She stood, gathering her things. "I'm sure you have the means to turn with your sister. I've no doubt she may be easier to convince to leave Copper now."

Marcia blocked her path. "Wait, what about your payment? As I said, I am good for the paper. I'd rather not owe you a favor."

She had done her research on her preferred fee. Fiona pursed her lips. "Paper is not what I want actually. In fact, what I want might be more valuable than you want to give, but it's the only thing I desire."

"What is that?"

"An introduction to the Binder."

Marcia tilted her head, assessing Fiona. After a moment she gave a curt nod. "I'll see what I can do. He doesn't just meet with anyone."

"I know," Fiona said and opened the door, waving off the running house steward, "but that's what makes it worth the ask."

Marcia nodded and closed the door behind her.

The light of day began fading away as Fiona made her way back to Thorne Investigations.

She opened the back door and walked into the kitchen area. Gaili was there putting together an odd assortment of beads on a length of rope. Fiona wasn't sure what it was supposed to turn into, but she was sure when it was finished it would be magical. Though she favored her unaged hand, the aged one was no less nimble. Perhaps they could rectify what had happened when they visited Mac for dinner.

"Oh, Fi, you're back already. How were things with Elinor? Did she admit she was a hag too?"

"More or less," Fiona said, lowering herself down to the bench. "It seems her host Marcia has made a full recovery as well. Miraculous how those two things work together."

Gaili tilted her head and then her eyes went wide. Fiona nodded and laughed. She picked up the cup of coffee Gaili had pushed toward her. Fiona inhaled deeply the heady aroma of her favorite brew. A perk that had been lost on her before without anyone in the house was coffee made for her.

"Well, I'm sure that's just one more secret you're going to keep, isn't it?"

"Yes, but technically I never said a thing."

"You've been around the faekin too long now." Gaili laughed.

"Well, I'll take a good long break from Copper as long as you stick around."

Gaili looked at her hands and then back at Fiona. "I think I will stick around, if the offer still stands. You could certainly use the help. How else will you get on through the various pages? Your Aguan was atrocious."

Fiona laughed, not at all needled. "I'm glad. I think we make a fine pair of investigators. Oh, and this belongs to you." She pulled out a small paper envelope with the crest of the Order of Seven and handed it to her. "Dorin saw fit to give it to me while they were arraigning Clara. Your half is in there."

Gaili frowned and opened it up. Inside was a small fortune of paper. "This is more than I've made in the shop in a week!"

"Yes, well, don't expect it every time. Our normal clientele are much more apt to pay in books or information." In truth she had wanted a favor of some sort, but a favor from the Seven was more than they were willing to part with unfortunately. Money was much less contentious. "But this should be enough to make times when you have to be away from the shop a little less stressful, so you don't overwork yourself."

Gaili nodded. "Thank you, Fiona."

"You have nothing to thank me for, friend." Fiona stretched. "You earned it yourself."

"Did they find Jacopo safe?"

Fiona frowned. "Yes, he was fast asleep in the Pavilion. Luckily that had never happened to him before." Without an option to take on Clara's persona again, Sadie took a gamble changing into Jacopo. A gamble that paid off, giving her the crowns. Or some of them. Fiona had alerted Olea and Dorin afterward, but a city search turned up nothing. The Rise authorities as well had no clues as to the whereabouts of Mistress Sadie Stoneguard.

Fiona had so many questions about the illustrious hag. Why did she take them? She no longer thought she had actually been working for Clara as she had let Fiona believe. Another duplicity. The Book of Larrakane was fast becoming stacked with clever people who had dubious agendas.

Fiona took another sip of coffee, thinking hard as the pull chain bell rang. She groaned. "I literally haven't finished a nibble between one thing and the next." Gaili got up, but Fiona waved her back down. "No, you sit. I can get the door myself sometimes. We're equal partners here."

She traipsed to the front door and peeked out the glazed window. No one was on the porch, but there was a wrapped box. She opened her door, waved to her nosy neighbor, and grabbed the box before coming back inside. A letter was adhered to the top. The outline of a fox was stamped in the blue wax seal. She broke it open and pulled out a single printed page.

Fondest Fiona,

Much appreciation for all the work you did on the retrieval job from Clara. Though I did have to help a little along the way, you fared better than I expected. You truly are worth the ink fit to print your likeness. A little shorter of course, but I digress. I'm sure you're upset by now about my wordplay in our little game, but needs must when there's a deadline. Feel free to keep the dagger as payment. Even if I'm short one crown, it won't be for long.

No doubt you'll return the items enclosed. Your type tends to do those things. Till we work together again in the future.

Sincerely,

Sadie

Fiona threw open the door ignoring the cries of Gaili and ran outside. People milled everywhere; children laughed in the streets. Her neighbor called her name, alarmed. Fiona ignored them all. She couldn't pinpoint a single thing that stood out. Not one person.

Sighing she went back into the house. Gaili had opened the package, discovering a bell, watch, and four copper crowns.

"What happened? Who sent these?" Gaili asked.

"Who indeed," Fiona said, picking up the letter and slamming the door.

If you enjoyed your latest D. Hale Rambo fantasy adventure, spread the word by writing a review! Reviews really help my books get into the right hands, so I'm super grateful for every single one.

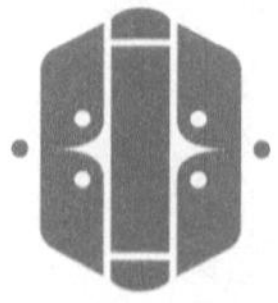

EXPLORE MORE OF THE Planar Pages for FREE by signing up for my <u>newsletter</u>.

Not only will you get me in your inbox with news and giveaways, you'll also receive The Planar Pages prequel HIDDEN WORDS

About *HIDDEN WORDS*

Life flourishes in the Book, a world of stacked realms spanning the ages. Those who can travel between them are page turners, blessed with the power to go from one page to the next.

For investigator Fiona Thorne, turning the page is normal life. Solving mysteries is where the excitement lives. No case is too small to ignite her curiosity, no page too familiar to explore.

Hired by her charming, gossipy neighbor to track down a shipment of rare books, Fiona thinks it'll be easy. She'll search for clues, sort out the issue, and be back in time for her nightly cup of coffee. And her reward? An introduction to one of the most reclusive leaders in Spine, the Druid Elder.

But that dream slips through her fingers as she realizes there's little evidence. She'll have to kick this investigation into high gear if she wants to impress her neighbor and earn her way into a privileged connection.

You can only read HIDDEN WORDS by signing up online for my newsletter at www.dhalerambo.com/newsletter/

Glossary of The Planar Pages series

Find expanded lore, world information and more at
https://go.dhalerambo.com/tpp

Spine: A realm connected to every page in the Book. All page turners live here and can suffer ill effects for being gone too long. Split into over a dozen districts.

<u>Seven Known Pages (as stacked in the Book)</u>

Elemental Chapter

Blaze: page of fire, contains salamanders, flarions, ragnis, and other fire elementals

Depths: page of water, contains water elementals, merfolk, turtles, and more

Mistral: page of air, contains sylphs and other air elementals

Cobbles: page of earth, contains gnomes and other earth elementals

Mortal Chapter

Restless Rise (Rise): page of humans, contains a central mountain with floating islands all round it

Kerus: page of smilodon, elephas, and ursidon

Court of Copper (Court): page of faekin: fairies, fae, fauns, centaurs, and nymphs

<u>Terms</u>

Aer: language from page of air, Mistral
   Aguan: language from the Depths

the Binder: leader of the Guild

the Book of Larrakane (the Book): all the known pages of the universe

bookmark: token from a page, used to travel there by a page turner

the Card: a free leaflet by the Travel Guild

the Church of Larrakane: organization devoted to worship of Larrakane

Claire: a language from page of fire, Blaze

Depth's Door: a lake in Spine

diamonnette paper (papers): universal currency

dusty: used to described a page turner who's ready to retire

elephas: like elephants standing on their hind legs, from Kerus

faekin: fauns, fairies, pixies, centaurs, all from the Court of Copper

Fallen Bubble: a cocktail

flarion(s): fire elementals who live in pools of magma from page of fire, Blaze

the Followers: a subset of the Church of Larrakane

format: slang for rumor

the Gilded: six leaders in the Travel Guild, including the Binder

the Hinge: Travel Guild headquarters

inked: blessed by Larrakane with the ability to turn pages

the Inking: historic event that created page turners

jacket(s): slang for officers of the Guild

kora: fish with an oily excretion from page of water, Depths

Larrakane (she/her): bestows the ability to turn pages and creator of the Book

La'mior: a fire forest in Blaze

pagemark(s): safe places where turners can move between pages

page turners (**turners**): people who can move between pages

Pestles and Mortar: smithy in the Spine

pulp: slang for creatures from various pages who are not page turners

ragnis: metallic-boned quasi-flame creatures from page of fire, Blaze

ripper(s): slang for thieves and smugglers across pages

Schiflan: a language spoken from page of humans, Restless Rise

skimmer(s): slang for tourists visiting other pages

skips: slang for criminals on the run

smilodon(s): catlike people, from Kerus

Sod: language from page of earth, Cobbles

spotter(s): cartographers

sylph: stark white air creatures from page of air, Mistral

the Towers of Calistino (**the towers**): prison in Copper

the Travel Guild, the Guild: organization that regulates all the comings and goings of page turners in the Book

the Trussadary Inn: hotel in Court of Copper

the Waterfall Palace: hotel in the Depths

unread turner: slang for someone new to being a page turner

ursidon: bearlike people, from Kerus

Pressed, Book 3

Step into the next Page and pre-order Book 3, *PRESSED*
www.dhalerambo.com/pressed

THE YEARLY ATTENDANCE WITH Queen Brilliance of Rise is upcoming, and wouldn't you know it, Fiona is dreading it. All human page turners assembled together in one place is not for the faint of heart. Between the tangled politics of home and facing her overbearing mother, she counts herself lucky it's only for a few days. But this year, the Queen presses Fiona with an unexpected request—find the mythical Guardian of Restless Rise.

Can she discern true intentions amid obscured agendas? Is the Queen's desire sincere or does she, or the enigmatic Painted Edge, seek control over the Guardian's power?

Fiona soon finds herself joined by a sharp-tongued gentleman whose verbal sparring belies an undercurrent of something more. Can he be trusted or is he another hidden player? Amid schemes and betrayals, Fiona must piece together palace intrigues and a myths to discover if the Guardian truly exists.

Continue your adventure and purchase PRESSED in your preferred format at www.dhalerambo.com/pressed

Also by D. Hale Rambo

A SERIES OF DECISIONS ON KAIRAS

A cozy high fantasy trilogy set in the world of Kairas where the deities may be sealed away but their troubles are not.

Book 1, TOOLS OF A THIEF

How do you stop being a thief? Zizy Zakar assumed quitting her job, stealing from her boss, and teleporting hundreds of miles away was one way to give it a go.
Buy it now: teleport yourself to books2read.com/toat

Book 2, COMPONENTS OF A CASTER

Laysa has always vowed to do whatever it took to learn magic. Can Laysa keep her friends alive and survive uncovering the depths of the unknown? Does she have what it takes to be a Caster?
Buy it now: cast your coins at books2read.com/coac

Book 3, ROUTES OF A RANGER

A family under threat. A perilous journey home. Skinny has spent her life running from her past. Now she must achieve the destiny she was denied before she can defeat the enemy at her doorstep.

Buy it now: steer yourself towards go.dhalerambo.com/roar

THE PLANAR PAGES

A historical fantasy mystery series with investigator Fiona Thorne and her motley crew of friends.

Life flourishes in the Book, a world of stacked realms spanning the ages, like the pages of an epic chronicle. Those who can travel through them are page turners; blessed with the power to go from one page to the next. For investigator Fiona Thorne, being a Turner is normal life. Solving mysteries is where the excitement lives.

Book 0, HIDDEN WORDS (newsletter exclusive prequel)

Cases are ramping up in the Spine and Fiona is in the middle of the action. Hired by her charming, gossipy neighbor to track down a shipment of rare books, Fiona thinks it'll be a piece of work.

Read it for FREE by signing up for my newsletterat go.dhalerambo.com/freestory

Book 1, BETWEEN THE LINES

Blaze, the page of fire, is wasting away. Fire elementals are being smuggled out in waves, but by whom? Fiona is on the job and nothing will hold her, not even the overbearing Travel Guild.

Read BETWEEN THE LINES and buy it now at: go.dhalerambo.com/tppbtl

Book 2, HARD BOUND

Someone has stolen from the Court of Copper, the illustrious fae page nestled within the Book. Is it a member of the fractured counsel, the fabled Order of Seven, or could the thief be much closer to Fiona than she realizes?

The fae realm is only a step away. BUY HARD BOUND at: go.dhalerambo.com/tpphb

Book 3, PRESSED

Between the tangled politics of home and facing her overbearing mother, Fiona counts herself lucky the yearly attendance with Queen Brilliance is only for a few days. But this year, the Queen presses Fiona with an unexpected request—find the mythical Guardian of Restless Rise. Amid schemes and betrayals, Fiona must piece together palace intrigues and myths to discover if the Guardian truly exists.

Join the investigation. BUY PRESSED at go.dhalerambo.com/tpppressed

About the Author

D. HALE RAMBO IS a historical fantasy author whose books transport readers to wondrous worlds filled with magic, mystery, and humor. With compelling and memorable characters at the heart of her stories, Rambo weaves tales to entertain and enthrall.

A lifelong storyteller, she's been writing and creating other worlds since she was old enough to mark them on her bedroom wall.

When she's not writing, you can find her enjoying a stiff cosmopolitan while reading mysteries alongside her favorite pet companion.

Discover more about her wondrous worlds, the versatility of gnomes, and fun fae cocktails at www.dhalerambo.com

www.ingramcontent.com/pod-product-compliance
Lightning Source LLC
Chambersburg PA
CBHW061610190726
48288CB00007B/2254